FAMILY PORTRAIT

VICTORIA CONNELLY

Cover design by Jane Dixon Smith
Author photo © Roy Connelly

ISBN: 978-1-910522-24-0
Published by Cuthland Press.

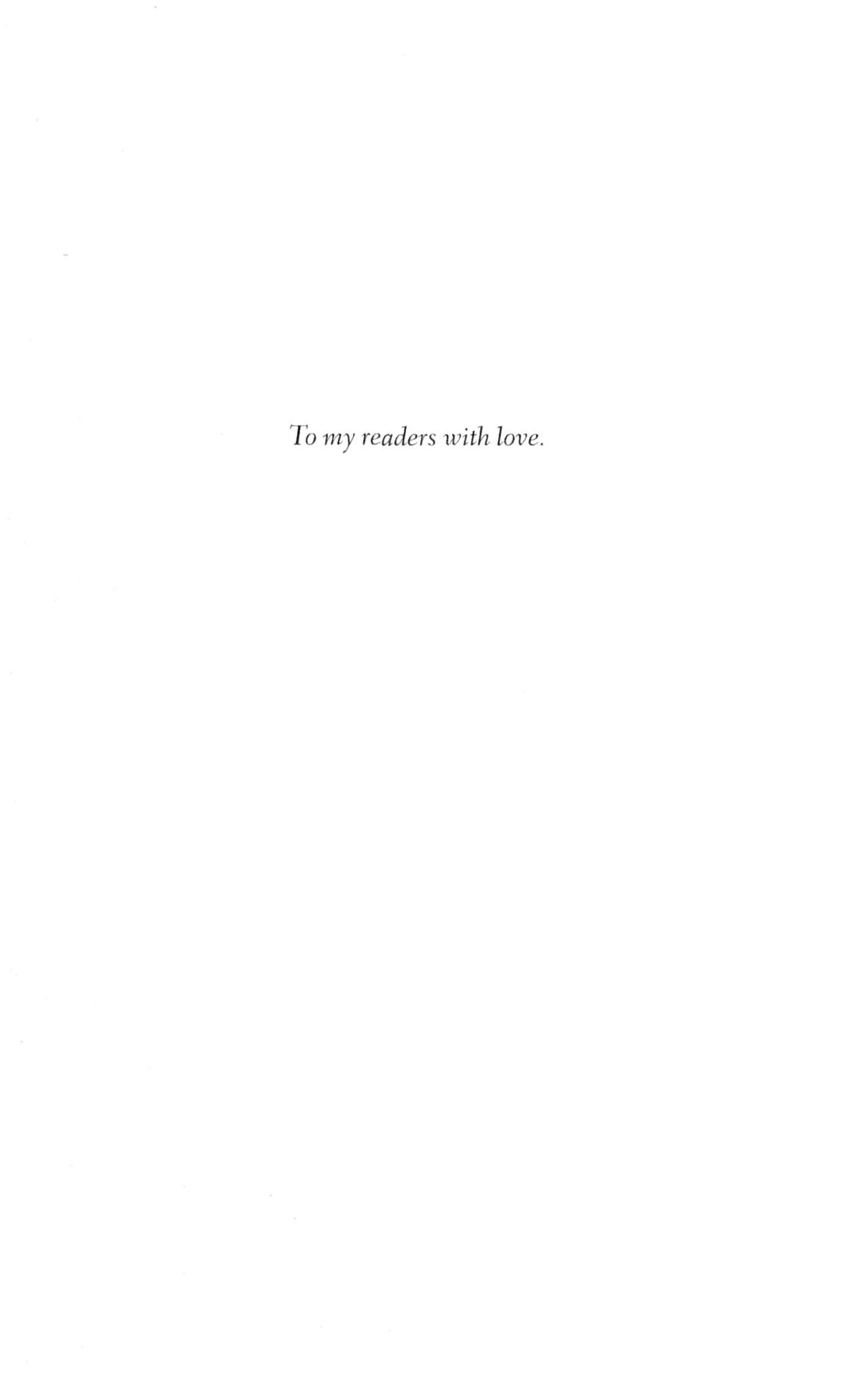

To my readers with love.

CHAPTER ONE

Brenna Bellwood did not want to go home. At least not to the family home high in the hills above Grasmere in the Lake District. She was happy in her modest terrace in the Yorkshire Dales and had been for some years. It was a sweet and simple cottage with two rooms downstairs and three rooms up. After growing up in a large and draughty country manor, it had been a relief to find a home that didn't have more rooms than a person had fingers to count them on. No, her cottage, with its low ceilings and woodburning stove, felt like a hug in stone form, and she hated to leave it.

She'd already packed her bags and told her neighbours she'd be away for a little while and – no – she wasn't quite sure when she'd be back. Family business, she'd told them, without going into detail. She couldn't face the detail. Not yet.

Leaving her cottage and getting into the car, she still didn't feel ready. Indeed, as she later crossed the border from Yorkshire into Cumbria, she deliberately slowed the car down, delaying the moment of arrival as long as possible. She got caught up in traffic in Windermere and, a few minutes later, she parked, gazing into the blue depths of the water and watching a white boat as it sailed by. But the moment came when she couldn't put it off any longer and she drove on to Grasmere, skirting the water and heading into the gentle hills above it towards home.

It felt strange being back even though she'd visited many times over the years since she'd left home. But this visit was different. This was the first since her father's death. And, depending on what was decided, it could be the last time too. The thought was a sobering one, and one she didn't feel ready for even though she was thirty-two. The truth was she'd thought her father still had years ahead of him. He'd been in his forties when he'd met her mother and had Brenna and her brother Alex, and he'd been in his fifties when their sister Cordelia had arrived. But, even though he'd died a little shy of his seventy-fifth birthday, Brenna felt cheated. People lived so much longer these days, didn't they? It was quite commonplace to live well into your eighties or nineties, and reaching one hundred no longer seemed miraculous. So Brenna couldn't help feeling upset that her father had been denied so many years that others were freely given. Especially when she knew that he'd have used them well, creating works of art that gave pleasure and added to the sum total of beauty in the world. And yet seventy-four was a good age compared to what some people got, she knew that. She'd recently lost a friend from her village – a forty-one-year-old mother of three. What would she have given to have reached the age of Brenna's father and to have seen her children grow up, to have watched them find partners and have children of their own? Life could be so very cruel sometimes.

Brenna slowed the car for the final bend in the road and

pulled up at the beginning of the driveway. The large ornate gates were closed and she got out of the car to open them, the weight of the metal and the eerie creak so familiar. The driveway was a long one, winding through the extensive grounds which were filled with rhododendrons, camellias and hydrangeas that flourished in the Cumbrian soil. Her mother had hated those monstrous bushes, preferring the more delicate beauties of jasmine and honeysuckle, and the tender annuals she'd grown from seed. As she drove slowly through the gates now, Brenna remembered one Sunday lunch when her mother had dared to ask Father if she could dig up the great bushes and create new beds. He'd stared at her with that intense green gaze of his, his knife and fork pausing for the briefest of moments before he'd resumed the business of eating.

'Sorry,' her mother had said in response to his silence. 'Sorry.'

And that one word had said it all. The house and the grounds were Father's.

'But not anymore,' Brenna whispered as she stared at the hydrangeas that still lined the driveway; their large pink and blue mopheads didn't seem real and she could understand why her mother had never loved them. They were too big and showy, and the colours seemed unnaturally strong. There was nothing delicate about them – they shouted their presence and her mother had preferred flowers that whispered.

Slowing the car still further, she braced herself for the first view. And there it was – Slate House – sitting in the lush green landscape like a malevolent dragon. There was something deeply unsettling about the Victorian gothic mansion and Brenna, like her mother, had never been able to disguise her dislike of the place. Made of traditional Lakeland stone with a slate roof, it was almost completely grey. Even at the height of summer, the house looked so dark and foreboding with its pointed gables and towering chimneys. It seemed to suck all the light out of the landscape.

Brenna had often wondered why her father had bought it. For a man obsessed with light, it seemed like an odd choice with its dark floorboards and panelled rooms. But then he'd lived almost permanently in the downstairs room with the largest windows which looked out across the lawns towards the mere. Whenever Brenna thought of him, she pictured him in this room, surrounded by his paintings. Her mother had loved the garden. Even if she hadn't always been allowed to put her own stamp on it, Lydia Bellwood had spent many hours outdoors – if only to get away from her husband, Brenna couldn't help thinking.

She parked her car and sat for a moment listening to the engine cool down. The car, like her cottage, was old but she loved it and couldn't bear to part with it, even though common sense told her it would be better if she bought a newer model. She was the first to arrive. She'd known she would be because she was the closest geographically. Cordelia was in London and Alex in Greece. But they had all agreed to meet here. Well, she assumed Alex had agreed. The reply she'd got after sending him a fifth email had been short and a little evasive. But he'd be here. It was his duty as much as hers.

Taking a deep breath, she got out of the car. She still had her house key, but it seemed strange to use it and to enter what she would always think of as her father's home. There was some post on the floor which she scooped up, giving it a cursory glance. It was mostly junk. She'd deal with it later.

Junk mail didn't care that you were dead – it still kept coming.

She glanced up the staircase, wondering if her old room was still as it always had been. Of course it would be. Her father wouldn't have had any need to change it. But she didn't feel ready to go upstairs yet. Instead, she wandered through to the living room. It felt cold in the September afternoon even though it had been a warm day. The cool of the house was pleasant during the long hot days of summer, but it wasn't quite as welcome in the throes of winter, and even the addition of shutters hadn't done much to keep the cold at bay. Her father had never seemed to notice it nor the discomfort of his family. As long as the studio was kept at a constant temperature – for the paintings – that was all that had mattered.

Brenna left the living room and walked across the hall towards her father's studio. She hesitated by the door, remembering the time she'd visited on his seventieth birthday. It had been an awkward visit with stilted conversation. He was working, he'd told her shortly. He didn't want a fuss. He wasn't sure why she'd made the journey. Lunch? No, he didn't want to go out for lunch. He had work to get on with. But, if she was going into the village, could she make herself useful and take some post for him?

Brenna wasn't sure why she'd bothered trying to plan something nice for him. Why had she imagined that a landmark birthday would suddenly make them comfortable with one another, able to chat and laugh at shared memories? She didn't know what she'd been thinking when she'd arranged the day off work to take him out and, even though it was five years ago, she could still feel the sting of his rejection. She'd left Slate House in a fury, and had driven across to Langdale and marched up a couple of pikes, her anger palpable in every single stride.

The truth was, they'd never been close. They'd never shared confidences or revealed anything of themselves to one another. Brenna knew as much about her father as anyone who had access to his Wikipedia page. And yet they'd spent so many years of their lives together. How could you do that and yet feel that you didn't know someone?

Taking a deep breath, Brenna opened the door and stepped into the studio. It was pretty much as it had always been – the wide wooden floorboards splattered with paint, and the huge window at the end looking down to the mere. There were canvasses everywhere – some finished, some not. Brenna wondered what he'd been working on the week he'd died. She had no doubt that he had been working for true artists rarely retired unless their health prevented them from doing what they loved. She wouldn't have been at all surprised if he'd been clutching a paintbrush in his hand when the heart attack took him. The housekeeper, Mrs Jackson, had been the one to find him, but she hadn't told Brenna the details and Brenna hadn't asked because she hadn't wanted to picture her father in any particular place as his life ebbed away.

She walked further into the room, glancing at some of the recent landscapes that were stacked against the wall. The moody fells, meres and tarns of the Lake District had been endlessly fascinating to him. They were subjects he'd never tired of, painting the same scenes over and over again – in different weathers with different light, and in different seasons. Brenna recognised some of his favourite views now. There was beautiful Buttermere with its distinct line of trees; there was Catbells – the stunning peaks above

Derwentwater; and there was Wastwater with its dramatic scree slopes falling into the dark water below. Each place had a distinct personality and communicated something different to the viewer. That's what Brenna loved about paintings – they made you *feel* something.

There were some smaller paintings on shelves – unfinished pieces – sketches really. And there were others that had been framed, possibly to send to galleries or customers. Brenna wondered for a moment if, perhaps, there were clients out there waiting for commissions that would never be completed.

She moved towards the window, the light and the view drawing her. She loved the panorama you had from this spot. On days when it was too wet to paint on location, her father had often set up his easel by the window and painted this view. From the first stirrings of spring in the garden, through the lushness of summer and the rich tapestry colours of autumn, to the frosts and snows of winter, this scene had been committed to canvas countless times. Today, the view of the lawn and the mere was in the muted colours of early September. Everything was slightly damp around the edges as it so often was in the Lake District for rain was rarely far away. She stared at the lawn, recalling summer days from her childhood when she and her siblings would run across it, calling to each other in playful abandon. There'd been picnics too where an old tartan blanket would be laid on the grass and a proper picnic hamper was packed even though they were only going in the garden

'It's important to do things properly,' Brenna's mother would say, and Brenna loved the meticulous attention to detail. Her mother would never compromise with plastic cups or sensible melamine plates. Real glasses and china were always used. She would even insist on napkins – fine embroidered linen ones, neatly pressed and folded.

Brenna felt tears pricking at her eyes as she thought about her mother now. How could both she and Father be gone? She didn't feel ready to have lost them both. Was she now an orphan? Could you be an orphan as a grown-up? She felt sure there had to be a word for the children left behind even if they were now adults, because the loss was so great.

Turning back to the room, her vision softened on the worn floorboards and the little patches of paint on them. She wondered how old they were. Possibly decades. Possibly new. She couldn't help thinking that they might soon be gone if she and her siblings sold the house. Nobody had dared to mention it yet; it felt too early. But it would come up at some point. And what would happen to everything? The beautiful pieces of furniture her parents had spent years gathering together. The art. The *life*. For she could still feel her father's presence in the house. He might have gone, but there was something of him still here. But, if they sold Slate House, which surely they must for none of them could afford to buy the other two out, then a new owner would come in and... what? Brenna felt faint at the thought of this sacred space of her father's being lost forever. She couldn't bear to imagine it stripped of its paintings, the floorboards mercilessly sanded until not a drop of paint remained – unless another artist bought the place and used the same space as their studio.

It was as she was about to leave the room that she saw him. Her father. Larger than life and staring right at her. Or, at least, his self-portrait. It was obviously a recent work, showing his steel-grey hair, thick eyebrows and that intense stare of his, made even more so by the wrinkles around the green eyes. Brenna took a step towards the image. The paint still looked wet and her fingers itched to touch it – as if she'd be able to feel flesh instead of paint. And there in the bottom right-hand corner was the name he always wrote in white paint. *Nicholas Bellwood.* Her fingers hovered over the familiar shapes of the letters. When had he painted it? Perhaps it was his last work. Had he known that? He wasn't famous for his self-portraits. He'd painted other people's including those of Brenna and her siblings. As children, they'd hated being forced to remain still for hours while their father committed them to canvas.

Brenna left the studio, carefully closing the door behind her even though there was no artist now to disturb. She walked around the rest of the ground floor rooms. The house smelled a little musty and Brenna decided she'd need to open some windows and let a bit of air in from the fells at some point. Mrs Jackson had always made sure the place was neat and tidy at least but, with her position being part-time and with just Mr Bellwood living here in recent years, it was too much to expect that rooms were kept aired or maintained. The building was over a hundred and fifty years old. The windowsills and frames were rotting, the guttering needed replacing and the chimneys would no doubt need sweeping. But they weren't jobs for today. She had to focus on the essential things because she knew she didn't have the energy for anything else.

One of the first things she needed to do was to go shopping and she was dreading it. Although September wasn't the height of the tourist season, Grasmere would still be busy and Brenna had never enjoyed pushing through crowds. She'd only brought a little food with her and would need some more bits and pieces with Alex and Cordelia arriving soon. But she felt too tired now. Her journey had only taken a couple of hours, but it had taken its toll emotionally.

Standing in the living room, she glanced out of the window, across the lawn towards the dark waters of the mere. It was beautiful in that slightly menacing way in the early evening, once the sun had slid down behind the hills and the clouds had begun to bank up. She turned on a few of the lamps scattered around the room and that's when she heard a car pulling up outside.

Running into the hallway and opening the front door, she saw a taxi.

'Cordy!' Brenna cried as her sister finished paying and got out of the car. The driver handed Cordelia a small suitcase from the boot and Brenna ran across the driveway to greet her as the taxi pulled away.

'Come on in. You look exhausted,' Brenna told her.

'You wouldn't believe my bad luck with trains today.'

'Well, you're here now.'

They entered the house together, Cordelia put her suitcase down and they embraced, locking together in silence for neither quite knew what to say next. But the hug was enough.

When they parted, Brenna saw tears in Cordelia's eyes and remembered just how young she was – a full ten years younger than herself. Cordelia had only recently graduated from drama school, but she looked even younger than her twenty-two years. Her mother had called her 'a delightful surprise' and it hadn't only been her and Father who'd been surprised. Alex had been a very mature twelve-year old at secondary school and the thought of having a baby sister had been quite shocking. Brenna had been a little gentler in her response, welcoming the little pink baby who'd smiled and gurgled whenever Brenna had held her.

'I can't believe Father's gone,' Cordelia said at last.

'I know. Me neither.'

'I only spoke to him last week. He seemed... fine.'

'It feels too soon, doesn't it? I thought...' Brenna's voice petered out.

'What?'

'I thought we'd have longer.'

Cordelia nodded. 'When did you last see him?'

'Not since we were all here at Christmas.'

'Oh, Brenna!'

'You know how it was between us.'

'But you spoke to him since then?'

'I think so.'

'You're not sure?' Cordelia asked gently.

Brenna shook her head. 'I did try over the years – you know that!'

'I know.'

'But he never made it easy and I kind of gave up.' Brenna could feel that she was on the verge of tears and she really didn't want to cry in front of Cordelia. She was the stronger, older sister. That was her role. But the thought of not having spoken to or seen her father for so long, and the helplessness she felt at not being able to do anything about that upset her.

'Let's make some tea,' Cordelia suggested and Brenna was glad of the distraction.

The kitchen was at the back of the house. It was a long narrow room full of dark wooden cabinets. Their mother had hated it, but Father had refused to update it. Brenna switched the lights on, but it didn't seem to make much difference.

'I love this kitchen,' Cordelia said.

Brenna blinked in surprise. 'You *do?*'

'Don't you?'

'No!' Brenna cried. 'I was just thinking how dark it is. The whole house is dark, don't you think?'

Cordelia shrugged. 'It's the style,' she said as she filled the kettle. 'All part of its charm. It has a kind of timeless quality.'

'You're so like Father.'

She smiled. 'Possibly. It's just, well, this house is special, isn't it? It has soul.'

Brenna frowned. Although they were sisters and had both grown up in the same house with the same people, they obviously felt things very differently. Where Cordelia felt a beautiful soul, Brenna felt nothing but darkness.

Tea made, the sisters walked through to the living room and Brenna was glad she'd turned the lamps on earlier because it made it feel cosy. It was a grand room with an enormous feature fireplace, a baby grand piano which all three of the Bellwood children had been encouraged to learn to play with differing success rates, and, of course, many paintings including the ghastly triptych of the three of them. Well, Brenna thought the image of her was pretty ghastly and had managed to avoid looking at it up until this point. She'd been a self-conscious fifteen-year-old when her father had painted it, with Alex looking very mature at seventeen, and Cordelia looking like a flower fairy at just five years old. Alex, Brenna and Cordelia. A, B, C. Had that been deliberate? It always felt as if it had. Her father liked order and something like that would have appealed to him.

The sisters sat on one of the large sofas together and sipped their tea.

'We should have hunted for biscuits,' Cordelia said.

'I doubt there would have been any. Father never liked them.'

Cordelia frowned. 'He always liked the ginger ones I bought him.'

Brenna didn't say anything, but had her suspicions that their father had enjoyed them because they'd been a gift from his favourite child. She still remembered the time she'd made chocolate chip cookies at school and the excitement she'd felt when offering them to him when she got home.

'I don't rate your school's hygiene standards,' he'd told her harshly, making her think that her cookies were somehow horribly contaminated. She'd been about to tip the whole lot in the bin when Alex had swooped in.

'I don't care about hygiene,' he'd told her, making her laugh.

It was odd how a moment of pain from childhood could still sting after so many years.

'Are you going to see him?' Brenna dared to ask her sister now.

Cordelia's eyes widened at the question. 'I... don't know.'

'You don't have to make your mind up straightaway.'

'No,' Cordelia said, and Brenna saw her swallowing a lump of emotion.

'I've been reading about it. You know – seeing the body. Some people find it cathartic. Necessary. But others... well, don't.'

'Let me think about it.'

Brenna nodded. So many decisions – big decisions – had to be made all at once after someone died, and it was so hard to know if you were making the right ones.

'I'm so glad you're here and that I didn't have to spend a night in this place on my own,' Brenna confessed.

'You'd have been all right, wouldn't you?'

'I'd rather not find out.'

'When's Alex arriving?' Cordelia asked.

'I've no idea. I've sent five emails and rung him three times now and it just goes to voicemail,' Brenna said. 'But he knows we need him here. It's not right that we're left to sort everything out on our own.'

Cordelia hugged her mug of tea tightly in both hands. 'We're going to be okay, you know?' she said softly. 'Whatever has to be done. Whatever decisions have to be made. We'll do it together.'

Brenna nodded and smiled, desperately willing herself to hold it together, but her sister's sweetness unlocked her emotions and tears were soon coursing down her face.

'I'm sorry,' she cried as Cordelia closed the space between them and hugged her. 'I'm okay!'

'No. No, you're not. And neither am I. We've just lost our father. We're not expected to be okay,' Cordelia said, sounding so much older than her years. 'But we *will* be. Not today, perhaps, but at some point. I promise.'

CHAPTER TWO

The sweet, clear notes of a song thrush woke Brenna up the next morning. She lay in her old childhood bed, staring up at the ceiling rose and the pretty chandelier that hung from it, the clear glass beads so perfect. It had been a gift from her mother the Christmas Brenna had turned thirteen, and had replaced a very dull lightshade. Brenna had been bowled over by the chandelier's beauty and sophistication and had felt very grown up having such a thing in her bedroom.

For a few minutes, she looked around the room from the cocoon of her pink and yellow patchwork bedding, thinking about the childhood and teenage years spent here. She clearly remembered the tears she'd wept when James Webster had broken her fourteen-year-old heart, and the angst she'd felt each night before her school exams and that almost sleepless night before her first – and second – driving tests. So much of her life was wrapped up in this room. It held a hundred secrets and a thousand memories. But what would happen to it now, she wondered? Should she take the beloved chandelier down? She didn't think it would suit any of the modest rooms in her cottage. Yet the thought of leaving it for some stranger taunted her. And what about everything else? The sweet little dressing table, the book case that had housed first children's adventures, then pony stories, then romances and classics. The truth was, she didn't know what to do.

Getting out of bed, she drew the curtains back and stared down into the dewy loveliness of the garden. The hydrangeas were at their colourful best with dusky pinks, deep creams and sky blues vying for attention. They'd been another favourite subject of her father's and he'd painted them over and over again, committing their colours to canvas so that they would live forever. Brenna often wondered where all his paintings were now. Vignettes from their home were hanging on the walls of complete strangers. All over the world, there were people gazing at little scenes her father had painted from their family home and garden.

The thought of all the paintings and the rest of the contents of the house weighed heavily on her. Even with Cordelia and Alex to help her, she still fretted over what was to become of everything for they surely couldn't absorb it all themselves. Alex was renting in Greece and she doubted if he'd take more than a few tubes of paint and a selection of paintings, and Cordelia was in a flat share in London with limited space. Brenna could take a little of the furniture. Her home was small and she didn't want to crowd it, but she would choose something. She felt it was important to have one or two things to remember the old place by, but she felt awful even thinking that way. The house and its contents didn't feel like hers and she suspected that Alex and Cordelia would feel the same way. It seemed like a kind of treachery to start dividing it all up and disposing of it. But who would do it if not them? They were the children, the heirs, the benefactors so, as painful as it was, it was something they had to get through.

Washed and dressed, Brenna left her room. Cordelia's bedroom door was firmly closed and Brenna couldn't blame her for having a lie in. She'd looked utterly depleted last night, exhausted by her journey from London and the emotions she'd obviously felt at being back home again.

Grabbing a slice of toast and a cup of tea from the meagre rations she'd brought with her, Brenna decided to have a walk to clear her head before the day began in earnest and so pulled on a pair of boots she found in the hallway cupboard and left the house. It had rained in the night and the air was fresh and cool, the autumn leaves a wondrous mix of greens and golds. The sky was promising, holding just a few clouds in its blue embrace, and the water of the mere was inky and placid.

It felt good to get out and breathe it all in. In the last few days since the call had come through about her father's passing, Brenna had forgotten how important it was to simply slow everything down, and to walk and breathe. She didn't really have a direction in mind, but she found herself in the narrow lane below Slate House. The hedges were high and stuffed full of ripe blackberries. Brenna picked a few as she walked, popping the juicy fruits into her mouth.

She wasn't thinking about where the lane headed until she rounded a corner and saw some Herdwick sheep in a field. She smiled at their distinctive dark coats and white faces. Icons of the Lake District. They belonged to Yewdale Farm and that's when she remembered that the lane ended at the farmyard. She was just about to turn around and double back when she spotted a young girl sitting on an old wooden gate up ahead. Thin bare legs poked out of a pair of shabby denim shorts and two red plaits fell down the front of her jumper. Brenna couldn't help thinking that there was something awfully familiar about the child, but she couldn't possibly know her.

'Hello,' Brenna said, approaching slowly. The child said nothing. 'Do you live around here?'

The girl nodded and then jumped down from the gate and ran along the lane towards the farm, her little boots kicking mud up the back of her bare legs. Brenna followed, remembering that she used to play here herself as a child oh so many years ago. She'd been friends with the farmer's daughter, Bluebell Daker. A romantic mother had named her Bluebell, but a prosaic father had insisted she be known as Blue. Brenna couldn't remember the last time she'd seen Blue. Probably the summer after they'd finished secondary school because life had taken them in different directions after that. Brenna had started sixth form and Blue had started work on the farm. It all seemed such a long time ago, yet Brenna's memories were fond ones. But was Blue still there? Farming was a tough profession and she might very well have packed it in.

And then it clicked.

'The girl,' she whispered as she entered the farmyard, spotting the child running into a barn just as a few red hens were running out. Brenna walked on past the barn and then got her first glimpse of Yewdale Farm. It was just as pretty as she remembered it – white-washed under its grey slate roof, it hunkered down low in the valley, looking cosy and inviting. Five windows winked in the morning light and a late summer rose climbed up around the porch, its red petals raining down onto the path below.

Brenna took it all in for a moment and then spotted a woman striding across a field to the left of the farm, a galvanised bucket swinging from her right hand. She had short, red hair which flew out from under a brown corduroy cap and she was whistling something that Brenna didn't recognise.

Climbing over a stile in a stone wall a moment later, the woman entered the farmyard, a huge grin on her face.

'I don't believe it!' she said.

'Blue?'

'Well, of course it's Blue!'

'I haven't seen you in years!'

Blue put the bucket down and hugged Brenna, and she could smell the soft mossy fells and the wild bracken in that embrace.

'You've met Linnet?' Blue asked.

'She's yours, isn't she?'

'Yep.'

'She looks just like you at that age.'

'Mucky and insolent, you mean?'

'No! Cute and – well, yes – mucky!'

'Not much has changed there then,' Blue said, gesturing to the mud-splattered overalls she was wearing.

'You look fabulous!' Brenna said and Blue gave a laugh that seemed to echo around the farmyard.

'So what are you doing back in these parts?' Blue asked.

Brenna paused before answering. 'My father's died.'

'Oh, hell. Recently?'

'A week ago actually.'

'I'm sorry, Bren, I hadn't heard. I don't get out much.' Blue swore and shook her head. 'That's tough.'

'Yeah.'

'How are you coping?'

Brenna kicked her right boot against her left one. 'I don't know. I'm just getting through each day at the moment. Responding to what's being thrown my way.'

'You on your own?'

'Cordelia's here at the house with me. And Alex will be arriving at some point. At least I hope he will. I might actually have to go and physically get him.'

'He never had an easy relationship with your dad, did he?'

'No.'

'And neither did you, as I recall.'

Brenna glanced at Blue who was looking at her intently. She remembered that way her friend had of looking at her – as if she could see into her very being.

'Your memory's much too good,' Brenna told her.

Blue removed her cap and scratched her head. 'You got time for a cuppa?'

'Sure.'

Blue led the way through the yard, passing a couple of large pigs in a pen who grunted happily at the sight of them.

'That's Wrynose and Hardknott,' Blue told her. 'Not had them long.'

'They're enormous!'

'And they're not done growing yet.'

Linnet appeared from the barn in front of them, smiled at her mother and then ran ahead into the dark interior of the house. They followed her inside and Brenna heard the little girl's feet on the stairs that led up from the hallway as Blue gestured to Brenna to go into the kitchen, flinging her hat on a wooden rocking chair beside an old kitchen range. There was a low beam above it from which hung a row of highly polished horse brasses, gleaming in the dim light.

The farmhouse kitchen was like something from a Beatrix Potter illustration with its friendly flagstone floor covered by a bright rag rug, and a bulky wooden dresser stuffed full of pretty china in pinks and blues – chipped but cherished. There was a fat stoneware jar full of wild flowers and a heap of post under a random piece of slate. And then Brenna noticed a little terrier asleep in a basket by the range. One watchful eye opened for a moment, assessing potential danger, and then closed again.

'That's Midge,' Blue explained. 'He's getting old now, but he can still nip an ankle if he needs to.'

'I'll bear that in mind.'

'Have a seat and I'll put the kettle on. Tea okay?'

'Tea's fine.'

'I'd offer you some chocolate cake, but me and Linnet have eaten it all. I made it for one of my guests, but she told me she doesn't like chocolate.'

Brenna frowned. 'Really?'

'I know, right? Weirdo!'

Brenna pulled a heavy wooden chair out from the kitchen table and plumped up the flattened cushion that lived on it. The table was one of those enormous scrubbed-pine affairs full of nicks and gouges. How different from the polished mahogany table at Slate House, she thought, where you dreaded dropping your cutlery even when a tablecloth was placed over it. This table was one to be used and she could well imagine generations of hungry, hardworking Dakers eating here. She suspected that even the odd muddy-footed chicken would have found its way onto it and nobody would have minded.

Brenna didn't really remember the kitchen from her visits as a child because they'd mostly played outdoors or had charged into the hallway and gone straight up the stairs pretty much as Linnet had done a few minutes before. But it was a lovely room – colourful and comforting.

Blue was whistling again as she filled the kettle and brought two sturdy pottery mugs out of a cupboard, and the oddest feeling came over Brenna. She felt completely at home here with her childhood friend. They hadn't seen each other for years, but that didn't seem to matter. They were easy in each other's company and Brenna felt her whole body soften, the tension of the last week slowly dissipating. Perhaps being in the farmhouse had something to do with it. The interior was dark owing to the small windows, which probably dated back at least three hundred years, and the walls were thick and the ceiling low. The room could have felt awfully oppressive, but it didn't. There was a warmth about it – a charm even – which Brenna had never felt at Slate House, and she could feel the tautness in her shoulders and the tightness in her chest easing just a little.

Blue brought the two mugs to the table together with a jug of milk and a bowl of sugar and two spoons.

'Tell me what you're up to these days,' Blue asked as she heaped a teaspoon with sugar.

'I've got a little shop in Skipton.'

'You're in Yorkshire now?'

'For some years.'

'Traitor!'

Brenna grinned as she stirred milk into her tea and took a sip. 'I know. I escaped across the border.'

'So what's your shop?'

'Picture framing.'

'Still in the art world then?'

'Yes, but I'm not actually creating anything.'

'Well, it sounds pretty creative to me.'

Brenna shrugged. 'I guess it is a little, but it's not creative in the way that Alex and Cordelia are. He's a true artist – like Father. And Cordy's acting now.'

'Is she?'

'Well, she's looking for acting work. She's had a couple of stage roles off the West End and was in a commercial for an online bank.'

'Sounds exciting.'

'It is. I'm really proud of her. I really think she could make it big.'

'Wow! You're all leading such amazing lives.'

'Yeah?'

'Yeah!' Blue said, her eyes wide in admiration. 'I've never so much as stepped foot outside this valley. Well, I had a day trip to Carlisle once, but it was much too noisy. Even Windermere's too much for me.'

Brenna laughed.

'Hopeless, aren't I?'

'No, not at all! You know what makes you happy.'

Blue nodded. 'That's true. This place – I really can't imagine a life outside it. I think it's in my DNA or something.'

'Are your parents still around?' Brenna asked.

Blue shook her head. 'My dad died eight years ago and Mum two years next month.'

'I'm sorry.'

Blue glanced out of the window. 'You know, I still think I catch a glimpse of Dad up in one of the fields every now and then. It was a favourite haunt of his in the summer evenings. He'd sit on top of a stile and watch the sun setting over the fells.' She sighed. 'I miss him and Mum like crazy, but at least Mum got to know Linnet.'

'And is Linnet's father on the scene?'

'No.'

'Oh, I'm sorry.' Brenna bit her lip, suddenly feeling awkward at having asked the question, but Blue seemed happy to talk about it.

'Don't be,' she said. 'It was all planned that way. I wanted a child and we came to... an arrangement.'

Brenna frowned. 'Really?'

'Well, don't sound so shocked!'

'Sorry. I didn't mean to.'

Blue shrugged. 'It's just that, well, you can't do these things on your own, can you? I mean, the conception bit. I can raise her alone. That's no problem. I love that.'

Brenna took a sip of her tea. 'You always were an independent soul.'

'Yeah?'

'And you run this place by yourself?'

'Mostly. There's Jake who comes in part-time and I started taking bed and breakfast bookings a few years ago and Sophie from the village helps me with that at weekends. It's actually a bit of a pain having people staying here because it means I have to be a lot tidier about the place than I am naturally. But the income is welcome and it's nice to have someone to talk to other than a six-year-old girl and a pair of pigs.'

Brenna smiled. 'I guess conversation with them is somewhat limited.'

'And guests bring the outside in. It's easy to become

something of a recluse in a place like this that's literally a dead end.'

'Yes, I guess,' Brenna said, thinking of her father who had holed himself away at Slate House. He had always been known for being reclusive and it was something that had become progressively worse the older he got. Brenna couldn't blame him. Artists, by nature, were naturally introverted, happiest when alone, creating. The outside world could be forgotten for weeks at a time.

'So tell me more about your job,' Blue said.

'Well, I love being my own boss,' Brenna admitted with a smile. 'And every day is different. I can be working on frames for an artist's exhibition or doing something much simpler but equally important like helping someone choose the right frames for their wedding photos. It's also nice to be able to take time off. Like now. When I need to.'

Blue nodded. 'That's something a farmer knows nothing about, I'm afraid. There are no days off here. There's always something that needs feeding, fixing or mucking out.'

'But you love that, don't you?'

'I do.'

They smiled at one another and Brenna could sense the deep peace in her friend and that much longed for quality of being settled.

'I guess I should get back to Cordy,' Brenna said, finishing her tea and standing up to go.

They walked out into the farmyard and Brenna heard the sound of singing from one of the upstairs windows which was wide open.

'That's Linnet. She suits her name, doesn't she?'

Brenna listened to the sweet notes for a moment and nodded. 'She's good.'

'She sings and I whistle.'

'You're the Lake District's own von Trapp family.'

Blue laughed and even that sounded melodious. 'Well, don't expect to see us on one of those talent shows.'

They passed the pigs and walked to where the farmyard turned into the lane.

Blue cleared her throat. 'I'm really sorry about your father. He might not have been an easy man to get on with, but he was always a good neighbour. Let me know when the funeral is, okay?'

'I will.'

'It's really good to see you, Brenna.'

'You too.'

'You'll pop by again, won't you? You're welcome any time. I might be out in the fields, but just wait for me here. Or come and find me if you like. I'm never far away. We could have lunch or, better still, dinner. Evenings are usually easier when you farm – once it's dark and the animals are resting.'

'I'll do that,' Brenna promised and then she left, the smell of the pigs, the mud and the sweet breeze from the fells filling her senses, and the dulcet notes of Linnet's song echoing in her ears.

When Brenna got back to Slate House, she found Cordelia in the kitchen sorting through the cupboards.

'I thought I'd make a start on something easy,' she said. 'You know – slinging out of date food isn't as emotive as going through clothes or photos.'

Brenna nodded, impressed by her vigour, watching as

her sister brought out tins and packets, placing them on the kitchen worktops.

But then Cordelia stopped, her eyes filling instantly with tears.

'What is it?' Brenna asked, stepping forward. And then she saw the tin of pineapple rings. In itself it shouldn't have had the power to evoke tears, but Brenna instantly understood the full weight of its meaning. Their father had loved pineapple, but he'd had a horror of the whole fruit with its hard scales and spikiness. He'd always bought it tinned and in rings. Rings were important. He never bought the pineapple pieces which were too small and fussy. He liked to cut his own into more appropriate sizes and he liked it served in a very particular glass bowl. All this the sisters saw as they looked at the innocuous tin of pineapple rings.

'I'll keep it,' Cordelia said at last. 'It's still in date.'

Brenna reached out and squeezed her shoulder. 'This isn't going to be easy, is it? Not any of it.'

Cordelia shook her head. 'I've never had to do anything like this before.'

'Why don't you take a break? It looks like you've done plenty already,' Brenna told her, nodding to the bin bag that was already full.

'I'm okay. I just have to resign myself to crying a lot.' Cordelia gave a gargantuan sniff as she put the tin to one side and delved back into the cupboard. 'Why has he got so many spices when he never cooked with them?'

Brenna smiled, surmising that they were going to learn a lot about their father over the next few days. The thought made her sad. It felt so horribly wrong and intrusive to be opening cupboards and drawers and to be making decisions about the worth of things and ruthlessly disposing of items that weren't wanted. A life, she realised, was made up of an awful lot of stuff and, sooner or later, somebody would have to sort through it all.

It was sad to see her little sister so upset. Cordelia always reminded Brenna of springtime. Her fair skin and hair, the blueness of her eyes and the way she just seemed to bounce with life. Even now, in the midst of this sad duty, she radiated an energy that Brenna just couldn't muster.

'There's a lot of mugs and cups,' she said now as she opened another kitchen cupboard.

'Keep whatever you want. I'll choose a couple too. We can box the rest up for charity.'

Cordelia took out an old mug featuring Winnie the Pooh. 'I'm keeping this one.'

'Is the blue and white china set still here?'

'In the other cupboard.'

'Remember how Father would roar if you dared to take any from that set out into the garden?'

'Yes,' Cordelia said. 'There was a strict hierarchy, wasn't there? And you'd never give the blue and white to builders or plumbers either.'

'Although Mother once did, didn't she?' Brenna recalled.

'Oh, yes! That electrician from Kendal. He dropped one of the cups in the sink and chipped the handle. Father was furious.'

'I sometimes think he cared more about things than us.'

'Don't say that!' Cordelia cried. 'It's not true.'

'No, you're right. It was only *beautiful* things,' Brenna corrected herself. 'I think we possibly rated higher than the more mundane items.'

Cordelia chose to ignore this statement. 'Have you heard from Alex yet?' she asked.

'No.'

'What are we going to do?'

Brenna had been thinking long and hard about this. 'I'm going to go and fetch him.'

'You're going to Greece?'

'I don't see that we've got a choice.'

'He won't like that.'

'Then he should answer his phone, shouldn't he? He's got to be here, Cordy. We can't do this on our own. It's not fair.'

'I know.'

'He needs to be a part of this. He might think he doesn't want to be, but he'll regret it in the future if he isn't here now. Anyway...'

'What?'

'He's the artist. We need him to guide us. I don't want to make any wrong decisions, you know?'

Cordelia nodded. 'I know.'

'It's too much responsibility.'

'Do you want me to come with you?'

'No. You're better off here – as long as you don't mind being on your own for a couple of days.'

'I don't mind. It'll give me a chance to sort my head out a bit.'

Brenna smiled. 'Well, ring me if anything – you know – comes up. If you hear from the funeral directors or solicitors, or make any strange discoveries.'

'Don't worry,' Cordelia said. 'If I hear or find anything difficult, awkward or sinister, you'll be the first to know.'

CHAPTER THREE

There was a part of Brenna that hated her big brother for forcing her to get on a plane because she hated flying, but another part of her was glad to get away from Slate House for a while. Cordelia hadn't seemed overly perturbed about being there on her own. She'd told Brenna not to worry, but Brenna had felt a little anxious. After all, *she'd* always been the organiser in the family. It had been a very specific role her father had given her. Brenna the administrator. That's how she'd always thought of herself in terms of her relationship with her father. Alex had been the rival – the budding artist always in their father's shadow. And Cordelia? That was easy – she'd been the muse. The favourite. There was never any doubt about that. It would have been easy for Brenna and Alex to have hated their little sister. She seemed to swallow up all of their father's affection. And yet they adored her. She just had that sort of personality that was impossible not to love. They couldn't really blame their father and yet it had always felt unfair and unbalanced. She wished she didn't have to think about all this, but her father's death was dragging all sorts of memories out of the depths of her psyche. Well, she'd do her best to shut them off while in Greece and pretend – if only for a couple of days – that she was on holiday.

After one taxi, two trains, one flight another taxi and a ferry ride, Brenna finally arrived on the island. She'd texted Alex several times and had finally heard back from him the night before. He'd sent some directions and told her not to bother coming which seemed contradictory. She only hoped he'd be there when she arrived.

Skopelos.

Brenna smiled as she whispered the name to herself. How did a Cumbrian end up in Skopelos? How did *anyone* end up in Skopelos? As she walked off the ferry and into the town, she answered her own questions and couldn't really blame her brother for choosing to live here. After the greyness of Cumbria, the Greek island seemed like paradise. Everything was light, bright and beautiful.

Skopelos Town was a wonderful jumble of white houses with red roofs which wound up the hill from the bluest of seas. And, somewhere in that jumble, was her brother. He was renting rooms in a villa and she pulled out her phone now to read his directions. It seemed easy enough to find.

After the misty coolness of an early morning wake-up in Cumbria, Skopelos felt wonderfully warm and Brenna rolled up her sleeves as she started up a hill. There were pots of plants everywhere – on the pavement outside old wooden doors, on deep windowsills and spilling over balconies. There was the occasional chair outside a property too where a resident might bring a cup of coffee and sit in a patch of sunshine.

As she continued up the hill, glad she'd only brought a

very small overnight bag with her, she caught glimpses into tiny courtyards where olive trees shared their shade. She spotted a pretty Madonna in a tiny alcove with an offering of flowers in a jam jar, and she caught the scent of jasmine from a secret garden. And there were bell towers high above the streets and sleepy cats curled up next to terracotta pots.

And, everywhere, there was white.

For a moment, Brenna wondered if it had been the white that had attracted Alex to the island. All the buildings seemed to be painted white, the steps and walls too. The Lake District had its share of white-washed homes, but it had so many grey ones too, including Slate House. Perhaps Alex had renounced grey completely and had made an artist's pact with white.

Stopping by a tiny shop opposite a church, Brenna read Alex's text again. She was to take the next left. And there it was – the villa. Sugar white with cerulean shutters. The door, up a few shallow steps, was open and Brenna walked inside, instantly embraced by the coolness of the room. She let her eyes adjust and saw that there were canvasses everywhere – some complete, some left woefully unfinished. She'd come to the right place.

'Alex?' she called, feeling sure he must be at home otherwise his door wouldn't have been left open.

There was a murmur from the next room and, a moment later, her brother emerged, his clothes rumpled, dark hair dishevelled, and his face obliterated by a horrible beard.

'Bren!' he said as if surprised to see her there.

'You were expecting me, weren't you?'

'I guess.'

She put her bag down and crossed the room, wrapping him in a hug he clearly didn't want.

'You smell awful,' she told him.

'Yeah? Well, you smell...' he paused and gave a long, audible sniff, 'of home.'

'Is that good?' Brenna asked tentatively.

'I'm not sure.' Alex broke away from her and ran a hand through his hair, making it stick up in a different direction.

'What's through there?' She nodded to the room he'd walked out of.

'Bedroom. It's one of those upside-down places with the bedroom on the ground floor to keep it cool.'

'Were you asleep when I arrived?'

He shook his head. 'Just resting.'

'Are you okay?' She glanced around the room again and noticed that there were empty beer cans and wine bottles among the canvasses.

'Don't start,' he warned her and she watched as he headed upstairs.

Brenna followed.

The upstairs room was one big open plan space with a tiny kitchen at one end, and a sofa and table in the middle. The rest of the space was being used as Alex's studio and, like the downstairs room, was full of canvasses at various stages of completion. A large easel stood near a window that opened out onto a balcony with a view across the town and out to sea. Instinctively, she walked towards it. She'd always been one of those people who walk into a room and go straight towards the window to see the view, and this one didn't disappoint.

'I bet you've painted this scene a few times,' she said with a smile as she walked out onto the balcony.

Alex followed her. 'Once or twice. Not recently.'

'What have you been painting recently?'

He shrugged.

'You haven't been painting?'

'Not since – you know...'

Brenna nodded. She felt lucky that, since the news of her father's death, she'd been able to distract herself with her work. She guessed that wasn't so easy when you were an artist. That sort of work was tied up so much with your emotions and, when they took a hit, work was often neglected.

But it wasn't only his work he'd been neglecting, Brenna couldn't help feeling. His place was a mess. There were plants drying out on the balcony and the room downstairs had been in a sorry state. He'd been neglecting himself too judging by the look of him.

They left the balcony together and she glanced around, fearful of what she might find and was pleased to see some really beautiful paintings stacked against the walls. She picked one up at random. It was a study in blues and greens. Was it the sea or the sky or both? She couldn't tell, but she liked it.

'This one's good,' she told him.

He glanced at the canvas. 'You've got it upside down.'

'Oh.' She flinched. 'Well, I like it this way.'

There was an awkward pause between them.

'Go on,' Alex said at last.

'What?'

'Say it.'

'Say what?'

'That I'm not as good as Father.'

'I wasn't going to say that!' Brenna said, appalled that her brother should think so little of her.

'Weren't you?'

'No! I'd never say something like that.'

'But you were thinking it.' Alex said this matter-of-factly.

'No! Alex – I've never thought that! I love your work. You know that surely!' She looked closely at him. 'Well, you obviously don't if you're saying things like that. But I'm your biggest fan. I've got your paintings all over my house. I even bought one of your first – remember? The fuzzy sheep? I think we called her Fenella, didn't we?'

She saw Alex raise a tiny smile. 'You were only ten when you painted it and I bought it with three weeks' pocket money. Wasn't that what you charged me? Anyway, I remember being so amazed by your talent. I was a bit jealous too, truth be told, but I never compared you to Father. Your paintings are quite different – they're looser, lighter. I've always thought so. You have your own distinct style.'

'Father never thought so.'

'Alex! That's not true.'

'No?'

'No! Why would you even say that?'

Alex turned away, staring out of the window. 'You were never there when he was attacking me. You didn't hear his comments.'

'No, perhaps I didn't. But I had a fair few fired my way, so I can imagine.' She put the painting down. 'Are you selling well?'

'I do okay. Could be better.'

'Are you trying to sell more?'

'What's that meant to mean?'

'Well, are you?'

'Not really.'

'Alex!'

'What?'

'You're really not making an effort at all, are you?'

'It's enough effort just to get out of bed some days.'

'Are you drinking again?' Brenna dared to ask. 'Silly question. Of course you are.'

'Have you come all this way just to pick a fight with me?'

'No, of course not!'

'Then stop baiting me. I've got enough to cope with without an irate sister. You do know Aimée left me, don't you?'

'Yes. And I can't say I blame her.'

'Gee, thanks!'

'Well, look at the state of you! And you have rather isolated yourself here. I can't imagine that makes things easy. A Greek island isn't for everyone, I guess.'

'She said she preferred Birmingham. Can you believe it?'

Brenna tried to hide a smile. 'She's obviously crazy. You're well shot of her.'

He didn't reply.

Brenna sighed. She was secretly sad that Aimée was no longer on the scene. She'd been a wonderfully calming presence. Brenna had instinctively felt that even though she'd only met her once, and Alex had clearly been besotted. But maybe he was fated never to settle down. He'd had a few partners over the years and they never lasted long. Still, there was no point dwelling on those romantic failures now.

She cleared her throat. 'Alex, why didn't you answer my messages about Father?'

He gave a grunt and a little shrug.

'This isn't something you can ignore, you know? It's not fair on me or Cordy. We can't sort everything out on our own. Besides, you're the artist.'

'What does that mean?'

Brenna bit her lip. What did she mean by that? She had to be careful with her answer. Alex was in an odd enough mood as it was and she didn't want to make it any worse and tip him over into one of his ice-cold silences.

'I just think that you'll be able to make some decisions about the art more easily, that's all.'

'You want to sell it all?'

'Well, that's it – I don't know what we should do.' She paused. 'You know, I had a message from a complete stranger via my Instagram account saying that they were sorry to hear of the loss of my father and could they possibly buy one of his paintings?'

Alex snorted. 'What did you say?'

'I deleted the message and blocked them.'

'Anyone else been scavenging?'

'No, thank god.'

'They will. Everyone comes out of the woodwork at times like this, wanting a piece of something.'

'That's why you should come home. We need to be in charge of it all.'

'Is that what the will says?'

'I don't know. The solicitor's coming over in a couple of days. So we should go home tomorrow. There's room on the plane so you just need to pack.'

'What's the point?'

'The point? Because you've got a role to play in this.'

'Role! You sound just like Father when you talk like that.'

'Don't say that!'

'Well, you do. Isn't that how he saw us? We all had our places, our roles.'

Brenna swallowed hard, not confessing that she'd been having the exact same thoughts on the journey here.

'That's just how he processed the world,' Brenna said, her words far more magnanimous than she felt.

'And what if I don't want to go home?'

Brenna sighed. 'Don't sulk. You're a grown man.' As soon as the words were out, she regretted saying them because he seemed to somehow shrink within himself and she couldn't see the man at all. All she could see was the boy. Her little brother. She'd always thought of him as that even though he was older than her. And now, more than ever, she could feel her sister gene kicking in.

'How have you been?' she asked gently.

'How do you think?'

She nodded. 'Me too.'

It was then that he seemed to acknowledge her for the first time. 'It's not easy, is it? I mean...' He stopped, his voice catching in his throat.

'No. I don't think it's meant to be.'

'It's all too soon,' he told her.

'Yes. I know.'

'I thought we'd have more time.'

'I thought that too.'

Time seemed suspended for a moment as they stood gazing at each other across the mess of the room, the white curtain at the balcony window blowing in a light breeze and the strange weight of their grief settling between them.

'Do you mind if I have a drink?' Brenna asked, her throat suddenly feeling very dry.

'Tea or something stronger?'

'Tea would be lovely.'

She watched her brother move around the small space of the kitchen, pulling something ghastly out of the sink and she grimaced at the state of the mugs on the draining board.

'Listen,' Brenna said, 'why don't you go and have a shower? I'll make myself a cup of tea, okay?'

He frowned, knowing she was up to something, but too tired to protest. Instead, he nodded and took his cue honourably.

Brenna waited a moment and, as soon as she was quite sure it was safe, she went into the kitchen, found the bin, took the liner out and started tidying the place, picking up discarded food wrappers, empty cans and bottles. The eco warrior in her was desperate to recycle what she could, but she knew she'd only have the five minutes Alex was in the shower to clean up and, if she made a fuss about bottle banks, he'd probably throw her out. So everything went into the black bag for speed and efficiency.

There wasn't time to clean much, but she managed a quick wash up and wipe down of the main kitchen worktop as well as giving the plants on his balcony a good watering before switching the kettle on and actually making herself the promised cup of tea. Alex appeared a couple of minutes later and she could tell from the look on his face that he'd clocked what she'd done, but he didn't say anything. It seemed the fight had gone out of him.

'When do we leave?' he asked in a resigned voice. Brenna told him the travel details and he nodded which was a relief to her. 'And the funeral?'

'We don't know yet.'

'I really don't want to go back.'

'I know you don't.'

He gazed down at his bare feet. 'What's it like?'

'The house? The same only... empty.'

'Was it a mess?'

'No. The housekeeper's kept it pretty straight but there are all the same old repairs that need doing.'

'Bloody old house. I don't know why he bought it. I've never liked it.'

Brenna gave a little smile. She felt the same way.

'Do you know what's going to happen to it?' he added.

'I guess we'll find out when the executor comes round.'

Brenna had had the good sense to book a hotel room for the night, knowing that Alex's housekeeping might not be up to her own standards. It was a relief to close the door later that evening. She found Alex's company draining at the best of times, but the situation they now found themselves in had made him particularly morose. He'd taken her out to dinner at a little place on the harbour that he liked. The food was delicious and the soft breeze from the sea felt like a balm. Brenna totally got why Alex had come here and why he was so reluctant to leave. She was beginning to fall under the island's spell herself. How easy it would be, she thought, to forget about the flight home tomorrow and to stay a while longer. But that wouldn't be fair on Cordelia.

Brenna didn't sleep well that night; she never did the first night in a new place. There were always too many stimuli: strange sounds coming from other rooms and the street outside, the smell of detergent on the bedding when she climbed under the duvet, and the alien space around her with its high ceiling to accommodate a fan. On top of all this, there were her worries about the journey itself. Brenna was an anxious traveller at the best of times, but having Alex in tow added another dimension. He clearly didn't want to leave his beloved island and return to Slate House and he'd no doubt sound off about it on the way home. And what awaited them when they got back? She'd been texting Cordelia to keep updated, and to tell her that she and Alex were heading back together, but they couldn't really make any progress until the executor had spoken to them all.

Death was never just about the loss of a person. It was a loss of a way of life. Everything changed. Your mind had to find a new way of thinking as you coped not only with the physical loss, but with all the unexpected emotions that went with that.

As Brenna stared into the darkness of her hotel room, she knew that something fundamental in her was changing. What was it, she wondered? Was it a kind of acceptance? The precursor to letting go perhaps? She felt horribly different – a little flat. Lethargic. She hoped it was just the day's travelling and the stress of seeing her brother under such sad circumstances, but she suspected it wasn't.

She turned over in bed, her face against the cool pillow that smelled of somebody else's detergent. She wished she was in her own bed at home while also wishing that she could hide away in this hotel room forever. Anything but face the days that were coming.

Mercifully, Alex was ready and waiting for her when she called round the next morning. He looked smart in a blue shirt and jeans and she saw that he'd packed a small suitcase, but there was something decidedly odd about him. He looked just a little bit blurry around the edges.

'Alex, have you been drinking?' Brenna dared to ask.

He shuffled his feet from side to side as he'd always done when he was caught out.

'Oh, Alex! It's not even ten in the morning!'

'Yeah, well.'

She sighed. This was worse than she'd imagined if he was drinking during the day. She only hoped it was manageable.

'You're ready though?' she asked.

'No.'

She reached out towards him, touching his arm lightly.

'Come on. Let's get down to the ferry.'

The journey home allowed them time to talk in a way that they might not have had they been sat together in a room. The forced proximity and the boredom of a flight meant that conversation opened naturally and Brenna was surprised when Alex broached one particular subject.

'Do you think he had dementia?' he suddenly asked somewhere over mainland Greece.

'What makes you ask that?'

'Just the way he talked the last time I saw him.'

Brenna shifted in her seat, feeling uncomfortable. 'How did he talk?'

'He never seemed to finish his sentences. His mind would seem to wander off.'

'He's always been like that with me,' Brenna confessed. 'I used to think it was because he got bored of his sentences and assumed whoever he was speaking to would know what he meant without finishing his train of thought. He'd moved on, you know?'

'You're saying he couldn't be bothered to finish his sentences?'

'Yes.'

'That sounds like Dad.'

'But I don't think he had dementia,' Brenna said. 'Just an artist's temperament. He was always focused on it, wasn't he? Anything else, any*one* else, was merely a distraction.'

Alex seemed to take this in. 'When did you last speak to him?'

'I can't remember.'

'You can't remember?'

She sighed, having already gone through this with Cordelia. 'You know how it was between us. I can't be sure. It was always so sporadic anyway.'

Brenna looked down into her lap. She could feel Alex's eyes upon her and it made her feel awkward.

'What?' she said at last.

'I'm sorry, Bren.'

'Sorry for what?'

'That it was – you know – difficult between you. I mean, it was for me too, but in a different sort of way.'

Brenna gave a sad smile of acknowledgement.

'I often wonder what it must be like to have a normal family – if there is such a thing!' she said. 'I think there must be though because I have friends who talk about theirs and I find myself listening to them, observing them, like I'm some kind of anthropologist.' She gave a nervous laugh. 'They talk about getting together at a family home. Just imagine that – a home where they all grew up as children and where their parents are still living together, happily!'

Alex guffawed.

'And they all get along. They buy silly gifts for each other and take endless photos and upload them all onto every single social media site. It's quite sickening really.'

'If it's any consolation, they probably secretly hate each other and are only putting on a show. You do know that anything you see on social media is a highlight and has been edited? Nobody confesses to the really gruesome stuff that's going on.'

'I'm don't know,' Brenna said thoughtfully. 'I think happy families do exist.'

It was something of a relief to make it back to Cumbria, Brenna thought, although her brother didn't seem to be happy in the least.

'This is the last time I'm coming back here,' he told her as the taxi wended its way up into the hills above Grasmere.

She glanced at him as they approached the final bend. He looked half dead, his skin pale and his eyes bloodshot from lack of any decent sleep anytime recently. He'd had a drink on the plane too when the flight attendant had come round. Brenna had attempted to stop him but Alex had been insistent and she hadn't wanted to cause a scene.

'It takes the edge off,' he'd said.

'The edge off what?' she'd asked, wondering if he was a nervous flyer too.

'Life.'

Finally they reached the entrance to Slate House.

'God, I hate these gates,' Alex complained as the taxi drove through them.

'How can you hate gates?' Brenna asked.

'They're so pretentious. And so typical of Father, aren't

they? It's like he's saying, "This property is mine. I'm important enough to have gates this big and this fancy and your place is the other side of them."'

'I never thought of them in that way.'

'One day, I'm going to walk out those gates and never come back,' Alex vowed.

'One day, perhaps,' Brenna said. 'But not today.'

CHAPTER FOUR

Alex remembered the first time he'd realised that there was a world outside the gates of Slate House – a world beyond home and school. He'd been seven years old and his father had taken him to one of his exhibitions in London. It had been a rare trip. Nicholas Bellwood didn't like the capital and he was moody and reticent for most of the journey down on the train. But Alex had been captivated by it all – the sights, the sounds, the smells. Everything was new and *not home*. He watched people interacting with one another on the train. They weren't all arguing and they seemed to be happy for the most part. That was odd, Alex remembered thinking. At Slate House, there were always arguments and happiness was a fleeting thing.

Once at the show, Alex had been told to sit on a chair and not move and he'd stayed there for a while, his eyes roaming the crowded room. There were so many people and he didn't know any of them. Did his father know them? Alex looked for him in the crowd and saw him talking to a woman who was wearing a lot of sparkly jewellery. She seemed to be excited about something and kept pointing to one of the paintings, but his father seemed to be bored by the whole thing.

Alex was getting bored too so he left the chair he'd been made to sit on and wandered into the crowd. A few people nodded and smiled, but he was mercifully invisible. He heard words like 'enchanting', 'genius', and 'unique' and he knew they were talking about his father's work and he allowed himself to feel a moment of pride as he looked for his father in the room. Only he couldn't see him. He'd been swallowed up by all the other people.

'Hello, young man!' an elderly gentleman said, placing a large, heavy hand on Alex's slender shoulder. 'Past your bedtime, I'd say.'

'I'm allowed to be here. It's my father's show,' Alex said defensively.

'So you're the Bellwood boy, are you?' The man took a swig from his glass. 'And what do you want to be when you grow up, eh?'

'I'm going to be an artist too,' Alex declared.

The man laughed and Alex hadn't been able to understand why because he'd not said anything funny, had he?

'Well, you've a lot to live up to, son,' the man said at last. 'A hell of a lot.'

That had been the first time Alex was told that, but it was by no means the last. It was something he'd grown up knowing. As certain as he was that he wanted to be an artist himself, he was even more certain that he would never live up to the legend that was his father. It would have been far easier for Alex to have become something else – a teacher, a doctor, an electrician – anything. But art was part of his DNA. He just couldn't help himself.

From the moment Alex could hold a brush, he'd started to paint, daubing great blobs of primary colours onto paper with happy abandon. The colours had always fascinated him. They were like pure emotion distilled. Of course, he hadn't been able to understand the concept of that when he was young, but he'd somehow felt it. Colours were a way of communicating. Even if he wasn't able to create anything resembling a shape, the colours themselves still seemed to say something to him.

Alex had never forgotten the first time he'd finished a painting. A proper painting on a board. Not one of those juvenile attempts on paper with stick figures standing in a row on green grass with a blue sky above and a huge white blank in the middle where the grass and sky refused to meet. This had been a Cumbrian landscape with a bridge across the river in the foreground and mountains in the distance. It had taken eight-year-old Alex an intense amount of concentration to get it to his satisfaction but, finally, he had something he was proud of. And he remembered the tight feeling of anxious excitement he'd had when he knew he was going to show his achievement to his father.

Nicholas Bellwood picked up the board which was still wet, taking it to the window where he stared at it for a long time. Alex could feel his heart thud-thudding and felt quite sure his father would be able to hear it too. Finally, he spoke.

'Of course, your perspective is out. You need to pay attention to that.' And he'd handed the painting back to him before picking up a stack of brushes to wash. 'Maybe stick to painting on paper for a while longer,' his father had added. 'We don't want to waste boards.'

Alex had watched him as he'd moved to the sink and turned the tap on. Was that it? Was that the sum total of time he was going to get from his father? Were there no words of encouragement? No, it seemed not. He'd zoned straight in on the fault and had demoted him from painting on boards.

Alex had carried the sting of that moment with him for years. In fact, he still suspected that it resided somewhere deep within him alongside all the subsequent put-downs from his father – of which there'd been many.

It had always been a strange dynamic between them. Alex clearly sought his father's approval and sincerely wanted to be an artist and learn from him. His father had taught him in a roundabout sort of a way – not through encouragement but through criticism.

'You haven't got that line right.'

'So you weren't trying to capture the light in that moment?'

'You should try that view again on another day.'

These were just a few of the classic comments Alex remembered from his apprenticeship as an artist. He wasn't quite sure what had kept him going and what had made him study art. It would have been so much easier to simply put his brushes down and walk away from his easel. But there was a compulsion in him. A *need* to paint. He was clearly cursed by the genes he'd inherited.

When he'd started to paint full time, finding his way around his home county, setting up his easel in the verdant valleys and scree-strewn mountains, he'd been so fully aware that the Lake District was his father's domain. It seemed unreasonable that one person could so completely own a place, but that's how it had felt to Alex. Every lake, beck and tarn, every pike, ghyll and mere belonged to his father. They were his subject matter and his name was as closely associated with the place as William Wordsworth, Beatrix Potter and William Heaton Cooper. Alex felt like an interloper.

Even the colours of the Cumbrian landscape seemed to be owned by his father and, every time Alex used them, he felt as if he were competing in some way. Indeed, that's how others often saw his work too.

'Ah, yes – that's a favourite view of your father's, isn't it?' buyers would say if Alex dared to exhibit his work.

It certainly hadn't been a good idea to have some of his early work in one of his father's shows. But Nicholas Bellwood had encouraged it so the work itself must have been up to standard. Unfortunately, its reception had been lukewarm at best. The paintings had been hung on a separate wall. Every gallery had a bad wall – the one next to the stock room or behind the till or where the lighting isn't quite right. Alex's wall was en route to the toilets and customers rushed by it after their second glass of wine. Few stopped to look at the work and fewer commented on it. One out of the six paintings had sold.

Perhaps that's why Alex had flown south at the first opportunity. Escaping the long shadow cast by his father, he'd followed in the footsteps of painters like Van Gogh and Cezanne and moved to Provence, leaving the moody grey skies and cold climes behind.

Provence meant a whole new palette. The colours, at last, were his. They were lighter and brighter than his father's. They sang from the canvas in a way that the muted northern colours of the Lake District never could. Alex had found a palette of his own and, for a while, he had flourished, producing some of his best work.

And then he'd discovered Greece and its islands. Alex had to admit that it had felt good to have put over two thousand miles between himself and his father.

All these memories came flooding back in a crushing rush as he stepped into his father's studio shortly after arriving home. Brenna and Cordelia had left him to it and he appreciated them giving him some space.

He walked straight to the window and looked out over the garden, taking in the familiar view and the lush greenness of the landscape beyond. It was as far from Skopelos as you could imagine and, as his eyes adjusted to the difference, he found himself remembering how much he'd enjoyed painting it once upon a time.

He turned into the room and slowly worked his way around the paintings that were lined up against the walls. Idly, he picked one up. It was a landscape. Of course it was. A recent work, he judged – the paint was still drying. It was beautiful. It had such depth. The eye was led in so effortlessly that the viewer almost became the painting.

Alex put it down and got his camera out, taking a quick photo of it. The picture didn't do it justice, of course. One needed to see it in the flesh, so to speak. Still, it looked pretty amazing trapped in his phone.

While he had hold of his phone, he couldn't resist a quick visit to Instagram – the social media site popular with artists, photographers and creatives. Just before he'd left Skopelos with Brenna, Alex had uploaded a photo of his latest canvas. Truth be told, he hadn't painted anything for a little while, but the landscape he'd shared had been painted in a wild moment of freedom when he'd been between drinking bouts and he'd felt the need to create something. He remembered the feeling still – the mad rush to grab his paints and brushes and to head somewhere – anywhere – and capture the scene.

He went to his page now and looked at the startlingly low number of likes and a darkness swelled inside him. All the old voices surfaced again.

Why do you bother?

There's no point.

You should just give up.

It was the same appalling dialogue in his head where he spoke in the second person, berating himself as if he were both angry teacher and naughty pupil.

Then, to compound the torture, he visited the page of an artist friend. Well, not a friend exactly – he'd never met the man. In fact, he thought of him more as a rival for his work was similar in style. Like Alex, he'd moved from the UK to the south of France and painted the landscape there. His Instagram feed was full of lavender fields and hill-top towns, market squares with fountains, boulangerie windows and picnic rugs casually thrown down in olive groves. His fans could never get enough.

Alex clicked on the latest painting on his rival's grid. It was a white track leading through a rural landscape. As a study in light and shade, it was okay. Well, perhaps a bit better than okay, but it wasn't spectacular, Alex thought. Certainly not spectacular enough to warrant all the likes and comments he'd garnered. How had he managed that when Alex's own feedback was so meagre?

Because you're not as good as him.

There was that voice again: the critic that had first materialised as his father but, slowly, had become an internal soundtrack.

He took a few deep breaths, trying to calm himself

naturally rather than with alcohol. He knew it would be harder to drink while he was at Slate House although he did happen to know where his father hid a bottle of whisky in his studio.

He glanced back at his father's painting, idly speculating what it might be worth. Four figures for sure – possibly five. He took another photo of it and, almost without thinking, uploaded the image onto his Instagram feed.

Unfinished work by Nicholas Bellwood, he wrote before choosing a few choice hashtags for extra reach.

He put his phone in the pocket of his trousers and glanced across the room at the shelves filled with art books and folders. It was a bit of a mess, but Alex knew where to look. It was somewhere behind the paint-splattered copy of a book called *Painter's Progress*. It didn't take him long to find and, pulling the huge tome out, he grinned as he saw the secret bottle and a single crystal glass. The whisky was a good one and, taking the lid off, he sniffed it appreciatively before pouring himself a generous measure. Then he raised his glass to one of his father's unfinished self-portraits and downed it in one.

Glancing at the door as if expecting Brenna to enter at any moment, Alex poured himself a second glass. The already half-empty bottle wouldn't last long at this rate, he thought, wondering if there might be another secret stash. Alex pulled a neighbouring book out from the shelf, but there wasn't anything behind it. He'd search the place properly later. He couldn't be expected to deal with the death of his father and not have a friendly bottle or two to help him through. He was a bit anxious about that, knowing that Brenna disapproved of him drinking. But she wasn't completely without compassion. She knew he liked the odd drink. It's just that the odd drink had turned into a few more than strictly necessary in recent weeks. Well, recent months if he was being perfectly honest with himself.

It was since the break-up with Aimée. That's what it was. He wasn't dependent on alcohol. He simply used it as a way to blur the edges of life a little. That's what it was meant for, right? Still, he'd have to find a way of topping up his supply if he couldn't find anything else at Slate House.

He walked around the studio, pulling books from the shelves and examining more paintings. There was a lot of stuff in here – stuff that they'd have to sort out. The task was daunting and he wasn't looking forward to it. Indeed, he'd hoped he'd be left out of it and that his sisters would do what needed to be done. He knew that wasn't fair, but he couldn't help how he felt. It was one of the reasons he'd left the country – to be as far from his family as he could be. He'd so desperately tried to find an identity of his own. And yet he was still trying to emerge from under the Bellwood name. It was recognisable wherever he went. Even in the far reaches of the Mediterranean, people had heard of Nicholas Bellwood. It was quite remarkable really and yet it baited Alex. Perhaps he should have changed his name. But that would have been unfair. He was a Bellwood. It was as much his name as it had been his father's.

It was all so exhausting. He cleared a stool of old newspapers and sat down for a moment, pulling his phone out and checking his page of Instagram. It was a horrible addiction and, as with the alcohol, he knew he should wean himself off it.

He groaned as he looked at the photo of his father's painting he'd recently uploaded. Unsurprisingly, the number of likes and comments had flooded in, surpassing anything he'd ever posted of his own. He read some of the comments.

This is sublime.

Is it for sale? DM me!

Just wow!

Alex felt hot with rage. Even beyond the grave, his father was still eclipsing him.

He was just contemplating removing the photo of the painting when Brenna burst into the room.

'Alex! What were you thinking?'

'What?'

'The painting! Father's painting!'

'What were you doing on Instagram?'

'Messaging a client. And then up you popped! You can't just upload images like that.'

'Why not?'

'Because they're not yours. They're Father's. Where is it, anyway?'

'The painting? Here.' Alex got up off the stool and crossed the room, pulling it out and showing it to Brenna. She approached it almost cautiously, as if afraid.

'It's beautiful.'

'So everyone's said.'

'What have they said? I only read the first few comments.'

Alex handed his phone to her and watched as she read the myriad messages.

'Don't worry, I'll delete it,' he told her.

Brenna shook her head. 'No, don't.'

'But I thought you–'

'It seems a shame to take it away from people now it's out

there.' Alex watched his sister's expression soften and sadden. 'They've missed him.'

'They haven't had long enough to,' Alex pointed out.

'That's not true. Haven't you been following his account? He'd not posted for months.'

'It wasn't him that posted anyway. Didn't he have a virtual assistant?'

'Well, his *assistant* hadn't posted for months. I expect Father wasn't easy to work with towards the end. Or maybe he hadn't produced any new work for a while.'

'There's lots here that seem new.'

Brenna slowly walked around the room, bending to examine the paintings.

'I'd love to frame some of these,' she said.

'Why didn't he ever use you as his framer?'

Brenna looked surprised by his question. 'You know Dad. Set in his ways.'

'But it would have been a great way of supporting you and keeping things in the family.'

'I don't think he liked my frames.'

'He said that?'

'He said it by not using them, didn't he?'

Alex shrugged. 'Who knows?'

'I know. If I'd made the best frames in the world at the best prices, he still wouldn't have used them. We just weren't a good fit.'

It was then that Cordelia popped her head around the door.

'You okay in here?' she asked.

Alex threw his little sister a poor attempt at a smile.

'I've just had Simon Grant on the phone. He'll be here around twelve.'

'With the will?' Brenna said.

'Yes.'

'I suppose it would be good to get it over and done with,' Alex said.

'That's what I was thinking so I said yes.'

'I think we pretty much know what we're in for anyway,' Brenna said.

'I guess,' Cordelia agreed.

'Why can't he just email the will to us?' Alex asked. 'Why does he have to come to the house?'

'I guess it's what Father wanted,' Brenna said.

'It seems a bit old-fashioned, doesn't it?' Alex went on. 'A bit dramatic.'

'Like one of those scenes from a film,' Cordelia said. 'You don't think it's going to be like that, do you? Some awful revelation that will have us all at each other's throats before teatime?'

Alex couldn't help smiling at the image painted by his sister. 'Nah,' he said. 'It's just Father being as pompous as ever.'

CHAPTER FIVE

Cordelia had hated watching her sister leave in the back of the taxi for her trip to Greece but knew she had to go. She'd felt a little lost for the first couple of hours and had drifted around Slate House like a ghost. Finally, though, she'd got herself into a rhythm and made good progress sorting out the kitchen and had worked her way through a heap of post too.

Then, in a moment of bravery, she'd dared to enter her father's bedroom. The curtains had been closed and she'd opened them, allowing the soft September light to bathe the room in gold. The lyrical beauty of the scene hadn't helped and she'd felt tears in her eyes before she'd even opened the wardrobe door. But she'd been determined to make a start at least and had pulled a few items out that she knew her father hadn't worn for years – the crisp, smart shirts and the tailored suits. They'd been for gallery events and he hadn't done one of those for some time. He'd preferred a soft blue denim shirt when at home – something with a bit of age and a bit of give. A shirt that wasn't too concerned if it got paint splattered on it. Cordelia had already found one in the laundry basket along with the last of the things that hadn't been washed. It had been a sad undertaking to load the washing machine with the clothes he'd last worn and she'd carefully folded them and taken them to his bedroom once they were dry.

By the end of the morning, she'd managed to collect three bags of clothes for charity. The denim shirts were still in the wardrobe and the soft wool round-neck sweaters he'd loved remained in the old chest of drawers that wobbled. She'd ask Brenna what to do. She couldn't take on the responsibility of parting with them. As she'd picked up one of the navy sweaters and held the soft material to her cheek, she could visualise him wearing it on a crisp autumn day as he marched through the garden, looking up at the sky, examining the view.

Later, she'd found one of his favourite winter scarves in the cupboard under the stairs and, in a moment of weakness, had wrapped it around her neck.

Father.

But having his clothes hadn't made her feel any closer to him, had it? He was gone and these clothes were just things. They weren't *him*. Some of the items seemed more intimate than others. His shoes for example. Cordelia picked up a pair. There was a little mud from the garden on the sole. Good old Lakeland mud. A part of her wanted to wash them and perhaps even give them a polish, but that seemed pointless when she thought about it. Or was it? She'd stood looking at them for a long time, stuck in indecision. Did the shoes really need cleaning or was it a strange need in her that wanted to be fulfilled?

The phone ringing had broken the solemn spell. It had been a wrong number, but it had been enough to shake her out of her mood and she'd made a little progress clearing the cupboard of old newspapers, carrier bags and tins of dried out shoe polish. She'd then opened every single drawer in the chest in the hallway. It was full of all the bits that accumulate over time: receipts, rubber bands, leaflets stuffed through the letterbox by local tradesmen, greeting cards, stationery and other detritus. She'd binned most of it, leaving a few items to go through with her siblings.

Cordelia felt like she'd made good progress during the time Brenna was away. But it was just the tip of a very large iceberg, she knew that.

And now Brenna was back and Alex was with her. Brenna was making a cup of tea in the kitchen, fortifying herself before the arrival of Mr Grant with the will. Alex was still in Father's studio. There'd been a fair bit of clattering around in there and she hadn't wanted to disturb him. Cordelia had only briefly entered that room the morning Brenna had left, but it had been too unspeakably sad to see it without her father standing at his easel and she'd quietly closed the door on it.

After popping into town in Brenna's car to buy some essentials, she'd returned home and made a sandwich, taking it out into the garden to eat on a bench which had the best view across Grasmere. Of course, she couldn't look at such a view without a thousand memories flashing before her: playing hide and seek with Brenna and Alex, learning to cartwheel and accidentally crashing into one of her father's favourite hydrangeas, and walks around the mere. It was one of the smallest in the Lake District and had a wonderful intimacy about it. It might not have the same appeal to tourists as Windermere or Ullswater, or the stately gravitas of Wastwater, but it was a friendly mere – a place where one felt safe and comforted.

It wasn't ever going to be the same now. First Mother and then Father. Could you still call a place home when your parents were no longer there? And what would actually happen to Slate House? Cordelia knew they'd have to wait for the executor to let them know her father's wishes, but she couldn't imagine that the house would remain in their family if it was, indeed, left to them. Brenna would never want to live there, Alex was happier abroad these days, and Cordelia's place was London.

She got up off the bench and turned to look at the imposing façade with its steep gables and tall chimneys. She knew it was a house which Brenna had never loved, but Cordelia couldn't help adoring it. Perhaps she had similar sensibilities to her father whereas Brenna had taken after their mother. Cordelia had always been drawn to the dramatic, the gothic, the imposing. She loved the ornate chimneys and the arched windows. It was all like a film or stage set. Maybe it was the actress in her that responded to it so much. Anyway, whatever it was, she loved the place and it broke her heart to think of it being sold as surely it must be. It felt much too soon in her life to lose the family home.

As she returned inside, she saw the pile of bin bags she'd filled and felt guilty, traitorous for throwing her father's things away. But that's what she was here for. She and her siblings had to sort things out, as painful as that might be.

Cordelia went upstairs to her bedroom to freshen up before Mr Grant's arrival. Their father had never talked openly about finances and nobody had even thought to broach the subject with him. They'd never been spoilt growing up, but there was always enough. Each of the Bellwood children had been encouraged to go to university and to take driving lessons. Independence of thought as well as spirit was deemed important. However, Nicholas Bellwood hadn't gone as far as to buy any of his children their first car. They'd each been expected to save up their own money from jobs they found for themselves.

Cordelia looked around her bedroom now. It was still filled with all her teenage collections of books, clothes and jewellery. There was a poster of a band who'd long gone out of favour and a selection of cheap perfumes she no longer used. She'd have to sort it all out, she thought, feeling a pang that this friendly little room at the top of Slate House was fast disappearing from her and that she wouldn't be able to return to it whenever she felt like it. During her student years, it had been a relief to leave the capital during the holidays and journey back to Cumbria. For those precious few years, she'd had Father to herself. Brenna had moved to Yorkshire to start her picture framing business and Alex was living a nomadic life in Europe.

It had been a time of relative calm because there wasn't the friction that came from her siblings' relationship with Father. She'd sometimes felt guilty for enjoying being the only one of them still at home and it made her sad when she thought about how awkward they'd both felt around him and how very happy she'd always been in his company. It was hard when the ones you loved didn't love each other.

She glanced out of the window down into the garden. Her room overlooked the sweep of driveway and the mere beyond. It was the view she'd grown up with and it had changed very little over the years. The rhododendrons were a little bigger but, otherwise, it was the same.

It was as she was daydreaming, her gaze soft on the mere beyond, that she saw a black BMW coming up the drive and she knew she could hide in her room no longer. It was time to hear her father's will.

Simon Grant was a short, neat man in his fifties with close-cropped hair, a large pair of glasses and the shiniest shoes Cordelia had ever seen. Had he stood still long enough she would have been tempted to check her reflection in them, but he had an anxious sort of twitch about him and, after he'd declined a cup of tea, Brenna quickly led him into the dining room so they could get down to business.

He walked to the head of the table, his back to the large mullioned window as he sat down and placed his briefcase in front of him, opening it with a professional click and pulling out a manila file. Cordelia turned on a lamp in the corner to cheer the overcast afternoon and watched as Brenna and Alex took seats either side of Mr Grant. She couldn't help feeling glad that she didn't have to sit next to him herself.

There was a bit of throat clearing before he began.

'First of all, may I offer you all my sincere condolences on the loss of your father,' he began.

Brenna thanked him politely. Alex rolled his eyes. He'd always hated perceived false politeness such as this.

'I think, perhaps, you'll have some idea of the contents of the will. It is fairly straightforward and I have made copies for each of you which I'll let you see once I've had a chance to go through things. Foremost, of course, is Slate House. Your father has left it in equal shares to the three of you so it's up to you whether you keep it or sell it and divide the money.

The bequest also includes all the contents including furniture, fittings, and art works – finished and unfinished.'

Cordelia nodded and looked at her brother and sister. She could see Brenna's hands nervously twisting around themselves in her lap and Alex looked pale and tired.

'There are also considerable savings,' Mr Grant went on. 'ISAs, various bank accounts and shares which will need to be liquidated and divided between the three of you.'

Mr Grant then went on to list a few other sundries, but it seemed to Cordelia that the main business of the day was done.

'Any art currently out with galleries?' Alex asked.

'That will be returned to the estate and it will be up to the three of you to decide what to do with it. You may want to speak to a professional – a colleague in the art world – to advise you.'

'Or just sell everything on eBay?' Alex said with a laugh.

Cordelia gasped and Brenna shot him a look across the table.

'What? It was just a joke!'

'Well, of course, it's up to you how you proceed,' Mr Grant said.

'I was just joking!' Alex repeated.

'Anyway, moving on to the more delicate part of the will...'

Mr Grant paused, pushing his glasses as far up the bridge of his nose as they would go. Cordelia suddenly felt nervous.

'Your father also wanted me to tell you this. I did advise him that he should discuss it with you himself.'

'What is it?' Alex asked, his voice clipped and hostile.

'There's another property. In Cornwall. Your father may have mentioned it perhaps?'

Brenna glanced at her siblings. 'No, he never did.'

'He went to Cornwall a lot,' Cordelia said. 'For work. He loved to paint there.'

'Yes, of course,' Mr Grant said.

'I thought he stayed in some hotel,' Alex added.

Mr Grant shuffled his papers and pushed his glasses up his nose again even though they hadn't slipped down. 'No, he owned a house there, and he's leaving it to Daisy Bellwood.'

'Who's that?' Alex asked. 'Some relative we've never heard of?'

'Does she live in the house?' Brenna asked.

Mr Grant cleared his throat. 'Yes.'

There was a horrible silence as Mr Grant stared down at the papers in front of him, seemingly reluctant to go on.

'What are you not telling us, Mr Grant?' Brenna pressed.

He looked at her. 'Daisy Bellwood has lived in the house since birth.'

'How old is she?' Cordelia asked.

Mr Grant glanced down at his papers as if searching for the answer. 'She's nineteen.'

Cordelia tried to work out what exactly was being said.

'Who is she?' Alex demanded.

'She's your father's daughter.'

The words hung in the air for a moment, alien and absurd. Daisy Bellwood. Father's daughter.

Cordelia felt as if she'd been pinned to her chair by the words and she surprised herself by being the first to speak.

'We have a sister?'

'I suppose she would be your half-sister,' Mr Grant pointed out.

'Is her mother living at that house too?' Brenna dared to

ask and Cordelia immediately tried to picture this other life her father had been living.

'I believe so.'

'What's her name?' Cordelia asked.

'Angelina.'

'Not Bellwood, surely?' Brenna said.

'No. Hone, I believe.'

'I don't believe a word of it,' Alex stated.

'I know it's a lot to process,' Mr Grant said, leaning forward slightly in his chair. 'But you'll each have the will to read through in your own time and I'm always available to answer any questions, although I fear that my knowledge about private matters is limited. As you know, along with Brenna, I'm your father's executor and it's my responsibility to see that everything is handled as swiftly and smoothly as possible.'

'Does Daisy know about all this?' Brenna asked.

'She knows about you and your siblings, but she doesn't know the details of the will yet. I was instructed to let you know first.'

'Oh, good for Father – to let his *legitimate* children know of his wishes first!' Alex said, bitterness fuelling his voice.

'Alex, that's not going to help,' Cordelia said.

'No?'

'We might as well deal with this calmly.'

Alex glared at her. 'Calmly? How can you be calm about this? Our father had another family that he kept hidden in Cornwall!'

Mr Grant opened his brief case and retrieved three manila envelopes which he handed to each of them.

'Fantastic!' Alex said. 'Do we have contact details for this *relative* of ours?'

'The address of the property in Cornwall is in the will.'

'No phone number?' Alex asked abruptly.

Mr Grant shook his head.

'So what are we meant to do with this information?'

'Alex, let's just let this settle, shall we?' Brenna said and Cordelia nodded in agreement, aware that Mr Grant was now standing up, eager to leave.

'I'm sorry if this has come as something of a shock,' he said, not looking at any of them in particular. Cordelia couldn't help feeling sorry for the man and wondered how often he had to handle awkward situations like this.

Brenna stood up and led him out of the room, thanking him politely. Cordelia and Alex stayed seated for a moment.

'He's gone,' Brenna told them a moment later from the doorway.

'Thank god that's over with,' Alex said, getting up at last and pushing past her. 'I need a drink.'

'I'll put the kettle on,' Cordelia said, joining him and Brenna in the hallway.

'Not *that* kind of drink!' He stalked through to the kitchen and Cordelia and Brenna followed him. For a few minutes, the three of them busied themselves – the sisters making tea and Alex banging cupboards.

'There must be at least *one* bottle of wine in this house!'

'I don't think there is,' Cordelia said.

'Most of these cupboards are empty.'

'Cordy and I have been clearing things.'

'And you're telling me there wasn't any wine?'

'Yep.'

Alex cursed.

'I'll make you a strong tea,' Cordelia told him, taking pity on his nerves which seemed to be completely shredded. She had to establish how she was feeling. The words of the executor were still hovering somewhere beyond her.

'Ridiculous man!' Alex said.

'Who?' Brenna asked. 'Mr Grant?'

'No. Father. Fancy not having a proper drink in the house.'

'Wasn't there anything in his studio?'

Cordelia saw a sly sort of look cross Alex's face.

'No.'

Brenna popped tea bags into the mugs that Cordelia had placed on the countertop. 'I thought he always kept a bottle in there.'

Cordelia glanced between her brother and sister. Alex was visibly twitching.

'I can run out and get some supplies if you like.'

'You don't have to do that,' Brenna told her.

'I don't mind.'

'Alex can manage, I'm sure, can't you?'

'Do I have a choice?'

Tea made, they each took a mug and sat at the table. It was covered in odd items Cordelia had pulled out of the cupboards and which she hadn't been sure what to do with. There was a brand new tin of jasmine tea from Fortnum and Masons, a pair of Laurel and Hardy salt and pepper shakers and a vintage jug she remembered from childhood. It was a pretty thing with a floral design. It had been Mother's and she'd always been upset when Father insisted on having it in his studio as part of a still life.

'It always comes back paint splattered,' she'd complain, but he never listened. Indeed, Cordelia could see a distinct flake of green paint marring the cream glaze of the jug's neck. There were also a few packets of food which were still in date including a surprising number of sweets. Had Father developed a sudden taste for them? Alex eyed them up now, reached for a bag of strawberry bonbons and ripped them open.

'In the absence of wine...' He threw one into his mouth. Brenna grimaced and then took the bag from him and did the same.

'What are we going to do?' Cordelia asked.

'About this Daisy person?' Alex said.

'Will she be at the funeral? Are we going to meet her?'

'I've no idea,' Brenna said.

Cordelia reached for the bag of bonbons. 'Why didn't Father ever tell us?'

'I honestly don't know.'

'And to have a house down there. Do you think there are photos of it somewhere?' Cordelia said.

'I doubt it,' Alex said. 'They're probably all down there in Cornwall. Father was always good at compartmentalising, wasn't he?'

Brenna popped another bonbon into her mouth. 'Did Mother know? Or did he hide it from her too?'

Alex frowned. 'How old did he say Daisy is?'

'Nineteen, I think.'

'Then he was obviously seeing this Angelina woman while Mother was still here with us at Slate House.'

They all took a moment for the weight of this to sink in. Had Mother known and challenged her husband? Or had she turned a blind eye? Was Daisy ever mentioned at all? There were so many questions and it didn't seem likely that they'd find the answers now.

'I'm not the youngest,' Cordelia blurted out.

'What?' Brenna looked confused.

'I always thought I was the youngest child, but I'm not. She is. Daisy.'

'She's not a real Bellwood,' Alex told her.

'She's our sister.'

'Half-sister. *If* we're to believe all this – which I don't!'

'Why would Father lie about this?' Cordelia asked.

'He wouldn't,' Brenna said.

'God! What a mess!' Alex exclaimed. 'I don't know what to believe.'

'What are we going to do?' Cordelia asked again.

'I don't think there's much we can do,' Brenna said.

'If she's Father's child, don't you think it's a bit rough that we've got to split Slate House three ways while she gets the whole of this place in Cornwall?' Alex pointed out.

'Well, trust you to think of that,' Brenna said. 'Anyway, we don't know how big it is.'

'And we do get all the paintings he left.'

'Except whatever's down there in Cornwall, I'm guessing. We could contest all this, you know.'

'We'll do no such thing,' Brenna warned him.

There was a moment's silence when the only sound was the chewing of bonbons.

'D!' Alex cried.

'Pardon?' Brenna narrowed her eyes at him.

'Daisy – D!'

Cordelia cottoned on. 'A, B, C. And now D.'

Brenna sighed. 'Good grief! At least he was consistent.'

'I wonder if there's an E somewhere too. Or even a bloody F!'

'Alex!' Cordelia felt shocked by the implication.

'We never saw many of the paintings he did in Cornwall, did we?' Brenna said.

'No, they went straight to the gallery he had down there,' Alex confirmed.

'I'm trying to remember how he was when he used to come home from those trips. Leaving one family for another,' Brenna said.

'Don't! We've enough to process with losing him without this sort of...' Cordelia paused.

'Complication?' Brenna finished for her.

'I wonder what she knows about us,' Cordelia said. 'She's on her own down there. At least we've got each other.'

'She lives with her mother, doesn't she?' Brenna pointed out.

'Oh, yes.'

'*Angelina!*' Alex spat the name out. 'How pretentious is that?'

'It's no more ridiculous than my name,' Cordelia said with a tiny smile.

'Who wants the last bonbon?' Alex asked.

'We've never eaten the entire packet?' Brenna's face filled with disgust.

'I guess we're all emotional eaters,' Alex said. 'In the absence of alcohol at least.'

'I've only had two,' Cordelia protested and Alex handed her the bag. 'No, you can have it.'

Alex threw the final sweet into his mouth.

'Remember that painting Father did of us all in the garden?' Cordelia asked.

'Which one? There were a lot of them,' Brenna said.

'Mother was in it.'

Brenna nodded. 'Holding you as a baby? That one?'

'What happened to it?'

'Probably long gone. I don't remember seeing it much after he painted it.'

'I thought it was just another family portrait. He used to make us pose for so many, but now I think...'

'What?' Alex and Brenna asked together.

'It might have been different.'

'What do you mean?' Alex sounded frustrated and grabbed the bonbon bag, licking his finger and sticking it inside in an attempt to retrieve any candy dust. 'What's so special about that painting?'

Cordelia paused before answering, trying to bring the details of the image before her. 'I think we're all together in it.'

'Er – yeah – that's what a family portrait is,' Alex said.

'I mean with Daisy.'

Brenna frowned. 'He painted us with Daisy?'

'I think so.'

'That's a twisted thing to do, isn't it?' Alex cried. 'And how do you remember this when we obviously don't?'

'I'm not sure, but something keeps nudging me. I can see little fragments of it in my mind. I'd really like to try and track it down.'

'Well, good luck with that,' Brenna said as she got up. 'I'm going out.'

'Where are you going?' Cordelia asked.

'I need some air. I'm going for a walk.'

'Want some company?' Cordelia followed her to the front door and watched as her sister pulled on a pair of boots.

'No thanks. I just need some space, okay?'

Cordelia nodded, recognising her sister's mood.

CHAPTER SIX

Brenna had to get out into the open air. It was early afternoon and the light was gold and glorious. A recent light shower had made the blackberries in the hedge shiny and irresistible and Brenna's fingers nipped a few from their thorny stems, enjoying the natural sweetness after overdosing on bonbons.

She hadn't planned to walk to Yewdale Farm, but her feet had somehow taken her there. She stood for a moment at the entrance to the yard, the soft sound of the pigs' grunts her only greeting. Blue was probably in a faraway field and Linnet at school. She sighed, wondering what she should do when she heard a series of expletives coming from the nearest barn. Brenna grinned. It was definitely her friend and, like her name, her language was pretty blue too.

'Blue?' Brenna called. 'Are you okay?'

'Bren?' Blue joined her in the farmyard, blinking in the sunshine after the dark interior of the barn. 'What brings you here?

'If you've got a mo, I'll tell you.'

Blue nodded, wiping her hands on the khaki overalls she was wearing. 'Trying to fix an ancient machine with ancient tools,' she said, nodding back to the barn.

'Sounded painful.'

'Yeah, but I'm not giving up. I'll get there. Come on – let's put the kettle on. I've been meaning to take a break for the last four hours.'

A few minutes later they were sitting on a bench in a small garden at the back of the farmhouse which looked out over the fells. The garden comprised of a rough lawn, some wildflowers and a lot of brambles.

After taking a sip of her tea, Blue nodded towards the brambles. 'Plenty of fruit this year.'

'I had a few in the lane. They're so sweet.'

'Plenty of apples too in our orchard. I'll be filling the freezer with apple and blackberry pies and crumbles to see us through the winter,' Blue told her. 'But enough about pies. What's going on with you?'

Brenna took a deep breath, inhaling the sweet Lakeland air and wishing she could float away on it, high above Wordsworth's clouds. But the reality of the situation she found herself in meant that her feet had to remain very firmly on the ground. 'We've just had Father's executor round to read the will.'

'Oh, heavens! And how did that go?'

'One or two surprises.'

'Yeah?'

Brenna nodded, her gaze fixed on the middle distance as she sounded out the strange sentence for the first time. 'We have a half-sister we knew nothing about.'

Blue spluttered her tea, soaking her overalls. 'What?'

'Our father had a family down in Cornwall that he never told us about. Nice, huh?'

'What kind of a family?'

'Some kind of lover and their daughter.'

'You're kidding me!'

'I wish I was. But the daughter's nineteen now. Her name's Daisy and she lives with her mother, Angelina, in a property that we knew absolutely nothing about.'

'How did he keep all that hidden from you?'

Brenna shrugged. 'It was just his way, wasn't it?' she said, hearing the bitterness in her own voice and not liking the sound of it. 'He rarely spoke of anything of importance. At least not to me. But even Cordelia had no idea about any of this and she was the closest to him. It's come as a bit of a shock.'

'I bet!' Blue whistled and shook her head. 'Are you going to meet this Daisy?'

'I don't know.'

'What do Alex and Cordelia think?'

'Alex is emotionally eating his way through anything he can find and Cordelia seems fixated on some painting she remembers from childhood.'

'What's so special about the painting?'

'She reckons we're all in it. All four of Nicholas Bellwood's children.'

'Really? He painted you all together?'

'I don't think so. But Cordelia seems convinced. I can't remember any painting like that and that's something you'd remember, isn't it?'

'I don't know. I sometimes can't even remember where I've left my slippers,' Blue confessed.

'It's just so hard to imagine that he could switch between two families so easily and none of us ever saw it.'

'So this other woman – she came after your mother left?'

'No, not if Daisy's nineteen.'

'Did your mum know?'

'I've no idea.'

'Blimey.'

'We just thought he was working in Cornwall. We didn't think anything of us not going with him. It was his work place. At least, that's what we all thought.'

'Wow!' Blue said. 'That's some bombshell.'

'I know.'

'How are you feeling?'

Brenna shrugged. 'Shocked. Numb. Angry. I don't know.'

'Does this sister – *half*-sister – know about you and Alex and Cordelia?'

'Yes.'

They sat together, gazing into the golden afternoon, listening to the bleat of the nearby sheep and the happy grunts of the pigs in the farmyard. It was so easy to forget about the outside world when at Yewdale Farm. It was a perfect little bubble of a place. No wonder Blue had never left, Brenna couldn't help thinking.

'What's the time?' Blue suddenly said, looking at her watch. 'Ah, school's out.'

'Do you have to pick Linnet up?'

'The bus drops her at the end of the lane, but I always go and meet her there with Midge.'

The two of them got up off the bench.

'I'm sorry to come over and dump all this onto you,' Brenna said.

'Hey – don't apologise. We're friends, right? I'm here to

listen whenever you need to talk.' She smiled. 'Want to walk down the lane with me?'

Brenna shook her head. 'Actually, I think I'll take the footpath over the fell. Delay my journey back home a little bit longer.'

Blue nodded. 'Look out for the blackberries by the old barn up there. Sweet as candy. But don't pick them all,' she warned.

'I promise!'

They laughed and said goodbye and Brenna took the path that led from the back of the farm – the one she'd used to take as a child. It wasn't open to the public and it was a longer route back to Slate House than the lanes, but Brenna needed the extra time to herself. It began with a steep climb and, once at the top, she turned back to look down on Yewdale Farm. How pretty it looked from above, she thought. It had a charm about it that she'd never found at Slate House and, for a moment, she couldn't help envying Blue's relatively uncomplicated life there. She'd had her share of sadness of course, losing both parents quite close to each other, and the life she'd chosen for herself, taking on the running of the farm as a single parent, wasn't an easy one. But, if anyone could make it work, it was Blue.

Brenna walked through a little wood, a distant view of Grasmere strobing through the slim tree trunks. There was nobody else around. No hikers to disturb her peace and she was thankful for it. The Lake District tourists could sometimes be overwhelming if you wanted to find a little bit of space and freedom. Hikers, bikers and Instagrammers were everywhere these days and it was often difficult to escape them all.

When she got back to Slate House, the door to Father's

studio was open. Both Alex and Cordelia were in there and they seemed to be hunting for something.

'It was done in the garden,' Cordelia said. Brenna sighed. She was still going on about the mysterious portrait.

'I'm back!' Brenna cried from the door.

'Oh good. You can help us look,' Cordelia told her.

'She's driving me crazy, Bren!' Alex confessed, standing back up to full height after being bent double over a stack of unframed paintings.

'Where have you looked?'

'Everywhere! I don't think it's here, Cordy,' Alex told her.

'Do you even know what you're looking for?'

'I know what a family portrait looks like!' Alex snapped back. 'And I've not seen anything but landscapes and self-portraits here.'

'Do you remember it, Bren?'

'Not really, no. Perhaps Father sold it.'

'Would he? I thought he kept all the family portraits. What would anyone else want with a painting of someone else's children?'

'You'd be surprised what people buy,' Alex said. 'I once painted this really enormous nude and it sold immediately. Imagine having a painting of a fat naked stranger on your walls.'

Cordelia's nose wrinkled in alarm.

'Well, I still don't remember the painting,' Brenna confessed.

Cordelia sighed. She looked exhausted. 'Would you mind if I visited Father's old gallery in Keswick to see if they remember it?'

'Why not just ring?' Alex asked.

'I think this kind of thing is better face to face – less chance of them brushing me off.'

'You're really serious about finding this, aren't you?' Brenna said.

Cordelia nodded.

'It was a long time ago, Cordy,' Alex said kindly.

'I know. But they might have a record of it in a catalogue or something.'

'What do you think it's going to prove?' Brenna dared to ask. 'We already know about Daisy and I don't put it past Father to have painted us altogether.'

'I just need to see it again.'

Brenna could see there'd be no dissuading her. 'Do you want me to run you into Keswick?'

'No, I'll get the bus.'

'Is there time?'

'The gallery's open until five thirty.'

Cordelia made her way out into the hall and Brenna followed her.

'Look, I know it seems as if I'm slipping away from all the chaos here,' Cordelia said, 'but I did a fair amount while you were away.'

'I know. You don't need an excuse or to ask my permission. Do what you need to do.'

Cordelia leaned forward and hugged her sister. 'Thanks.'

'And give me a call if you find anything, okay?'

Brenna watched as her sister grabbed her bag and coat from the hook by the door and left the house.

~

As Cordelia got off the bus in Keswick, she realised that she hadn't been to her father's art gallery for some years. It didn't take her long to find and, luckily, nobody had decided to shut up shop early. Suddenly, she felt nervous and rather childish in her mission, but she'd made an effort to come here and didn't want to back out now so she entered the shop.

Fenton Fine Art was a wonderfully light and airy gallery with shiny blond floorboards, white walls and comfortable chairs at convenient intervals. The space was mostly dedicated to paintings, but there were a few choice sculptures too – some in bronze, some in resin.

Being the daughter of an artist, Cordelia had visited her fair share of galleries over the years and yet they still weren't places she was completely comfortable in. She preferred the informality of an artist's studio over the pristine surroundings of a gallery. A painting still wet on an easel was far more approachable than one hanging spotlit on a white wall. Still, as galleries went, this was a rather beautiful one and she could remember the solo shows her father had had here over the years.

Her father had felt the same way as she had. He'd never been at home with a room full of people. People he was meant to be impressing. She could still see his tight smile and the awkward angles of him as he stood with a wine glass in his hand making small talk. He'd always hated small talk even when it was about his own work.

'The work should speak for itself,' he'd complain. 'I shouldn't need to be here.' But his presence did seem to add something, Cordelia had noted that even as a teenager. She'd seen the way patrons would sidle over to him, anxious to speak to the great artist. The women would flirt over their wine glasses and the men would vie with one another to buy the most expensive pieces in the exhibition. That's what it was all about really – those little red dots that paid the bills and allowed Nicholas Bellwood to go on doing what he loved most in the world. So he put up with the painful preview nights when he had to shave and dress up, swapping his big comfy boots for insubstantial shoes, and his big baggy collarless shirts for stiff white ones that choked him. And – the final insult – a tie.

Cordelia looked around now. The gallery was empty.

'Hello?' she called gently, making her way to the desk at the back. 'Anyone here?'

A young man appeared from the room at the rear. He was tall and slim, wearing blue jeans and a navy waistcoat. His hair was a mad mass of corn-coloured curls and his eyes were the colour of autumn chestnuts.

'Hello there,' he said with a wide smile that was so infectious that Cordelia couldn't help smiling back. 'Can I help you?'

'I hope so but... I'm not sure. I mean, I don't know.' Cordelia gave a helpless shrug and then felt even more childish than she had a few minutes ago. This was a terrible idea.

'Sounds... intriguing.'

She cleared her throat and decided to start again. 'I'm Cordelia.'

'I'm Dylan. Dylan Fenton.'

'You own the gallery?'

'No. I just run it for my father. He retired five years ago. He still has a hand in all the shows but the day-to-day running is down to me now.'

'I see. Well, my father died recently and–'

'I'm sorry to hear that.'

'Thank you. Nicholas Bellwood.'

Dylan's bright eyes widened when he heard the name.

'And you're Cordelia Bellwood?'

She nodded.

'I've seen a painting of you, haven't I?'

'That's very possible.'

'Yes, yes! I remember it quite well. You were running through the garden in a blue dress, chasing a butterfly.'

Cordelia felt tears pricking her eyes at the mention of the picture she'd long forgotten. 'How do you remember that?'

'I have a good memory for paintings.'

'That might be very helpful because it's a painting of my father's I'm trying to track down.'

'If I remember rightly, he left Fenton's, didn't he? Took his work to The Wentworth Gallery on Cork Street?' Dylan said.

'Yes, but there's a particular painting I'm trying to track down and I think it was sold through this gallery.'

'Do you know when?'

'I'd guess it would be some time in the early 2000's. I think it was called *Family Portrait*, but I'm not sure. That might just be the name I've given it over the years.'

Dylan nodded. 'Right. It might be hard to track down.'

'Do you keep records?'

'We do. And we did going back to the eighties when my dad first opened Fenton's, but I'm afraid all the catalogues from 2014 and before were destroyed in a flood in the basement.'

'Oh no!'

'Yes. It was a great loss. My father kept absolutely every catalogue of every single one of his shows. There was a lot of other stuff down there too – newspapers, art magazines. All sorts of interesting art memorabilia.'

'And you don't have any computerised records of the earlier shows?'

'No, my father was old school. He hates computers.'

'So there's no way of knowing if this painting was sold via Fenton's?'

'I'm afraid not,' Dylan said.

Cordelia sighed. She hadn't thought that she'd come to a dead end quite so quickly.

'Unless...' Dylan said, tapping the air with his right hand like a conductor leading an orchestra.

'Unless what?'

'Crompton!'

'What's that?'

'*That* is a *he*. Henry Crompton. He's one of our best collectors. He's got a fair few of our paintings.'

'You think he might have *Family Portrait*?'

'He's more of a landscape and still life kind of guy so probably not, but he might well have the catalogue it featured in if it was, indeed, sold through our gallery.'

'How do I get in touch with him? Is he local?'

'He's in Cumbria. He has one of those white stonewashed cottages in Langdale. It's a tiny place, but it's stuffed with art. I've delivered paintings to him a few times over the years and it's always a joy to see what he has in that tiny home. There isn't a single wall that isn't covered.'

Cordelia smiled. 'He sounds fascinating.'

'Oh, he is. I could give him a call if you like.'

'Really? That would be great.'

He looked at the clock on the wall behind the desk. 'Tell

you what – give me your number and I'll give you a call once I've got in touch with Henry.'

'It's really kind of you,' Cordelia told him as they exchanged numbers.

'It's my pleasure,' he said, looking up from his phone. 'Do you mind me asking what's so special about this particular painting? I mean apart from it being a family portrait by your father.'

Cordelia hesitated before answering, but the open expression of his face made her trust him somehow.

'I remember something about it. Something... significant. At least I think I do. But perhaps I'm wrong. It's been a long time since I last saw it and I was very young. I might be completely mistaken, but I'd like to see it again.'

'Are you hoping to buy it?'

'I don't think I could afford to.'

'You'll be inheriting something from your father's estate, won't you?' he asked. 'Sorry – it's none of my business.' He held his hands up as if shielding her from his question.

'No, you're right. But that takes time, doesn't it? Everything's all tied up.'

'Yes. Of course. I hope you don't mind me asking.'

'No. It's fine. And I'm sorry if I'm being a bit... odd. This is all so strange. I never thought I'd be going through this right now. It all seems too soon.' Cordelia stopped. She hadn't meant to say so much, to *feel* so much. Not in front of a stranger. But there was something about this man that made her feel instantly comfortable. Was that the right word? She looked at him for a moment and decided that it was. She'd thought she'd feel awkward and silly making such a request, but he'd put her completely at ease.

Suddenly, a wave of sadness engulfed her, taking her

completely by surprise, and she was crying before she could stop herself. Maybe it was his kindness. Maybe it was that he was a stranger and she had been holding herself together for her siblings since the reading of the will. Or maybe it was just time to cry again. She'd found over the last few days that she didn't have control of her emotions at all. Things that she'd thought might set her off like the reading of the will had been handled without so much as a single sob. Now, standing in an art gallery, her vision blurred and her body felt hollow and fragile.

'Hey!' Dylan scooted out from behind the desk. 'Come and sit down.'

'I'm okay!' she said, attempting to leave the shop, but stumbling as she crossed the floor.

'No. No. I don't think you are. Come and sit. Let me get you a tea or coffee, hey?'

She shook her head. 'I don't want to make a fuss.'

'It's no fuss. Really.'

She wiped her eyes with a tissue from her pocket. She'd taken to carrying at least half a dozen about her person recently and was glad of that now. Dylan's face came into focus and she nodded.

'Okay. A tea would be nice.'

'Good. Milk? Sugar?'

'Just one sugar please.'

He disappeared into the back room and she took the opportunity to blow her nose good and hard and mop her eyes again. She must look a state, she couldn't help thinking. She always did when she cried. She wasn't pretty when the tears came. Her eyes turned instantly red and her cheeks blotched horribly, making her look like an angry strawberry. She took a few deep breaths and hoped he took his time making the tea so that her face stood a chance of returning to something approaching normal.

'Hey,' he said a moment later, coming through with two teas. He handed a mug to her. It was made of slate-coloured pottery. Simple, elegant and beautiful.

'Thank you,' she said, without daring to look up at him.

'You're welcome. You okay?'

She nodded and sipped her tea. 'I'm sorry.'

'No need to apologise.'

'I don't usually cry in front of strangers.'

'Well, I'd say you're going through a rather unusual time.'

'I suppose.'

'Is there anything I can do to help?'

'You have already.'

He nodded. 'Good.'

She finished her tea and stood up. 'I'd better get going. I've taken up enough of your time.'

He took the mug from her. 'I'll give Henry a call this evening and let you know if he's got any of the old catalogues.'

'Thanks.' She paused by the door. 'For everything.'

'It was nice to meet you, Cordelia.'

'Call me Cordy. All my friends do.'

She was treated to one of Dylan's big, wide smiles again and she mirrored it completely.

Cordelia left the gallery. There was a light drizzle of rain and the sky had darkened, but she couldn't help feeling just a little lighter than when she'd entered Fenton Fine Art and she had Dylan to thank for that. He'd been so helpful. But more than that – he'd been kind.

~

Cordelia felt utterly exhausted by the time she got back to Slate House. Brenna was in the kitchen, stacking pans into a cardboard box. She looked pretty tired too. It had been a draining day for them all.

'How did you get on?' Brenna asked as Cordelia entered the room.

'Good. The owner – well, the owner's son – is going to try and help me track down the painting. They haven't got a record of it, though, because the old catalogues were lost, but he knows someone who may have some.'

Brenna nodded and gave a thin smile which didn't have half the wattage of Dylan's, Cordelia couldn't help thinking.

'I know you think I'm silly wanting to find this painting and I can't really explain why it's important to me.'

'I don't think you're silly at all,' Brenna declared. 'Listen, grief does weird things to a person and you have to find your own way through it.'

'Yeah?'

'Yes. For the first few days after we got the news about Father, I kept playing Mozart's piano concerto 27 on loop. The second movement – the larghetto.'

'His favourite?'

Brenna nodded. 'He used to play it when he was signing his paintings and listening to it kind of kept him close to me.' She paused. 'Even though we weren't that close in life, I still felt a connection to him when I played that music. Does that make sense?'

Cordelia nodded. 'You keep saying you weren't close, Bren, but you still carry him inside you. Without getting all scientific or anatomical about it, he's in your DNA. I even feel that sometimes. I often find myself knowing that he had a thought that I'm having. I just *feel* him inside my mind somehow! I see him too. Sometimes, I'll glance in the mirror and catch an expression that's pure him.'

'You have his eyes for sure.'

'I do?'

'Very expressive.'

Cordelia approached Brenna and gave her a hug. She wasn't sure if it was because Brenna looked like she needed one or that she needed one herself. And it didn't really matter.

'We just have to find our own ways through this,' Brenna told her. 'So do whatever you need to do, okay?'

'Okay.'

There was a moment's silence as they stood hugging in the kitchen.

'Where's Alex?' Cordelia asked.

'He's doing what he needs to do. Out buying wine.'

CHAPTER SEVEN

Daisy Bellwood had been twelve years old when she'd learned that she had a brother and two sisters. It wasn't a massive revelation that she remembered with clarity; it was a quiet, subtle moment that she might have missed if she hadn't been listening properly. The news had been imparted to her with such casualness that it had all seemed perfectly normal.

It was on one of those glorious summer trips her father made to Cornwall. She'd been sitting outside on the patio which overlooked the garden that sloped down to the river and the woods. They'd just finished a light lunch and were sipping ice-cold lemonade.

'It's raining in Cumbria,' Dad had begun. He'd had a slightly smug look on his face as if congratulating himself on having made the decision to be in Cornwall instead of the cold, damp north. 'But I guess I'll have to head back soon. Before the end of the school holidays at least.'

'Why do you spend so much time there and not with us?' Daisy had asked.

'It's where my family is.'

'But *we're* your family,' Daisy had told him as if he needed reminding.

'His *other* family,' her mother, had said. 'More lemonade?'

Dad nodded and Mum had poured him another glass from the jug, the ice cubes clinking and drowning the mint leaves Daisy had picked earlier.

At first, Daisy had thought they were talking about her paternal grandparents whom she'd never met. But Dad never talked about them.

'You have a brother and two sisters,' Dad said after he'd finished his second lemonade. 'Alex, Brenna and Cordelia.'

Her mother had got up from the table at that point, her lips tight, no words forthcoming. Daisy watched her as she went inside before her gaze turned to her dad again.

'How old are they?' she'd asked.

'Alex is twenty-seven now. Brenna's twenty-five and Cordelia is fifteen.'

Daisy sat with these three startling facts for a minute. She wasn't quite sure what surprised her the most: the knowledge that she had three siblings, two of whom were adults, or the way in which the information had been relayed to her so casually over the lemonade. Her dad seemed completely unperturbed. He might have been telling her that the sunny weather was about to break or that he'd run out of crimson alizarin paint.

Alex, Brenna and Cordelia. The names, particularly the girls', seemed positively exotic, making her feel deeply insecure about her own. Daisy. It was quite dull really when you thought about it. Weren't daisies one of the most common flowers? Pretty as they were, they had no scent and were really no more than weeds. And it didn't seem right that her mother whose own name was Angelina, seemed to chime, had chosen such a prosaic one for her.

Perhaps she should make up her own name. She really should be called something more beautiful as the daughter of an artist. But, sitting there in shock on that summer afternoon, she couldn't come up with anything. Anyway, her mind was too full of questions which cartwheeled through her mind one after the other. What were they like – these sisters in the north? What colour was their hair, their eyes? Did they like the same things as she did? Did the two older siblings still live at home? Did they have jobs? And did they know about her? If she'd only just found out about them, maybe they didn't. But what did dad tell them when he was away? And what about their mother? She presumed they had one. But maybe they didn't. And, if not, why hadn't he married *her* mother? Would they have been able to do that without the other family knowing? It was all so complicated.

Sitting there that afternoon Daisy had had so many questions and, as if anticipating that very thing, Dad had got up, mumbled something about the light on the river, grabbed his easel and paints and left. He hadn't come back until after dark and Daisy hadn't dared raise the subject of her siblings again.

Life in Cornwall was quiet. Almost too quiet at times. Daisy often thought about her siblings in the north. Was their life more interesting than hers? They had each other for company. That must be fun. Being an only child could get a little dull at times, she had to confess. She had friends, of course, but Creek Cottage was tucked down a long dead-end lane out on a peninsular and most parents didn't have the time to ferry their kids back and forth. So Daisy had learned to amuse herself, living a rich interior sort of a life which revolved around books.

Once in her teens, she'd dived into the novels of Daphne du Maurier, loving the Cornish settings and the romance of them. *Frenchman's Creek* was her favourite and she'd spent many happy hours wandering the footpaths along the river, but no handsome Frenchman ever came to make her life slightly more adventurous. There was a skinny Scottish boy who'd arrived on holiday one year, but his accent was so thick and he only ever talked about football. Daisy was quickly learning that life outside of novels could be a huge disappointment.

Growing up with her dad absent so often hadn't really bothered Daisy. To her, it had seemed normal and her mother had never seemed upset by it either. He'd always provided well for them both, showering them with gifts whenever he did manage to visit, and Angelina had her own work as a chef in a nearby restaurant so they never wanted for anything. It could be a little frustrating at times not to have her dad there. He'd missed countless school plays, parents' evenings, picnics and little days out and, more than once, Daisy's birthday. If he ever missed a special occasion like that, he'd send an extravagant gift like a huge teddy bear clutching a bouquet of flowers or a special piece of jewellery. It made it impossible not to forgive him, but she still felt miserable when he wasn't there to celebrate with her and eat the cake she and her mother would make together.

'You know how busy he gets with his work,' her mother would tell her. 'He's probably meeting very important people in London.' And that was it, Daisy had thought – those London people were more important than her. But it hadn't been London people at all – it had been Cumbrian people. *Family* people.

Once Daisy learned about the other family, she'd begun to feel a jealousy that she'd never experienced before. She found herself counting the days her dad spent with her and those he spent with his other children. Unsurprisingly, he spent far more time in the north, even though the two eldest children didn't need him anymore. Daisy felt as if she was now competing with this unknown sister called Cordelia. She'd done an internet search, finding just one photo of her in a gallery at a show. She'd had long fair hair that wasn't dissimilar to Daisy's own and her eyes were wide and expressive. She looked like someone Daisy could be friends with and it was impossible to hate her, but resentment began to build in her heart all the same. She couldn't help it.

Further searches on the internet threw up a few images of the portraits her dad had made of her three siblings. She'd studied them for hours, trying to work out their personalities from the expressions on their faces, the way they were standing or sitting and the clothes they were wearing. She'd looked each of them up on all the social media sites, wondering if she dared to befriend them or follow them, but deciding it was better not to. She had no idea if they knew of her existence and hadn't the nerve to ask Dad if they did.

Ever since that sunny day revelation, Daisy had felt an awkwardness around her dad, knowing that he had this whole other life away from her and her mother. She tried to find clues in his face that he was thinking of his other children and dared to look around his studio one day for something that might link him to this other family, but there wasn't anything to be found. It seemed that he kept his two lives completely separate.

One day, when she was fifteen, she and her mother had driven to the coast to walk along one of their favourite beaches where the Atlantic rollers brought in the surfers and the golden sands attracted the day-trippers. It was a favourite of Daisy's father too. He loved to paint the surfers and the swimmers and the stripy wind breaks of the tourists, and his paintings of this location always sold well. But he wasn't there that day. In fact, they hadn't seen him for several weeks.

'Do you miss him?' Daisy had asked.

Her mother looked surprised by the question. 'Yes. Of course.'

'And are you angry that he doesn't live with us?'

Her mother had stopped walking then and had turned to look at her. 'I'm not sure angry is the right word. Frustrated maybe. But I knew what I was getting into when I met him. He made things very clear.'

They'd walked on together, taking their shoes off and paddling in the shallows, craning their necks to watch the screeching gulls overhead before heading back home via their favourite fish and chip shop. And they hadn't spoken about Nicholas Bellwood again. Still, the phrase, *He made things very clear*, haunted Daisy. She and her mother would always be secondary, wouldn't they? Family number two. Even her name beginning with 'D' firmly placed her in the hierarchy, didn't it? Some days, when she missed her dad and was feeling melancholy, Daisy saw that 'D' like a failure grade at school. She'd just missed the mark.

And yet, when he was with them, they were the centre of

his attention. Well, when he wasn't painting. They would eat together, walk through the woods and swim in the sea, visit historic buildings, stone circles and deserted copper mines. And he would sketch and paint them both endlessly – sometimes together, often alone. Daisy always knew when Dad was painting her mother in the nude because he would tell her not to disturb him, clearing his throat noisily before firmly closing his studio door. Daisy had tried not to snigger although the idea of a nude painting of her mother seemed very silly indeed. Only once had Daisy seen one of *those* paintings. Her mother had been standing by the window, her back to the room, her long hair loose. It hadn't been remotely silly. It had been beautiful. There was love in each of the brushstrokes; she could feel it. Tenderness too. And a palpable connection between the artist and his model.

That was something else that had been lost when he'd died – that strange relationship of artist and sitter. Somehow, it fulfilled a need in both of them and Daisy's mother had confessed her insecurity the day after the news of his death had reached them.

'I don't have a purpose without him,' she'd said quietly. It was a dreadful thing to hear not least because it made Daisy feel as if she didn't count, but because it also diminished Angelina's own career as a chef to say nothing of the vibrant, kind and much-loved woman she was in her own right. Daisy had put it down to shock and hadn't said anything.

When the solicitor had informed them that Creek Cottage was theirs to keep, it had been a huge relief. Daisy could see some of the tension melt away from her mother's face. Although she had a good job, they wouldn't have been able to live somewhere like Creek Cottage if there'd been a mortgage to pay. Despite it being called a 'cottage', it was, in fact quite a large house with four bedrooms, two reception rooms and a garden studio all set within half an acre of prime Cornish countryside. The views alone were probably worth millions, Daisy couldn't help thinking. No, without Nicholas Bellwood's generosity, they would have had to have left the only home Daisy had ever known.

Daisy wasn't quite sure who it was who'd called to tell them the news about her father and the will. Her mother had been so distraught and Daisy hadn't asked. But she'd guessed that it was the solicitor. It certainly hadn't been any of the Bellwood family, she was sure of that at least. But would they reach out to her and her mother now? Or would they automatically hate her existence? She couldn't blame them if they did.

Daisy tried to imagine what would happen next. Would they all be at the funeral together: A, B, C and D? Nothing had been arranged yet, but it would probably take place in Cumbria rather than Cornwall. A through to C would claim him again, wouldn't they? Lowly D and her mother would most likely remain in the background, not being consulted on anything from flowers to music to burial site. Was he even going to be buried or had he wanted to be cremated? Tears pricked her eyes as she thought of the two ghastly options in relation to her beloved father.

She tried to remember the last time she'd seen him. He hadn't seemed ill, had he? A little tired perhaps, but that's because he'd been working hard. It was his default setting even though he could have retired long ago. But that wasn't what true artists did, was it? Art was a part of who you were. She'd seen that in her dad. He wouldn't be able to just step away from the easel, put his brushes down and sit in an armchair all day. He wanted to be outside, looking at the world and capturing its colours.

But they'd been captured for the last time. There would be no more new paintings. No more insights into how he saw the world. He had painted his last picture and it broke Daisy's heart.

CHAPTER EIGHT

Brenna still felt numb from the revelations of her father's will and she guessed Alex and Cordelia were feeling equally estranged by it all. The three of them had been moving around the house in uneasy companionship, finding it hard to settle to any particular job which was frustrating because there was so much to do.

Reality jolted her into action when an email came through from Mr Grant who was doing his best organising the funeral and, understandably, wanted their input. So Brenna had called Alex and Cordelia into the dining room and they'd sat with her laptop on the table, choosing three pieces of music together. One was a favourite Chopin piano concerto she knew her father had loved. Now, she'd never be able to listen to it again without associating it with this terrible time. Maybe she shouldn't include it. Father would never know, would he? But that would be rather selfish. As they went through the task of organising everything, it was quickly becoming apparent to Brenna that funerals were for the living, not the dead. It had nothing to do with the departed one. Unless they'd left specific instructions, they wouldn't know anything about the details.

Still, these things had to be got through and the three of them spent time carefully choosing photos of their father for the order of service. They then picked a local hotel for the wake, and a caterer and florist.

The list of possible attendees was being compiled from an address book that they'd found in Father's study. It was all fairly straightforward as he'd been an only child. His parents had had him late in life and had long since passed themselves. There were a handful of cousins in America and France but Brenna didn't expect that they'd make the journey. Still, she'd make sure they knew the arrangements.

It was all completely exhausting and there'd been a bit of bickering over the location of the wake because Cordelia had felt that Slate House was the obvious choice and that they could arrange some of Father's paintings for visitors to see. But both Brenna and Alex had felt it would be too intrusive and that the house wasn't in a fit state for visitors anyway.

Brenna was glad that Mr Grant was super-organised and confident enough to arrange so much of what was needed without reaching out to them with the minutiae. He'd obviously been a good friend to their father over the years and was really proving his worth now, which freed them up to sort out Slate House. Of course, with probate pending, it was much too early to put the house up for sale. But Brenna thought it might be worth getting a valuation and talking to an estate agent. She knew Alex would want to know what Slate House was worth. So she made a note of it on a list of things to do that seemed to be never ending.

After their morning's work, the three of them ate a piecemeal lunch in the kitchen as none of them had the energy to put anything proper together. They ate in relative silence, each consumed by their own thoughts. Alex finished first, throwing his plate and cutlery into the sink. Then Cordelia got up and left her things neatly by the side of the sink. Brenna sighed and went to wash everything. She took her time, wiping down the table and the worktops, refilling the kettle and straightening things that didn't need straightening. She longed to go for a walk, but knew she shouldn't. There was so much to do in the house and she really shouldn't keep leaving her post and going for long, leisurely chats with her old friend Blue.

For a moment, her mind drifted to Yewdale Farm and the little paradise Blue had made for her and her daughter. Life there had always stood in stark contrast to that at Slate House. But maybe that was a case of the grass seeming greener, she thought, remembering back to her childhood visits. For the most part, Blue's parents had made her welcome. Mrs Daker always seemed to have a tin of homemade cookies waiting to be plundered, and Mr Daker would often make time to introduce her to the new animals, from day-old chicks to squealing piglets. But there had been times when the Dakers had been a little gruff with her. Brenna had always shrugged it off, thinking that farm life could be pretty stressful. Still, it had seemed a far more welcoming place than her own home.

Whenever Brenna had brought Blue back to Slate House, her mother had done her best, but her nervous constitution was ever apparent, and her father would be hidden away in his studio. *Not to be disturbed.* It was never the warm welcome she wanted to give her friend. No, Brenna had rarely felt any warmth in her family home. Maybe that's why she was finding it so hard to be back. Every impulse was telling her to leave – to flee at any opportunity even if it was only for a few blessed hours. But she couldn't. She had to get on with things.

What was the best thing to do with everything, she thought, surveying the living room as she entered it? Should they all go through every single item individually as they'd begun to do? Or just pay for a clearance company to come in? That seemed so heartless. This wasn't an average sort of house either. It was an artist's home full of beautiful creations and collections, and Brenna was scared that something would be overlooked and thrown away by someone who didn't see its true worth or beauty.

She couldn't help wondering, however, what her father would have kept of hers if she'd been the one to die. She doubted very much if he'd even have visited her home. He'd only made the one trip to her little cottage shortly after she'd moved into it and had sniffed very loudly and made a comment about the garden not being large enough and facing the wrong direction. Brenna had told him it was all she could afford and that she adored the little patch of garden. It wasn't a sprawling time suck like Slate House's was. But he hadn't been listening. He'd been looking at his watch, mumbling something about leaving to beat the traffic.

No, Father wouldn't have wanted anything of hers. He'd never been a sentimental man. But that realisation didn't make it any easier for her when she was going through his things, even when it was only a drawer in the kitchen full of silly items like a wood and chrome bottle opener or a set of fancy chopsticks, because each was weighed down with memories. But the memories weren't in the things, were they? That's what she was trying to tell herself. The memories were within her and she didn't have to keep every single item, no matter how fancy or beautiful or expensive they were. She had to let things go. They had been his and they didn't have to become hers.

Leaving the kitchen for the time being, she walked towards the studio where she could hear Alex banging and crashing his way through the room. She dared to look inside and saw him shifting bits of furniture around.

'Are you okay?' she called, trying not to startle him.

He looked up and flicked his hair out of his face. 'No.'

Brenna sighed, wishing her brother would sometimes try and mask how he was feeling if only a little.

'I know it's not easy, but we've still got to get on with things,' she said diplomatically as she entered the room.

'I can't believe it,' he said, his face sulky and despondent. 'He was lying to us *all* those years.'

'Well, not lying exactly. He just didn't tell us the truth.'

'Isn't that the same thing?'

'I don't think so. I think Father was very good at separating things in his mind. When he was with us, he was our father; when he was in Cornwall, he wasn't.'

'A *sister*, Bren! A partner! He had this whole other *life!* How could we not have known about it? How did he hide it so well and not leave clues all over the place?'

'I don't know. He was very organised.'

Alex stared at her, a look of complete bafflement on his face. 'Aren't you *angry?*'

'I don't know – probably. But what's the point? He's not here anymore and it was his life anyway. He lived it how he saw fit.'

'Didn't he think about what would happen when he died? He knew what was in his will. He knew we'd find out.'

'He probably thought we'd just get on with it.'

She heard her brother curse under his breath.

'Really, Alex – there's no point in moping or getting mad. We've still got to sort all this stuff out.' She motioned to the stacks of paintings.

'It's insurmountable,' Alex said.

'No. Only immense.'

She watched him closely. It took a moment, but he seemed to be doing his best to pull himself out of his dark mood so that he could be a useful and functioning person again and Brenna was mightily relieved.

'What are we going to do with all these paintings?' Brenna asked. 'So many of these are unfinished.'

'Father didn't leave any instructions for them.'

'Are unfinished paintings worth anything? Should we try and sell them? Or would Father not want them to be seen?'

'I've no idea.'

'But you're an artist – how would you feel if they were yours?'

'You could burn the lot and be done with them.'

'Oh, Alex!'

'I wouldn't want unfinished work out in the world.'

'Okay, well now we're getting somewhere.'

'I think anything unfinished shouldn't be seen by anyone other than us.'

'Hang on – didn't you post one on Instagram?'

'It looked pretty finished to me.'

'All right, so we're not selling them. But are we keeping them? There are so many.' Brenna glanced around the room again and knew that she wouldn't want her tiny home crowded by her father's art. She had a couple of his small paintings and a few sketches and that, as far as she was concerned, was more than enough. She'd been spoilt having paintings around her growing up and, now she was an adult, she quite liked the walls uncrowded by art. But it seemed so heartless to just bin them or burn them. There were some lovely scenes – little cloudscapes and sunsets that weren't quite complete; a tree with half its leaves missing; a lake that was half water, half blank canvas. So much promise had now become so much clutter.

Alex stared blankly at it all. Truculent. And Brenna could see that she wasn't going to get any help from him.

'Listen, we're not getting very far, are we?'

'Sorry, Bren. I'm just not in the mood.'

'It's okay. Why don't you go out for a bit? Maybe paint something?'

He gave a weary sigh. 'I haven't got my stuff with me.'

'I think there's plenty for you to use here, isn't there?' Brenna glanced around the studio.

'Father *hated* me using his art supplies.'

'Yes, but they're yours now, surely.'

Alex flinched as if the thought hadn't occurred to him.

'I think it would do you good to get out for a bit even if you don't paint anything.'

'Yeah. Maybe you're right.'

She gave him a smile. She might be able to make more progress in the room with him out of it.

For a few minutes, Alex moved around, picking up brushes and tubes of paint, choosing a couple of blank boards and then reaching for one of his father's sketch easels. Brenna saw the choice he'd made and frowned.

'Didn't he always take that one out?' she said, nodding to the one Alex had ignored.

'Yes, but I don't want that one.'

'Why not?'

'It's got him all over it. This one's more...' he paused. 'It's less...'

Brenna nodded, understanding.

He left the room and the house and Brenna couldn't help wondering where he was going although she guessed he probably didn't know himself. It wasn't very likely he'd paint either. He'd most likely drive around ruminating. But the time away from Slate House would do him good.

Upstairs, Cordelia had been sorting through a huge wooden trunk in a spare bedroom. It was filled with old board games and jigsaw puzzles that hadn't seen the light of day for years. They'd all have to go, but she paused as she picked up the chess set her father had bought her for her tenth birthday. It hadn't been a gift she'd pined for and he had, at least, also bought her a new dress and a silver locket. But she recalled the evening when he'd taught her all the names of the pieces and showed her all the moves they made. She'd sat in a panic, believing that she'd never remember any of it and wondering why couldn't they play Snakes and Ladders instead? She liked that one. The board was full of coloured squares and funny illustrations. She liked the sound of the dice in the shaker and the anticipation of where your counter would land and that wonderful, comical moment when your opponent landed on a snake. Chess by comparison seemed so dull with its black and white board and complex moves. But her father obviously thought her ready to graduate.

She reached into the wooden trunk again and pulled out the Snakes and Ladders box, smiling at the memories it evoked. She knew that Brenna would probably banish it to the charity pile, but it was too precious to lose. As was the chess set. Cordelia realised that she was making quite a pile of things she wanted to keep and that her London flatmates wouldn't welcome the extra clutter in their small, shared space, but she just wasn't ready to let it all go yet.

It was as she was deliberating whether or not she really needed to keep an ancient jigsaw puzzle of Grasmere because it featured the bottom section of their garden that her phone rang.

'Cordelia? I mean Cordy? It's Dylan. How are you?' he asked in a sympathetic tone of voice.

'I'm good, thank you,' she said, her mood lifting instantly just hearing his voice.

'Listen, I rang Henry last night. He said he has every Fenton Fine Art catalogue ever printed.'

'Really?'

'Yep!'

'And can I visit him?'

'He'd be happy to see you.'

'Is he easy to get to by bus?'

'Not exactly, but I can run you over there if you like.'

'Oh, there's no need to go to any trouble.'

'It's no trouble. Anyway, it's always good to see Henry. If you let me know where you are, I can come straightaway. Does that suit you?'

Cordelia looked at the mess she'd made in the spare room and couldn't help wanting to get away from it all.

'Okay.' She told him how to get to Slate House.

Going downstairs a moment later, she found Brenna in the studio and explained what was happening.

'You're going now?'

Cordelia nodded. 'Where's Alex?'

'He went out to paint for a bit. He needed a break.'

'We're all deserting you.'

'It's okay. I deserted you for Skopelos, didn't I? Anyway, we need to ration this sorting stuff.'

Cordelia nodded in agreement. 'I promise I won't be long.'

CHAPTER NINE

The Lake District really was hard to beat when it came to landscapes. It was part Scandinavian with its deep waters and part Alps with its soaring peaks, but all British with its moody clouds and walkers dressed in heavy waterproofs.

Dylan chatted amiably as he drove down the twisting country lanes lined with stone walls and Cordelia tried to do her best to join in, but her mind was being pulled in different directions.

'Are you all right?' he asked at last. Perhaps he'd asked her a question and she hadn't responded. She wasn't sure.

She nodded. 'We all had a bit of a surprise when the will was read,' she said, instantly feeling traitorous for having divulged even that piece of information to an outsider. After all, she didn't really know this man at all. He might move in the same world her father had known, and might even have handled some of his work, but he was still a stranger. And yet there was something about him that invited familiarity. Perhaps it was just his open, friendly face and his easy smile.

'It's nothing,' she quickly added. 'Just...family stuff, you know?'

He nodded. 'We don't have to do this today,' he told her kindly.

'No, I want to.'

'You sure?'

'Absolutely. Anyway, we're virtually there now, aren't we?'

They'd driven into Langdale and Dylan slowed the car as they approached a rough track with a white stonewashed farmhouse at the end of it. Cordelia suddenly began to feel nervous. What was she doing? What was she hoping to find or achieve? And why had she roped in poor Dylan? He surely had better things to be doing.

'You're sure he doesn't mind us turning up like this?' Cordelia asked.

'He said he was looking forward to some company.'

Cordelia twisted her pale fingers together in her lap. She supposed it would be very rude to both Henry and Dylan if she backed out now.

'Well, here we are,' Dylan said a moment later as they parked in the farmyard. The old stone buildings opposite the main house looked in bad repair. They were shouting out for renovation but, from what Dylan had told her about Henry, it seemed every spare penny of his went on art.

They got out of the car and immediately saw the old man standing in his open doorway. He was short with a shock of white hair and he was wearing a checked shirt that swamped him.

'Mr Crompton!' Dylan cried.

'Henry. You know you can call me Henry.'

'How are you?'

'Very well, young man. So this is the Bellwood girl, is it?'

'Hello Mr Crompton. I'm Cordelia.'

'A beautiful name for a beautiful young woman!'

Cordelia could feel herself flushing at the compliment. 'I hope we're not disturbing you.'

'Not at all. I don't get many visitors. Tea okay for you both? The kettle's on and I've brought out all the catalogues for you so you won't have to risk the perils of the basement. Come in. Come in!'

They entered, mindful to duck their heads at the low entrance. The hallway was cool and narrow and every single wall was covered in paintings. Watercolours, acrylics, oils and prints in every conceivable size and shape. Some were in plain wooden frames while others hung in richly gilded ones that gleamed in the slant of light from the autumn sunshine that had followed them inside.

Henry led the way into the dining room and then excused himself to make the tea. As with the hallway, the walls were hung with paintings – so many that it was hard to tell what colour the actual walls might be behind them. But it was the table that caught Cordelia's eye. It was covered in heaps of catalogues from Fenton Fine Art. This man was serious when it came to collecting.

'Wow!' Dylan said. 'I haven't seen these for years.' He picked one up at random. It was a thick square catalogue printed on good quality paper and featured a portrait of a woman on the cover. 'I don't remember this one, but I do remember that one there.' He put down the catalogue he was holding and picked up another whose cover featured a beautiful painting of a Lakeland landscape. Cordelia gasped as she saw it.

'That's one of Father's.'

'Yes,' Dylan said. 'I recognised it immediately. Buttermere?'

'One of his favourite places.'

'Did he keep the catalogues himself?'

'I'm not sure. Probably,' Cordelia said. 'But there's so much stuff to sort through, I wasn't sure where to start looking.'

'Well, we know the rough dates to look for here. Shall we make a start?'

Cordelia glanced at the tottering piles of catalogues on the table and nodded.

'Here you go,' Mr Crompton said as he entered the room and placed two mugs of tea on a side table. 'I don't envy you this job.'

'Actually, I'm looking forward to it,' Dylan told him.

'Let me know if you find what you're looking for.' He left the room and the two of them sipped their tea and then began.

Dylan was a natural organiser and took the lead in pulling out all the catalogues with the relevant dates, and he told her little stories about the paintings he remembered as they worked alongside each other.

'It's always hard to choose just one for the cover,' he confessed, 'but it usually works out better to feature one standout image than several smaller ones. And you can just about guarantee that the painting on the cover will be one of the first to sell in the show.'

Cordelia was holding a catalogue with a still life of flowers and fruit on the cover. 'I wonder where this painting is now.'

'Yes. I often wonder where they all go to.'

'Father used to say that you can't become attached to a

painting. You have to set it free. It's an artist's job to simply do the work and put it out into the world. Of course, he kept quite a few too.'

'Of course. I guess it must be hard to let some of them go.'

'You can't keep them all, I suppose. Especially when you're creating new ones all the time.'

Dylan flipped through the catalogue he was holding. 'Here's another of your father's.' He showed her the landscape.

'It's beautiful. I can't believe there are so many I don't recognise.'

'He was prolific, wasn't he?'

She smiled. 'It was like a nervous sort of addiction. You could always tell if he hadn't painted for a day or so because he'd be all twitchy and anxious. Then, when he'd had a good session, you could visibly see that all that tension he'd been holding had simply melted away.'

Cordelia picked up another catalogue from the same period, trying not to lose hope because they'd gone through so many already.

'What if we don't find it?' she asked, voicing her fear.

'If it exists and he sold it through our gallery, we'll find it.'

'But I might have the title wrong and there might not be a picture of it.'

Dylan gave her a little smile. 'I think we've got all the catalogues from the time you think it was painted, haven't we? I've checked all the dates on them.'

'I think so.' Cordelia bit her lip, feeling so unsure. What if they'd missed one – *the* one? Or what if Henry hadn't got them all. It certainly looked as if he had, but how could they be sure? They could put them in date order and check, she supposed. Oh, this was such a silly idea, she told herself.

What did she think she was doing – coming into this stranger's house and turning everything upside down and taking up Dylan's precious time when she, herself, should have been helping at Slate House?

Suddenly, she heard Dylan gasp.

'What is it?'

'*Family Portrait.*' He tapped the open page.

Cordelia took the catalogue from him and looked. 'There's no picture.'

'No, I'm afraid not. I've looked. But we don't print an image of every painting in the show.'

'So how do we know this is the one?'

'It's the right title and the date seems right, doesn't it?'

Cordelia looked at the single line entry on the last inside page of the catalogue.

Family Portrait. Oil on canvas. 20" x 30".

'It's got to be the one,' she whispered. 'I wish I knew for sure. He might have given that title to a few of his paintings though.'

'How many family portraits did he do?' Dylan asked.

'A few. But not many from this date. I think he did more later on. I remember him painting me endlessly as a teenager. I was horribly self-conscious. You know how awkward you can be at that age.'

Dylan nodded. 'I had braces on then and lanky hair.'

Cordelia laughed. 'I was a skinny rake and had terrible skin.'

'I bet you didn't.'

They held each other's gaze for a moment and then Dylan cleared his throat.

'So what do we do now?' Cordelia asked.

'Shall we see if Henry remembers the show?'

'Do you think he will?'

'You'd be surprised at what Henry remembers when it comes to art.'

They left the dining room, Dylan carrying the tea things through to the kitchen where they found Henry.

'Did you find what you were looking for?' he asked.

'We think so,' Dylan said and Cordelia handed him the catalogue.

'We were wondering if you remembered this show,' she said.

Henry looked at the painting on the front of the catalogue. 'Nearly twenty years ago,' he said, tapping the image on the cover. 'Lovely painting, that one.'

'Esther Fielding, I think,' Dylan said.

'Yes. She didn't do many landscapes and she really should have,' Henry said.

'I agree.'

'Long gone, though, of course.'

'You remember the show?'

'I do indeed. And I'll tell you why. That was the year I lost my Fiona. Grew up with her. Met her on the first day of school and were never apart since.' He paused, a misty look clouding his pale eyes. 'That show was the first time I left my house since her passing and it took all my willpower to make the trip into town.'

Cordelia gently touched his shoulder.

'But you want to hear about the show, don't you?' He gave a sniff, as if holding back the emotion that had risen at his memory of that terrible year.

Cordelia and Dylan watched as Henry flicked through the catalogue. 'Ah, yes. Lots of colour, that year. Plenty of interest.'

'Did you buy anything?' Dylan asked.

'No. But there was a piece that caught my eye although I can't see it in here.'

'Which piece?' Dylan asked.

Henry turned to the back of the catalogue, scanning the titles of the paintings. 'There we are – this one.'

Cordelia looked at where he was pointing. '*Family Portrait*,' she said.

'That's the one we were looking for!' Dylan told him.

'Really?'

'We think so,' Cordelia said. 'What do you remember about it?'

'Well, it was a big painting. Set in a garden full of hydrangeas.'

'Slate House.'

'Your home?'

'Yes.'

Henry glanced upwards, his mind seeming to spiral back in time, trying to capture the details of something long since forgotten.

'It was more of the mood of the piece, I think. You'll know your father's work always had a certain quality about it – a *life*! Do you know what I mean? It's like he was able to capture not just a person's physical attributes but their character too. I know that's the job of a good portrait painter, but not everyone does it successfully. But your father had that gift and there was something about this family group that I connected with. Perhaps it reminded me of my own family.'

'What do you remember about the figures?' Cordelia asked, hope swelling in her heart.

Henry sighed. 'I'm afraid the details are a bit muddy. There was an adult. Or maybe two. I'm not sure.'

'And children?'

'Yes,' Henry said.

Cordelia swallowed. 'Do you remember how many?'

Henry gave a sad smile. 'My memory is good, but not that good.' He handed the catalogue back to her. 'Do you want to keep it?'

'May I?'

'Of course. I should really have a bit of a sort-out.'

Dylan's eyes widened at that. 'I can take them off your hands if you like.'

'You want the catalogues?'

'We lost a good portion of our archive a few years ago. We'd love to have these.'

'Well, you're welcome to them.'

'Wow, thanks, Henry. I'll make the arrangements and pop by when it suits you.'

'You know,' Henry said, tapping the air with a finger, 'I almost bought that painting of your father's.'

'Did you?' Cordelia asked. 'I wish you had.'

'But somebody pipped me to the post when I went off in search of the canapés.' He chuckled. 'Your father was there that night, though. I spoke to him.'

'Really?'

'I did.'

'What did you talk about?'

'Oh, the paintings, the crowd.'

'And what did he say?'

'It was a long time ago, my dear.'

Cordelia felt disappointed that the old man couldn't remember the actual words her father had said all those years ago. As if he'd carry them in his memory just for her. And what was she hoping for exactly? Did she hope to claim some little piece of her father she hadn't had before?

'Do you remember who bought the painting?' Dylan asked.

'Now, that I *do* remember. It was that nice old couple who lived in Eskdale.' He tapped the air again with his right index finger as if trying to conjure their names. 'Betty and... Arthur Dixon. That was it!'

Cordelia smiled, delighted that they now knew the names of those who'd bought the painting, but then her heart sank, supposing that they were no longer alive.

'I don't suppose you know if they're still around,' Dylan asked.

'I'm afraid not. But I did visit them once. They wanted my opinion on a painting they were thinking of selling. They lived in a big stone farmhouse by a little bridge over the river at the foot of the valley.' Henry gave them some directions. 'If they're still alive, that's where they'll be.'

'Well, you've been a great help, Henry,' Dylan told him.

'Yes, thank you so much for your time.'

'My pleasure. It's always wonderful to talk about art and – if I may – I'd like to say how sorry I was to hear of the passing of your father.'

Cordelia nodded, tears instantly springing to her eyes at the emotion in Henry's voice. She guessed Dylan must have told him the news.

They said their goodbyes, Dylan promising to come back for the catalogues in due course.

'How do you fancy trying to find Betty and Arthur Dixon in Eskdale?' Dylan asked as they got back in the car.

'Now?'

'I'm not doing anything else.'

'Shouldn't you get back to the gallery?'

'Nah! Dad's doing a stint. I don't want to take that little pleasure away from him.'

'But I've taken up so much of your time already.'

'Hey – I'm enjoying it. It's like a treasure hunt.'

Cordelia smiled. 'Well, if you're sure, but it's a long way round to Eskdale from here.'

'Not if we go over the passes.'

'You mean Wrynose and Hardknott?' Cordelia tried not to blanch with fear.

'I'm up for it if you are.'

'Have you driven them before?'

'Course!' he said. 'Piece of cake.'

Cordelia took a deep breath. 'Well, it's certainly quicker than going south and round. If we don't crash over the edge, that is.'

Dylan laughed. 'We won't crash, I promise. I've done it dozens of times.'

'Really?'

'Trust me.'

CHAPTER TEN

It felt good to get away from Slate House for a few hours. Alex had taken his father's Audi, driving over to a favourite view at Elterwater. The light was good and he could probably have got a painting or two in, but he didn't have the heart for it. Instead, he walked for a bit, watching a pair of swans on the water and gazing up into the peaks and pikes, summits and contours he remembered so well. But he didn't get very far along the footpath. He was wearing a pair of old trainers and it was horribly muddy and slippery underfoot so he did what he did best and found his way to a pub.

The pub was one of those wonderful old Cumbrian inns where you had to duck your head on entry. It was dark with oak beams and shiny wooden tables. The carpet was beer-soaked and food-stained and Alex felt right at home. He missed these old places. Greece was all very well with its sunshine and outdoor living, but it never felt cosy and comforting like this. No, he thought, nothing beat a warm pub on a cold autumn day.

He ordered half a pint, mindful of the fact that he was

driving, and took it to a seat near the fire which had been lit. There was just a handful of people in the pub – a few locals and a couple of walkers, and there was a distinct smell of wet wool, damp earth and old greyhound. It was heaven.

Alex settled back in his chair, stretching his legs out in front of him to make the most of the fire. He only felt a little bit guilty at not being out painting. He knew Brenna would be disappointed when he returned with nothing but a couple of blank canvases. He shook his head. That was his role in life, wasn't it? To disappoint people. First Father, then Aimée and now his sisters. And, if he was being absolutely honest, he'd disappointed himself too. He wasn't exactly where he'd imagined himself to be in his career now. At thirty-four, he felt as if he might have peaked already and that peak hadn't exactly been life changing. He'd had a show in London of his paintings of the Mediterranean. It had been timed well during a wet and miserable summer when everybody had been feeling fed up with the weather and had been dreaming of sunnier climes. But the follow-through hadn't been what he'd hoped for. The buyers hadn't gone on to become collectors and he'd slipped back into virtual obscurity. Just another fairly decent artist trying to make a living, but constantly worrying about how long the money would last.

He wondered if his father had ever struggled to make a living from his art. He somehow didn't think so; he'd been famous and successful for as long as Alex could remember, but it couldn't always have been so. There were very few artists who made a good living from the start. There was usually a torturously long apprenticeship. And had his father *always* been an artist? Alex seemed to remember him once talking about a job as some kind of rep, but he couldn't recall anything else about it. He supposed he'd never know now –

unless he found something in his father's paperwork about previous employment. It just went to show you how very little you knew about somebody.

Perhaps Alex should have reached out more, called more, visited more. But he'd thought he'd have more time. Perhaps that was the curse of life. You became so all-consumed by your own life that it was easy to overlook the lives of others, but they were all slipping by so much faster than you thought.

Mind you, his father hadn't exactly kept in touch with him, had he? He'd never shown any interest in his son's life in France or Greece and he'd certainly never visited. The truth was, and it made Alex intensely sad to think about it, that they had been two very separate people who were merely connected by DNA. Perhaps he'd been closer to his family in Cornwall, Alex mused. Maybe that's what had happened – his father had become disillusioned with his failed marriage in the north and had headed south to try again. Alex remembered those summers without his father. As he'd got older, he'd taken jobs during the holidays so hadn't been around the house much. They'd been looked after by Aunt Pippa. It was years before Alex realised that they weren't actually related to her and that she was being paid by their father to take care of them in his absence. She'd been nice enough and young Cordelia had adored her, but it made Alex furious now to think that he'd been with his secret family all that time. And there they'd been, imagining him working. Of course, he had been working, but that was a small part of his trips, it seemed. Alex wondered what had come first – the love of Cornwall or the new love of his life.

Alex took a sip of his drink and gazed into the orange flames of the pub fire. It was an awful thought to have, and he berated himself before it was even free-ranging in his head, but perhaps things might be easier now with his father gone. He didn't expect the art world or Father's collectors to suddenly turn their love and admiration onto his work now that Nicholas Bellwood was no longer around, but Alex himself might feel somehow freer to express himself. As much as he had tried to deny it, his father's existence had always cast its shadow over him. But would things change merely because Nicholas was no longer alive? Artists often became even more famous after they'd died. Perhaps there'd be a sudden wave of interest in his father's work. Maybe there'd even be a special retrospective show. Alex wouldn't be at all surprised. No, he wasn't going to escape his father simply because Nicholas no longer existed.

Still, he would always wonder if things might have changed if they'd had more time. He carried the same torment with him regarding his mother. Alex had been a teenager when she'd died and he remembered the hatred he'd felt back then – not because she had died, but because she had left them a couple of years before her death. But what he'd give to have her back again. Now that he was an adult, he could see what life at Slate House must have been like for her. He knew his father wasn't an easy man to live with, but Alex hadn't been capable of seeing that at the time. It hadn't been his responsibility to see his mother as a human being in her own right. He'd been her son – her one role on this earth was to take care of him and love him more than anything else in the world, and she hadn't; she'd failed him. She'd put herself before her children and had walked out on them. He'd despised her for years, carrying that weight of hatred inside him. But time had allowed those feelings to morph and mellow and oh how he wished he could talk to her now.

Perhaps that was the curse of being a child – one could never truly hope to understand one's parents because they would always be a whole generation away and that was a little like being from an entirely different planet. They were never really fully-rounded beings, were they? Sure, there was some acknowledgement that they must have been young once, although it was close to impossible to imagine his father as a boy unless he was some kind of prodigy, wielding a paintbrush from the age of three. But what had his parents *really* been like? Had they been happy? Had they felt fulfilled? Had they ever felt lonely or insecure? How he wished he knew a little more about the two people who'd brought him into this world.

It would have been so easy to have slipped into one of his drunken melancholias then, but the door opened and a man walked in wheeling a couple of boxes. He greeted the man at the bar and Alex frowned, recognising his old school friend, Marcus. However, instead of waving a hand in greeting, Alex found himself shrinking into his seat, trying to make himself invisible. The last thing he wanted was the agony of making small talk with an old friend. But it was too late. There was no escaping an encounter because Marcus glanced over and saw him.

'Alex?'

For one daft moment, Alex thought about shaking his head and saying, 'You must be mistaken', but Marcus had already crossed the room and was slapping him on the back.

'It *is* you! When did you get back?'

Alex sighed. The agony of small talk was upon him. Still, he could do his best to shut it down.

'My father died.'

'Oh, mate!' Marcus said and, instead of the news embarrassing his old chum, it had the opposite effect and he pulled a chair from behind him and joined Alex. 'I'm sorry to hear that.'

Alex nodded.

'Still, it's good to see you. You look well.'

'Liar!' Alex said. He couldn't stop himself. He knew he looked like garbage.

Marcus laughed. 'How are you doing?'

Alex shrugged. 'I don't know. Okay, I guess.'

'So you're home for a while?'

'Just to sort things out. The funeral and – you know – the house.'

'I'm really sorry.'

'But how are you?' Alex said, eager to change the subject seeing as his friend showed no signs of moving on.

'Yeah, good, good! Got my own business now.'

'Yeah?'

Marcus motioned to the bar. 'Just doing the deliveries now. Hey Tony?' he called to the barman. 'Chuck us a couple of packets over, will you?'

The barman opened one of the boxes Marcus had brought in, reached inside and threw a couple of packets over to them.

'Kirkstone Crisps,' Alex read.

'Best in the country. Try them.'

Alex opened the packet and took out a golden crisp, popping it into his mouth and crunching.

'Good?'

'Really good!'

Marcus beamed at him. 'A childhood dream of mine come true.'

'Impressive!'

'You still painting?'

Alex wasn't quite sure how to answer. 'When I'm not... you know... coping with all this.'

'Of course. Any family on the scene yet?'

'Kids?' The word shot out of Alex's mouth in surprise. 'No. You?'

Marcus got his phone out of his pocket and, quick as a flash, brought up a photo of a beautiful woman with two small girls. 'That's Olivia with the twins. Zara and Poppy.'

'Twins?'

'We don't do things by halves!'

'I can see that. They're lovely. You've – er – done well.'

'Thanks! It's a lot of work, of course. The business keeps me up some nights. Probably more nights than the twins as babies, but it's all good. We're getting there.' His phone beeped and he glanced down at it. 'Ah, rats! Look, I gotta go. More deliveries and an appointment with a supplier.'

'No worries.'

'It was good to see you. We should – you know – get together. Talk properly, yeah?'

Alex gave a half-smile, knowing it would probably never happen. Marcus meant well, but his life had moved on and Alex wouldn't feel right inserting himself and all his misery into it.

Marcus got up.

'Don't forget your crisps!' Alex said, motioning to the packet he'd left on the table.

'Keep them. I've got a few more where that came from!'

Alex watched Marcus leave the pub and he suddenly

wished his friend had stayed longer. He didn't often chat to people these days. He'd almost forgotten how to do it. Perhaps that's why he was such a grouch.

He finished his drink and glanced at the bar, his right hand tapping his knee in an anxious staccato. It would be so easy to order another one and to slip quietly away somewhere deep within himself. So easy.

He got up and walked towards the bar.

Brenna couldn't help wishing that Alex and Cordelia would hurry back to Slate House even though she'd told them it was fine to take a break. But, the truth was, she didn't like being in the house on her own. It didn't feel *right.* It wasn't that she believed in ghosts exactly, but there was a certain energy about the place that felt decidedly unwelcoming. Maybe it was the spirit of her father hanging over it. She'd never felt entirely welcomed by him even when she'd been a child. There'd always been distinct boundaries – places where she'd known she wasn't welcome.

'Don't go in there!' her mother would warn her about her father's studio. 'Not when the door is closed. Your father's working.' Or the constant reprimand from her father of, 'Don't touch that. I don't want fingerprints all over it.'

She often wondered why he'd had children. They were such a great inconvenience.

It was no wonder her mother had left. Even when Brenna had been very young, she'd felt her mother's unhappiness. Lydia had done her best to hide it, of course, but it had been all too apparent in her body language, the hushed tone she would talk in and the way she'd never quite express how she truly felt. She'd always had the supporting role. That's how Brenna interpreted it.

Father hadn't kept much of his wife around, but he'd never got rid of her beloved piano and Brenna approached it now and lovingly stroked the gleaming wood of its rosewood case. It was a beautiful object, dating from the 1890s. But what was to happen to it? It was just another bulky item of furniture that nobody would want to take home with them. She still remembered the beautiful music her mother would play. It used to drift across the garden when the windows were open during the summer. It had been one of the few ways her mother had been able to express herself in this house. Her music had been her true voice, showing how much real emotion she had locked away inside her.

Lydia had adored this piano and it must have been a wrench to leave it. Yet she had. Brenna could still remember her father standing by it, drumming angry fingers on the wood the day after his wife had walked out on them all.

'She'll be back,' he'd said. 'She won't leave this place.' He'd seemed so very sure of himself. He'd truly thought that a house, a garden and a family could hold a human captive – that all that was enough for a person to feel complete. But it hadn't been. There'd been something fundamental missing and she'd had to leave in order to find it.

Now they'd both left Slate House forever. Lydia and Nicholas. They must have loved each other once, Brenna reasoned. To get married and make a home and family. That took love and dedication, didn't it? So what had gone wrong? Had it simply been a mismatch? Two very different personalities that never should have been together? Brenna supposed she'd never know. Even if her father was still alive, she'd never have had the courage to ask him, and would he have told her anyway?

She was giving herself a headache with all the thoughts that were assaulting her so she determined to switch them off. She must focus on what she was here for. Dwelling on the past was no use. She had to focus on the present and that meant getting another bin bag from the kitchen to continue sorting through the mess in her father's study.

Cordelia and Dylan set off through Langdale towards the first of the passes. The road was picturesque, studded with the white-washed and slate roofed cottages the county was known for. The hedges were still high from their summer growth but the bracken was beginning to golden.

Cordelia remembered the one and only time she'd driven over the passes. Father had told them that they all had to have at least a year's driving experience before attempting it. Cordelia had taken a friend on her first attempt and could still recall the sick feeling in the pit of her stomach as she'd handled the hairpin bends. Still Dylan seemed to know what he was doing so she tried to relax and enjoy the scenery.

She'd forgotten just how much she loved the Cumbrian landscape, but how she missed the wild beauty of the fells and valleys especially on a day like today when the road was slick and glossy with recent rainfall and the sky was heavy with clouds. Indeed, the clouds were low and a menacing grey as they ascended the first pass. Dylan, who had been telling her about a recent show, suddenly stopped talking and Cordelia glanced at him. His face was serious as he concentrated on the road ahead. The landscape had changed from a gentle, verdant one to a barren bracken and boulder-strewn one.

You felt so very close to the sky up here. It was such an elemental place. The land dropped away to the left and Cordelia saw that the streams looked swollen. They passed a few brave walkers and a few even braver cyclists and Cordelia thanked her lucky stars that she was in the comfort of a car even though it was getting more hair-raising by the minute. They had to slow down a couple of times as a sheep wandered, quite unperturbed, across the road.

The moment when they began the descent and could see the road ahead snaking down below them was both inspiring and intimidating, but Dylan took his time, taking each bend slowly and with care, swerving gently around any potholes and rattling over the cattle grids. Cordelia glanced at him occasionally, noticing how his forehead creased in concentration.

For a while, the road followed the river. In some places, the river was wider than the road and the two came to within kissing distance of one another. One wrong turn and they'd be floating.

They drove on, passing a white farmhouse by a stone bridge, and Cordelia saw a road sign to Eskdale via Hardknott Pass. There were warning signs everywhere about weather conditions, prohibited vehicles and the gradient. Things were about to get serious. Wrynose Pass had just been the warm up.

Dylan glanced at Cordelia, his eyebrows raised. 'Ready?'

She nodded and they drove over a cattle grid and began the ascent. It was gradual at first and there were several moments when Cordelia wished they'd taken the long way round. The endless bends and the one-in-three gradient were taking their toll on her nerves. But then there was a wonderful moment when they reached the summit and the landscape opened up below them like a map of a mythical kingdom with the mountains in shades of blues and greens and the valley far below looking lush with trees.

At one point they passed a car that had careered off the road, perhaps taking a bend a little too fast. Its owner had abandoned it and Cordelia sighed in relief when they finally entered the safer lanes of Eskdale a few minutes later unscathed.

'Well done,' she told Dylan.

'I have a confession,' Dylan said, clearing his throat.

'What?'

'That's the first time I've driven those passes.'

'But you said...'

'Sorry!'

'How come you've never been over there before?'

'I don't know. Just never had a reason.'

'Me and my siblings couldn't wait to try it. I thought it was a rite of passage if you grew up here.'

'Well, I learned to drive in the north-east while at uni so I guess I missed it. But I might be hooked now.'

Cordelia couldn't help smiling at his enthusiasm.

It wasn't long before they saw a white stone farmhouse by a bridge and slowed down for the turn into the track that led to it.

'Is this it, do you think?' Cordelia said, noticing the sign. 'Henry didn't say anything about it being a bed and breakfast.'

'No, but lots of farms are diversifying now, aren't they?'

'I guess.'

They bumped along the track and parked opposite the

house, getting out of the car a moment later. There was a pretty bench outside the front door and large pots full of flowers which were still giving their all despite the cooler autumn weather.

Dylan knocked on the door and a woman in her forties answered, a tea towel in her hand and a smear of white flour across her left cheek.

'I'm afraid we're all booked up if you're looking for a room.'

'We're not,' Dylan said quickly. 'We're actually looking for Arthur and Betty Dixon.'

The woman shook her head. 'I'm afraid Arthur died some time ago and Betty went into a home three years ago.'

'Do you know which home?' Cordelia asked.

'One in Keswick, I think. I can't remember the name. I bought this place from her the year before.'

'I don't suppose she left a large painting here, did she? Of a family?' Dylan asked.

'No. Is that what you're looking for – a painting of a family?'

'Yes. Have you seen one?'

'I'm sorry, no, I haven't.' She gave an apologetic smile. 'You're going to have to excuse me. I've got a tray of scones in the oven. Good luck with the search!' And she closed the door on them.

Cordelia sighed. 'We've lost it, haven't we? It's gone forever.'

Dylan shook his head. 'Don't give up. Not yet.'

'But we haven't got any leads now.'

'Well, we'll try something else. A notice, maybe? Put a message up on the social media sites. Someone out there might know where the painting is.'

'But what if they don't? What if it's been auctioned or abandoned in an attic or just thrown away?'

'From what we've been told, it's too beautiful to throw away.'

They got back in the car and Cordelia felt her whole body sinking and slumping. It had been a silly thing to even think of doing, she berated herself, and she felt horribly guilty for having wasted so much of Dylan's time. She was quite sure he had better things to do than going on some wild goose chase across the passes of Cumbria.

Just as Dylan started the car, Cordelia glanced in her mirror and saw the owner appear in the doorway of the farmhouse. She was waving her tea towel at them and running towards the car.

'Dylan! Stop!'

'What is it?' he asked, hitting the brakes.

Cordelia lowered her window as the woman drew alongside them.

'I've just remembered – they had a son!' she told them. 'Michael. Michael Dixon. He lived in Windermere, I think. Ran a garage there. Of course, he might not still be there, but it's something at least?'

'Thank you!' Cordelia said as the woman returned to her scones once more.

'Told you!' Dylan said.

'Told me what?'

'Not to give up!'

She grinned. 'You did. But I can't keep involving you in all this madness.'

'What do you mean? What else have I got to do with my time?'

'Hundreds of things, I'm sure.'

'Yeah, but *this* is fun!'

'Is it?'

'Don't you think so?'

'I don't know. I'm worried that I'm using it as some kind of distraction from everything. I don't want Alex and Brenna to think I'm not pulling my weight – that I'm... what's that funny phrase?'

'Shirking your responsibility? They wouldn't think that, would they?'

'Probably not. But I want them to feel they can rely on me.'

'I bet they've got their own ways of getting through this, haven't they?'

Cordelia nodded. 'Alex is drinking. I think he's had a problem for a little while. This won't be helping, I'm afraid.'

'And what about your sister?'

'She's been walking a bit. Actually she's back in touch with a neighbour friend from her childhood.'

'That's good. We all need friends at times like this. I remember when my cousin died. He was just seventeen – two years older than I was at the time.'

'Oh, Dylan – that's awful.'

'It was. My dad was in pieces. He was really close to his sister and adored his nephew. And I wasn't much help. I was at that awkward teen age. But there was this neighbour friend. I'd always thought she was a busybody – poking her nose in where it wasn't wanted. But when she heard about what had happened and saw how it was affecting us, she was so kind.' He paused for a moment and smiled. 'You know in films where you see neighbours coming round with endless casseroles? Well, that was her. And they were much welcomed. I don't think we would have eaten much if it hadn't been for her. Mum had left by then, you see, so it was just me and Dad and we were both rather hopeless in the kitchen at the best of times. Anyway, Dad tried to bury himself in his work and I was permanently attached to my gaming console. But those meals kind of brought us together.'

'That was really lovely of her.'

'It was. I felt a bit bad about thinking of her as a busybody after that. She got me and my dad through a pretty tough time. And that's what you've got to do, I think – just find a way through all this. That's why I'm happy to help you now, you see?'

'Well, it's very kind of you.'

'I'm just sorry we haven't got any more time today,' he said. 'Unless we go back over the passes.'

'No way!' Cordelia cried in alarm.

'Only joking!'

'I'm voting for the long way round for sure. It's getting dark and those clouds look full of rain. Imagine if we got stranded up there.'

'Want to start again tomorrow? It shouldn't be too hard to find a garage in Windermere.'

'Okay. If that's all right with you?'

'I'll get Dad to do another stint at the gallery. He'll love it. He might actually come out of retirement if I'm not careful.'

'We could just ring round the garages first,' Cordelia suggested.

'Shall I do that in the morning? See if we've definitely got a lead?'

'That would be great.'

'Good. I'll get you back home then.'

Cordelia settled back in her seat for the journey, letting the pretty lanes of Eskdale ease her racing mind. The truth was she didn't want to go back to Slate House and everything that was going on there. She liked it here in this car with Dylan. She liked the way he chatted easily to her and how he smiled whenever he saw a sheep crossing the road, and how he'd point out favourite views that meant something to him. She liked it when he offered her a mint humbug from a paper bag in the glove compartment and she liked it even more when he told her about seeing her father's art for the first time.

'My dad was unwrapping some of the paintings your father had delivered and I'll never forget the first landscape. All these colours just seemed to explode from the bubble wrap! It was a view of Wasdale and it was so dramatic. You know what Wasdale can be like? Well, your father had captured it perfectly. It was all mist and mood and cloud and chaos. I wanted to buy it, but my pocket money wouldn't have been nearly enough!'

'Do you know what happened to it?'

'It was the first painting to sell in the show. Sold before the private view.'

'I wonder where it is now.'

'You want to chase after that one too?'

'No. I'd better not. Although it would be tempting just to see it'

'You should be able to see that one. It was definitely featured in the catalogue so I'll look out for it when I collect that huge stack from Henry.'

When they hit the main road, Cordelia began to feel sleepy and closed her eyes for a bit. Dylan put the radio on low. It was some classical music she didn't recognise but it was relaxing and she had the strangest sensation of floating somewhere above herself as he drove.

'Cordy?'

Someone was calling her name from a very long way away. Only, she didn't really recognise the voice. Perhaps she was dreaming. She'd just have to fall asleep again.

'Cordelia? We're here.' A light touch on her shoulder jolted her awake. 'I think you fell asleep somewhere south of Ravenglass.'

She yawned. 'I'm sorry. What a dull passenger I am.'

'It's been a long day.'

'Yes.'

They sat in the driveway for a moment, Cordelia delaying her entry for as long as possible. The lights were on in Slate House, but she rather liked the dimness of the car with the music on low and the heating on high.

'I'll make a few calls in the morning – see if we can find this Dixon chap.'

'Thanks. And for today. I hope...'

'What?'

'I hope I can repay you somehow.'

He shook his head. 'No need. Seriously. It's been my pleasure. And look – I've got all those incredible catalogues because of you. Dad's going to be thrilled.'

She smiled. 'Well, I'd better get going. Brenna will be wondering where I've got to.'

'I'll call you, okay?'

'Thanks Dylan.' She got out of the car and was making her way to the front door when he called to her.

'Cordy?'

'Yes?'

He smiled and he looked as if he was struggling to say something.

'What is it?' she asked.

He gave a little shrug. 'It's been a great day.'

She watched as he raised his hand in a wave and drove away and, even though she hadn't found her father's painting and there was no certainty that she ever would, it had, indeed, been a great day.

CHAPTER ELEVEN

'I could kill Alex!' Brenna cried

'I think one death in the family is more than enough to be coping with,' Cordelia replied.

'You didn't see him when he arrived back yesterday. He practically fell out of the taxi which *I* had to pay for! And he's left Dad's Audi somewhere in Elterwater so we've got to go and get that now.

'Oh dear!'

'Yes, oh, dear!'

'I'm sorry I wasn't here to help.'

Brenna softened a little at her apology. 'It's okay.' They were in the kitchen eating pasta. Cordelia had opened a packet of penne they'd found at the back of a cupboard and they'd teamed it with some vegetables Brenna had bought on a shopping trip.

'Where is he now?' Cordelia asked.

'Where do you think? Sleeping it off. And I'd hoped he was out painting all that time – doing something creative.'

'Poor Alex. He's not coping.'

'Well, he should try harder.'

They ate in silence for a few moments.

'Anyway,' Brenna said at last, 'you were going to tell me about yesterday.'

Cordelia told her about her adventures trying to track down the painting and how she and Dylan were now following a lead in Windermere.

'Sounds positive.'

'You think?'

'But you mustn't be disappointed if you don't find it. You seem to have set your heart on this thing.'

'I just need to see it again.'

'I don't know how you even remember it. You were so young.'

Cordelia smiled. 'It's funny, isn't it? But there was just something about it that... I don't know... caught my imagination, I guess.'

'And what does this Dylan think about it all?'

'He's really into it. I was worried because I was taking up so much of his time but he says he's having fun.'

'And are you? I mean *with him*?'

'What do you mean?'

'Well, you said he was about your age, didn't you? Is he cute?'

'Bren!'

'Come on! I want to know!' Brenna said. 'Cheer me up a bit.'

Cordelia sighed. 'He's tall and he's got fair hair which is kind of curly. And he's got kind eyes and he smiles a lot. I like that. And he...' she paused.

'What?'

'He puts me at ease.'

Brenna looked thoughtful at that. 'He sounds perfect.'

'Oh, Bren!'

'I mean, he's in the art world and obviously knows his stuff. What's his car like?'

'What's that got to do with anything?'

'You can tell a lot about a man from his car. Was it nice? Clean? Or was it full of burger wrappers?'

'You're terrible!'

'I'm just looking out for my little sis.'

'Well, I'm looking for a painting not a romance.'

Brenna tutted. 'Spoilsport!'

Lunch finished, Cordelia took the plates to the sink to wash up. 'Shouldn't we wake Alex?'

'I'll wait till you've finished the dishes then take the bowl of water up and throw it over him.'

'It would be kinder to take him up a cup of coffee.'

Brenna grimaced. 'I suppose.'

She crossed the kitchen to put the kettle on and, a few minutes later, walked up the stairs to Alex's room. She paused on the landing. Her brother's room had been a no-go zone when they'd been growing up. Not that she'd wanted to go into his smelly room. It was a known fact that all brothers' rooms smelt bad, wasn't it? And Brenna didn't think things would have improved now that he was an adult so she knocked on the door and braced herself.

The sight that greeted her of Alex sprawled under his duvet cover, one bare foot and a shaggy head of hair poking out from either end stabbed at her heart and she walked inside, placing the mug on the bedside table and gently opening the curtains before pushing the old windows open to let some much-needed air inside. It was just as she'd always imagined – a fuggy mess. Well, she wasn't tidying up after him here. She'd done her bit in his place in Skopelos and she had enough to cope with sorting through her Father's things without starting in Alex's bedroom.

'Hey!' she called. He didn't respond. 'Alex!' she yelled somewhere above his right ear.

He stirred. 'What?'

'It's the afternoon. It's time you got up.'

He groaned and mumbled something incoherent.

'We need you downstairs. I've made you a coffee, okay? Get washed, get dressed and get downstairs before I throw a bucket of water over you.'

She marched back out of the room and returned to the kitchen.

Cordelia turned around from the worktop she was cleaning. 'You were kind to him, weren't you?'

'Of course,' Brenna said.

It was mid-afternoon by the time Alex deigned to join them in their father's study. Brenna felt overwhelmed by the amount of stuff they had to go through. Just when she thought they were making good progress, she'd open another cupboard or drawer and discover another world of papers or documents, albums or receipts. She wondered if they should call in a team of professionals to help, but she didn't want strangers going through her father's things. That would make him too vulnerable, she thought – like a tortoise without its shell.

Although she had rarely felt close to her father, she felt him on a cellular level because she *was* him. She knew instinctively that he would hate strangers going through his personal items. Especially all the letters of rejection he'd kept over the years for jobs she hadn't known he'd applied for. He hadn't always been the renowned artist, she realised.

Once, he'd been a struggling artist doing his best to keep his family afloat by any means possible. There was one rejection letter from a building society in Carlisle. It sounded like a very dull job indeed and being rejected from that must have stung horribly. She wondered how he'd dealt with it. Alex gave an amused chuckle as she handed it to him.

'He certainly kept that quiet.'

'He'd lived a whole life before he had us,' Cordelia said. 'I wonder what he was like back then. Do you think we would have liked him?'

'What do you mean?' Alex asked.

'I mean, if you met your family out of context – if you had the chance to meet them as you would anyone else – would you get on with them? Would you want to be friends?'

'That's a weird question,' Alex said.

'I think it's rather interesting,' Brenna mused. 'So what's your answer?'

'We'd be friends – absolutely!' Cordelia said. 'Dad always knew how to make me laugh.'

'Huh! He always knew how to make me mad. I think he'd be the sort of person I'd cross the road to avoid,' Alex confessed.

'Oh, don't say that!' Cordelia cried.

'Well, you did ask!'

Brenna threw her hands up in the air as Cordelia turned to her.

'Don't ask! And don't pout like that. Come on. We've got to get on with this.'

The first thing they decided to tackle were the photos. They were everywhere – in albums, scrapbooks and loose in boxes. Masses of them. One drawer in the study had been crammed full and a tsunami of photos was released when Alex opened it.

'What are they?' Brenna asked.

'Mostly landscapes, I think,' Alex replied, scooping an armful up.

'Well, they can go for a start.'

'Doesn't that seem a shame?'

'But there are so many,' Brenna stressed.

'I know, but these photos – they're his vision of the world – they're what he saw.'

'Yes but only for a moment. A moment that's long gone. You can let them go, Alex.'

'I don't know if that's right.'

'He wouldn't expect you to keep them. You need to make your own moments.'

She watched as Alex sifted through a few of the coloured landscapes. They were mostly beautiful but some were a little more like reference shots their father had taken in order to capture the colour of the sky, perhaps, or the outline of a mountain.

'We really can't keep them all,' Brenna said gently. 'Unless you're going to cart them all back to Skopelos with you.'

Alex nodded, seeming to see sense, picked a couple of the photos he liked and then put the rest in the box for recycling.

Of course, it was much harder when the photos weren't of landscapes but of Father himself. Cordelia said she'd keep the albums from his childhood and Brenna said she'd take the wedding album, but what were they to do with all the loose pictures? They'd divided the family albums between themselves, but there were so many others of Father taken over the years – by his parents, their mother and others at his art events. They did their best to sift through them, pulling out the best.

'It doesn't feel right to put Dad in the bin,' Cordelia said as they worked through the pile.

'You really want to keep every single image of Dad ever taken?'

'Sure. Why not?'

Brenna could see that her sister was struggling with it all.

'Look at it this way, when will you have time to look at them? If you keep them all, just think of the time you'd have to set aside to go through them. How often do you think you'd do it? How often do you think Father did it? Judging by the way most of these were just crammed into a drawer or envelopes, I'd say it wasn't very often.'

'I know. But it still feels wrong somehow.'

'I think we keep a handful of the best and don't worry about the others. That way the ones we keep will really mean something to us and they'll kind of represent all the others.'

Cordelia nodded and Brenna was pleased that she'd helped her through the dilemma. They were making good progress physically, but it was certainly taking its toll emotionally.

'Look at this one,' Alex said, holding up a photo of their father as a young man.

'So handsome,' Cordelia said. 'We can't bin that one. He looks like a movie star.'

Brenna moved forward to see and barely recognised the man in the picture. It was so funny to see this incarnation of the man who'd simply been 'Father'. Here he was looking so young – younger than her and Alex were now – and obviously fashion-conscious. They'd been so used to seeing him wearing the garb of a northern painter – fleece shirts, jumpers and lined trousers. But here was the man he'd been before that. Father before he'd been Father.

'I'd like to keep this one,' Alex said. 'Unless you want it?' He nodded to Cordelia who looked a little unsure.

'You have it. I'll have this one,' she said, picking up a similar one from the pile.

And so the afternoon wore on as the three of them sifted through the decades of a life that had been captured on film and deciding what was good enough to keep for a few decades more and what would now be lost forever. As much as Brenna tried to distance herself from such enormous responsibility, she felt herself slipping occasionally and pulling discarded photos back out of the recycle pile. Thankfully Alex and Cordelia didn't say anything.

One thing they all agreed on was when it was time to stop for dinner. They were glad to leave the study. The kitchen felt relatively cosy by comparison and at least it was a clutter-free zone now that they'd sorted it out. The three of them got to work laying the table and prepping the food. Cordelia was making vegetable soup because it was cheap, quick and warming and she thought her siblings could do with getting more veggies into their diets.

It was as they were all finishing their meal that Brenna dared to raise a subject that hadn't been talked about yet.

'Have you given the money any thought?'

Neither Alex nor Cordelia responded to begin with.

'The money?' Cordelia asked at last.

'Yes. We don't know exactly what the house is worth yet, but we know roughly what's being left after Inheritance Tax.'

'I don't want to think about it,' Alex said.

'Well, I'm afraid you'll have to at some point.'

'It doesn't feel real, does it?' Cordelia said.

'No,' Brenna agreed.

'It's sad that a life so quickly becomes about the things you've accumulated. The *money*,' Cordelia said.

'And we're the ones who have to deal with it.'

Her sister sighed. 'I suppose I'll get a place in London.'

Brenna nodded. It was the sensible thing to do, wasn't it? To invest in property. And London property was always a wise decision.

'Actually, I've always wanted to do up an old place. You know – an abandoned building with a bit of history. Make it beautiful again, but make it functional too.'

'Develop and sell?' Alex asked. 'Smart move.'

'No. Not to sell,' Cordelia said. 'To convert into rooms to rent out.'

'Oh, you're going to be a landlady?' Brenna asked.

'I don't know. I suppose that's what I mean. But that's not really the aim. I might hand that task over to someone else. But what I'd really like to do is rent rooms to women in theatre who wouldn't otherwise be able to live and work in London.'

Brenna frowned and Alex looked equally confused by this notion so Cordelia continued.

'A few months ago, the film club I belong to had a little challenge – to research an old film star from the nineteen-thirties, forties or fifties and I chose Ginger Rogers.'

'As in Fred and Ginger?' Alex asked.

'Yes. Only, she wasn't just half of one of the most famous dance couples of all time. She was a pretty brilliant actress in her own right. Anyway, I found this film of hers called *Stage Door* from 1937. It's about a group of actresses all living together in a

New York boarding house. The rent is pretty cheap but some of the actresses even struggle to pay that. Anyway, I think it would be fun, don't you? To provide something like that?'

'I guess,' Brenna said. 'It's definitely original.'

The three of them sat musing this for a little while and then Cordelia spoke again.

'What will you do, Brenna – with your share?'

'Well, I don't want a bigger house,' she said quickly. 'I'll pay the mortgage off my place for sure. But I don't know. It's too early to make any big decisions. Maybe I'll take some time off.'

'Travel the world!' Alex said dramatically.

'I've always wanted to see Brighton.'

Alex laughed. 'Is that the sum total of your ambition? To see Brighton?'

'What's wrong with that? It's got a pier and a pavilion.'

'And chips and ice cream,' Cordelia added.

'Exactly!' Brenna said. 'So what about you, Alex?'

'I don't know. I'll invest in something.'

'You know, you have to make money work for you otherwise it's useless,' Cordelia said. 'I saw this story online recently about a father and son. The father owned this huge international company. It was making millions. He'd employed his son, but his son was going through some kind of spiritual awakening and hated the idea of all this wealth being held by one person and so he was giving the money away as fast as it was being earned.'

'Oh my god! I would've fired his butt!' Alex said.

'But what's the use of money just sitting in an account? Money's got to keep moving to be truly useful. It needs to be free. Like people need to be free.'

'Yeah, but people can't be free without money,' Alex pointed out.

'What about monks? Brenna said.

'They sell stuff, don't they? Honey and scary paintings of saints in gaudy gold frames,' Alex said. 'And someone must have earned all the money to have built their monasteries at some point. That son should have invested his father's money properly.'

'But he did,' Cordelia told him. 'He invested it in people and places he believed in. He gave it to charities who work to make life a little bit easier for others. That's *really* investing.'

Alex shook his head. 'We've got very different ideas about what constitutes investment.'

It would have been quite easy for a full-blown sibling argument to develop but, luckily, Cordelia's phone interrupted them and Brenna watched as her sister's face changed from tense to excited.

'That was Dylan,' she said as she hung up a moment later.

'About the painting?' Brenna asked.

'Yes. He's not been able to get hold of the garage owner so he thinks it best if we head over to Windermere tomorrow and try and catch him in person. Is that okay?'

'Of course it is,' Brenna told her.

'I don't expect it'll take long. It's probably another dead end anyway.'

CHAPTER TWELVE

The next morning, Dylan's car pulled up outside Slate House to pick up Cordelia. It was one of those bright September days when the sky was so clear and the view down to Grasmere was just the sort that Father would have painted. Cordelia took a moment to take it all in, the air edged with the scent of damp fallen leaves and rain-soaked earth.

Dylan gave her a big broad smile as she got into the car.

'Okay?'

'Yes. You?'

'Got woken up by a painting falling off the wall, but the good news is it was in a frame I hated and I was a bit bored of looking at it anyway.'

'Not one of my father's, I hope!'

'Certainly not. I'd never tire of his.'

Cordelia sensed the sincerity in his words and smiled.

'Well, it wasn't hard to find the garage,' Dylan told her, 'but, every time I rang, Mr Dixon, it seemed, was underneath a car or with a customer and I didn't really fancy trying to leave a message.'

'No, it might be easier to speak face to face.'

'That's what I thought. Anyway, I have a good feeling about this.'

'Do you?'

He nodded as they pulled out of the driveway.

It was a beautiful drive with stunning views down to Windermere. Even though summer was over, there were still plenty of boats. Cordelia had always liked the sailing boats so white against the blue water and she wished she'd inherited her father's talent for capturing such moments.

When they arrived in town, Dylan found somewhere to park and they walked to the garage. There was a small forecourt and a radio blasting from somewhere inside.

'Right, let's try and find this Dixon fellow,' Dylan said. 'You okay?'

Cordelia nodded. 'I'm suddenly nervous.'

'Maybe that's a sign that we're getting closer.' He smiled and that gave her courage.

It was then that a mechanic rolled himself out from underneath a Land Rover.

'Hello!' he said brightly. 'Pick up or drop off?'

'Neither,' Dylan said. 'We're looking for Mr Dixon.'

'You're looking right at him.'

'Oh, great! Mind if we have a chat about something?'

He frowned. 'What's this about then?'

'We were at your parents' old place in Eskdale the other day.'

'Oh, aye?'

'We're looking for a painting,' Cordelia told him. 'My

father was an artist and we were told your parents bought one of his paintings called *Family Portrait.*'

'Doesn't ring a bell,' he said, wiping his hands on an oily rag.

Cordelia knew her face wasn't doing a very good job of hiding her disappointment.

'Hang on a minute. I did find some paintings. Years ago, mind. I didn't know they had them. They were all wrapped up in the attic. Anyway, I couldn't justify keeping them. Not my kind of thing really and I've got this place to run.'

'So what happened to them?'

'Sold 'em.'

'Where?' Cordelia asked.

'Auction.'

'A local one?' Dylan asked.

He nodded and named an auction house in Kendal. Cordelia glanced at Dylan. He was frowning and she felt her heart plummet. This was it, she thought. This was the end of the trail. She didn't know much about auction houses, but she knew that purchases were often online or over the phone and, for the most part, confidential. Unless you happened to be in the room at the time of the auction and saw who'd made the winning bid, there was little chance of tracking down a piece after it had sold.

They thanked Mr Dixon and left.

'I know what you're thinking,' Dylan told Cordelia.

'What?'

'That that's it.'

'It is, though, isn't it?'

'Not necessarily.'

'No?'

'The auction house – there's just a chance I know

someone there and they might be able to tell us something about who bought the painting. If we can track down when it was sold. That shouldn't be too tricky with everything on computers these days.'

'Really?'

'Don't get too excited. They might not actually be allowed to give us the buyer's information.'

'No, I don't expect they will.'

'But I've got a good feeling about this.'

'You said that about Mr Dixon,' Cordelia dared to point out.

'Yes, I know, and that led us to this moment, didn't it?'

Cordelia couldn't disagree with that. 'And you think *Family Portrait* is among the collection he sold?'

'Well, it doesn't sound like he kept any and he was the one to inherit from his parents and we know they had the painting, don't we?'

She sighed. 'I wish we knew for sure. What if we're just following one dead end after another?'

'But we're not. Each lead has led us to another. We can't give up now.'

'Who knew a painting could have such an interesting life?'

'Yes. I've often wondered what happens to them after we sell them. Now I'm getting the chance to find out.'

'I hope we don't track it down to an owner who's just thrown it on a bonfire.'

'Cordy! You've got to have more faith!'

'Sorry. Bad headspace at the mo.'

'Listen,' he said, 'since we're here, how about getting a bite to eat?'

'If it delays my return home, definitely.'

A look of concern crossed Dylan's face. 'How's it going?'

'Okay, I suppose. Brenna's pretty tense and Alex – well – he holed up in a pub the other day and ended up with a horrible hangover.'

'And how are you coping?'

'I...' she paused, unsure that she was ready to address that question. Not many people had actually asked her. 'I'm okay.'

'Yeah?'

'I don't know. It's early days, isn't it? I'm probably building up to a magnificent breakdown at any moment.'

'I'll be on guard,' Dylan said and he touched her shoulder sympathetically.

They found a little café and ordered drinks and a light lunch. It felt good to sit down in a place she didn't have to sort through and organise – a place where the serious face of her sister and the sullen face of her brother wasn't hovering over her. As soon as she had the thought, she felt guilty. Her own face couldn't exactly be a picture of joy at the moment, she realised. But this was good, she thought. Dylan was an easy companion and she valued this new friendship which had arrived so unexpectedly.

It was then that she remembered something he'd said to her in passing and she dared to raise it now.

'You said your mum left when you were growing up. Is she still around?'

'Not really,' Dylan said. 'I mean, she's alive, but we don't see her. She,' he paused, 'she's kind of a nomad. Never settled. It was a wonder she was around as long as she was actually.'

'I'm sorry. That must have been tough.'

'I don't know,' he said with a shrug. 'I had Dad and we

were always good pals. Apart from a few awkward teenage tantrums of course.'

'Of course,' Cordelia said with a smile.

'I've got a few pictures of her with me as a kid and she always looks so happy in them that it's hard to work out why she left. I've often tried to understand. Do you think maybe she was one of those women who only like babies and young kids? And then – when I grew up and had a mind of my own – she just sort of lost interest? The maternal spark died.' He shrugged.

'People are complex, that's all I know,' Cordelia said. 'I'm not sure we should try to work them out although I guess that's what I'm trying to do with finding this painting.'

'So is your mother still around?'

'She died. She left then she died.'

Dylan frowned. 'Blimey! What happened? I mean if you don't mind talking about it.'

'I was very young at the time so I only know what I've been told. But she and my father were never an ideal match. And, one day, she just left. I think she'd been seeing someone for a while. I don't know the details. We refer to him as The Man Who Killed Mother.'

'What – he murdered her?'

'No! Nothing like that. It was an accident. On Derwentwater. I don't know much about it and I'm not sure I want to.'

'I'm so sorry.'

'It was harder for Alex and Brenna. They were teenagers. It was a lot to go through.'

'I bet.'

'And it's all being raked up again now for them – being

back at Slate House and going through old photos and just being in that space again.'

'It's a tough time for you all.'

Cordelia stirred her tea. She knew she was holding back a vital piece of information from Dylan, but she didn't know if she should share it.

'What is it?' he asked gently.

She looked up at him. He seemed so good at sensing her mood. But she reminded herself that, although they'd spent this time together and he seemed like a good person, he wasn't family and what she was going through was family business. She shouldn't be sharing such details. What would Alex and Brenna think? No, she couldn't tell him.

'We've just found out we have a half-sister,' she blurted.

'What?'

'It turns out Father was leading a double life. He had another daughter in Cornwall.'

Dylan looked shocked.

'I shouldn't have told you. Forget it. I've embarrassed you.'

'No. No, you haven't. It's just unexpected. I'm trying to imagine how that must have felt for you.'

'I'm still trying to work that out. It's one of the reasons I want to find this painting. I think he painted us all together, you see – as a family. Me, Alex, Brenna, Mother and Daisy.'

'Your half-sister?'

Cordelia nodded. 'I need to see it. I need to know.'

'What is it you're hoping to find out?'

'I guess I want to know how he saw us all. Did he think of us as a whole or as separate families?'

'And you think the painting might tell you that?'

She sighed and it felt like she was exhaling a world of

pent-up emotion. 'I really don't know. But it's nagging at me so I guess there's something in it. Anyway, I need to find out now.'

They finished their lunch, paid and left the café.

'I've been wondering,' Dylan began. 'Why would your father sell such a painting if it's so personal?'

Cordelia mused on this for a moment. 'Maybe it was too painful to have around.'

'I was so hoping Mr Dixon would have it today.'

'Yes, but I'm beginning to realise that you can't always keep hold of the things you've inherited. Things that are precious to one person might just be clutter to another.'

'Is that what you're finding with your father's things?' he asked as they crossed the road towards his car.

'Yes. It's breaking my heart every time I think about all the things we're going to have to part with. All the bits and pieces I grew up with. And it's silly really when you think about it. How can you be attached to inanimate things? How can parting with a wardrobe or a table lamp upset you?'

'I guess you're just sensitive? Maybe you appreciate beautiful things.'

'I think we attach far too much of ourselves to *things*, don't you?'

'How do you mean?' Dylan asked.

'Well, Brenna isn't sure what to do with our mother's piano. We'll have to sell it, of course, but she seems reluctant to. And yet none of us can keep it. I couldn't easily get it down to London even if I wanted to, and it would take up a whole room in the flat I'm in. Alex lives in Greece and Brenna's place is tiny so it's a really impractical thing to inherit. Anyway, none of us really plays it. Brenna used to enjoy playing, but she's not kept it up. But I can see her struggle to let it go because it's more than a piano, isn't it? It's a link back to our mother. It was her passion, you see? And I guess when somebody has poured so much passion into something, a little of that lingers on in the thing itself.' She shook her head. 'I don't know.'

'No, I think you're right. When my mum left us, she left behind all these hats. She loved hats. There were enormous sun hats in all sorts of gaudy colours and winter hats with felt flowers all over them. Anyway, one day when I came home from school, I saw Dad cramming them all into bin bags. I've never seen him look so mad. It wasn't just him making space or kindly donating stuff to charity – he needed to get those things out of the house because they were so linked to his memories of Mum.'

'I can totally understand that,' Cordelia said, 'but isn't it crazy to think that people are in their things?' She pulled at a silver and amethyst pendant she was wearing. 'This, for example. I love it and I wear it a lot, but I wouldn't want Brenna or anyone else getting all upset and emotionally crippled if I were to die and they felt obliged to keep it, because this isn't *me,* is it? It's just something I wear and, even if I wear it every day of my life, it still wouldn't be a fraction of who I really am because it's just a thing. A bauble.'

Dylan nodded in agreement and then smiled. 'I love this.'

'What?'

'That we're able to talk like this. I don't know – most of the time, people just skirt around subjects, skating over the surface of them. But this is good, deep stuff.'

She returned his smile. 'I'm sorry if I'm getting all heavy.'

'No. I'm really loving it. It's honest. *Real.* And you're right – people aren't in things. They're in our memories. The things – the hats, the piano, your necklace – they might evoke memories of the people they're associated with, but that's all. We don't have to keep the objects themselves, do we? We don't have to burden ourselves with it all.'

'So I can go back to Slate House and tell Alex and Brenna that we should get rid of everything and not feel guilty about it?'

'It could definitely be something they might want to consider.'

'I don't know!' She was still smiling. 'It would definitely speed everything up.'

'Yeah, but sometimes slow is good too. Giving yourself time to process your feelings. It's not just about the stuff, is it?'

'No. I guess not,' she said as they got in the car.

'Why is it all so complicated?' she asked a moment later as they left Windermere behind them.

'Because humans have an uncanny knack for making it so. Just imagine any other species behaving the way we do. Imagine a squirrel. A squirrel doesn't have any possessions, does it? The only thing it actually *squirrels away* is food. Animals don't go around collecting stuff. And, if they do, it's usually for a purpose – to build a nest or dam a river.'

'Dogs have toys though, don't they?'

'That's because humans are responsible for that.'

'We're pretty awful, aren't we? Filling the word with more and more stuff.'

'Now, don't get me wrong,' Dylan said. 'I like beautiful things. I'm in the business of persuading people to buy them from me, aren't I? So I can't talk.'

'But art is different, isn't it? It's life-enhancing.'

'But isn't your mother's piano? And my mother's hats?'

'So what are you saying? We *shouldn't* get rid of those things?'

'I don't know what I'm saying!' He laughed. 'I guess we have to work it out for ourselves. But I don't think that what one person thought of as being beautiful should be forced upon somebody else. Take Mr Dixon today. He didn't have any time for your father's painting. He'd rather pay a few bills with the money raised from it. But his parents loved it enough to part with their hard-earned money to buy it and to give it a place in their home.'

Cordelia mulled this over for a while as Dylan drove. By the time they reached Grasmere, she was more confused than ever about how she felt about things.

'Let me reach out to the auction house, okay?' Dylan said as he pulled up outside Slate House. 'I'll give you a call and let you know what they say.'

'Do you want to come in and meet Alex and Brenna? Maybe you could be the one to tell them your idea about getting rid of everything in one fell swoop!'

Dylan laughed. 'Maybe not! Anyway, I'd better get back to Dad.'

'Sure.'

'Another time, yeah?'

'Okay.'

Cordelia got out of the car and she had the oddest feeling of being stuck between two worlds. She didn't want Dylan to go and she certainly didn't want to go back into the house. She felt that she was kind of floating with no distinct place where she truly belonged. Perhaps it was only to be expected. This time – this twilight period after the death of her father – it was something she had to just get through. It wasn't something of itself. A transitory place. That thought was actually comforting. What was that famous saying? *This too shall pass.*

'You all right?' Dylan asked, jolting her out of her thoughts as she hesitated to shut the car door.

'Yes.' She smiled and nodded, trying to convince herself as much as him as she finally shut the door. He gave her a funny sort of salute and she watched as he drove away, and she couldn't help hoping that it wouldn't be too long before she saw him again.

CHAPTER THIRTEEN

'Sweetheart, will you *please* stop fidgeting?'

Daisy shifted on her tall wooden stool. Her legs had gone to sleep a long time ago and she knew her whole body had completely slumped in the last five minutes. She yawned and dared to glance out of the window. The sun had reached its zenith and she couldn't help thinking how beautiful it would be at the beach today. She longed to be there, wandering bare foot in that frothy heaven where the waves meet the shore, her toes disappearing and reappearing, the breeze blowing her hair out behind her as she gave her face to the sun. But she'd made a promise to sit for her father and, in fairness, he hadn't painted her in ages.

She glanced across at him. He looked so funny when he was concentrating. His eyes narrowed, his head nodding slightly, his steel-grey hair flopping across his face. His lips were pursed but they'd twitch every so often. Daisy giggled as she caught a twitch now.

'Daisy – *please!*' he cried.

'Sorry!' She giggled again and he sighed, putting his brush down in defeat.

'You're like a butterfly that's trapped indoors and needs to be released.'

'I'm fine.'

'No, you're not. And it's not fair to keep you in. Go on!' He nodded towards the door.

'Are you sure?'

'We can finish another time.'

Another time.

Daisy felt the full weight of guilt now because there would never be another time again. She'd denied him that feeling of accomplishing a finished painting and she'd also denied herself that precious time with him – that strange, indefinable bond between an artist and their model, made all the more precious by their relationship. She'd sat for him countless times over the years – at least twice each summer he'd spent with them and sometimes throughout the year if he was able to get away to visit them.

The early portraits had been sketches really. Charcoal or pencil drawings which had captured her youth and energy. There was one of her as a toddler racing around the garden, her smile wide and her hands reaching out to capture all that summer had to offer her.

A few had been framed and hung around the house much to Daisy's embarrassment. There was one in particular on the landing. He'd managed to catch every single one of her gawky, awkward teenage angles and the sulky curl of her mouth. She didn't know why her mum loved it so much. Daisy much preferred the one of her on the beach, her eight-year-old limbs tanned and silky with seawater as she waded through the rock pools. She could almost smell the ocean when she looked at it and feel the salt spray on her freckled face.

It was so hard to accept that this summer had been the last she'd ever have with her father. She tried to think back to how he'd been that day in the studio. Had he seemed older, frailer to her? She really couldn't say that he had. But how she'd wished she hadn't left when she had. The unfinished portrait made her heart ache when she looked at it now. He'd caught most of her fidgety frame and her hair looked finished, but her face was indistinct. It was just a ghost-like outline, undefined, eyeless, expressionless.

'I'm sorry,' she whispered into the silent studio as if her father might be able to hear her somehow.

Her mind drifted back to another day in the summer. Her mum had wanted to pack a picnic and head to the beach.

'No painting!' she'd said sternly. 'Just fun!'

Father had laughed and shaken his head. 'Actually, I was going to rest today.'

Daisy remembered the look on her mum's face. Bemusement tinged with concern. Father did not do *rest*.

But they'd shrugged it off. Her mum had made a flippant comment about him being so much older than her, but they hadn't thought anything of it. He'd fallen asleep in a deck chair in the garden as soon as they'd returned, the last of the sun streaking across the lawn, tickling his toes. He would normally have been painting during the glorious golden hour.

If only they'd known. Had they made the most of the summer together? Daisy berated herself now for having spent time away from him, but she'd recently got a summer job in a local craft centre and she'd enjoyed meeting all the holidaymakers. She'd known that her father had had her late in life and a part of her realised that he wouldn't be around forever but, when you're still so young yourself, the mind simply didn't dwell on mortality.

She left his studio, wondering what would become of the room now. Would they keep all his things as he had left them? Would one of his galleries want the paintings he'd left or would her mum claim them as hers? What happened to art once the artist had gone? Who was its rightful owner?

Her mum was in the living room, flipping through a photo album. It was like a relic from the past. Everything was digital these days, but her mum insisted on having all her favourite photos printed out and placed in albums and Daisy was glad of that now as she sat next to her on the sofa.

'Remember this?'

Daisy shook her head.

'Of course not. You were only two. We took you down to the sea for your first paddle.'

'Did I like it?'

'No! You screamed like a seagull!'

Daisy laughed, looking at the photo of her riding on her father's shoulders. His eyes were squinting in the sun and she could almost hear his laughter. Gosh, how she missed his laugh. He wasn't the sort to laugh all the time so, when he did, it really counted.

'And this was the summer we went to Dorset.'

'I remember that,' Daisy said. It had been unusual for them to leave Cornwall. Her dad had always favoured painting the beaches here so Daisy hadn't seen much outside the county. They'd never had anything exciting like a foreign holiday together. When her mum had once suggested visiting France, Dad had baulked.

'There's nothing I can find in France that isn't here.'

He could be extremely selfish like that, Daisy couldn't help remembering. He hadn't thought about how her mum might want to spend a holiday. For him, a holiday – if he absolutely had to leave Cornwall – was an opportunity to paint a new location.

Had it been the same for his family in the north, she wondered. Had they ever had holidays together? How had they spent the summers without their father? How had he explained his time away to them?

'I actually really want to meet them,' Daisy suddenly said.

'His other children?'

'Yes. Do you think I should?'

'It's your decision, Daisy.'

'Do you think they want to meet me?'

'I don't know. But if you want to meet them, they might be feeling the same way.'

'What do you think Dad would have wanted me to do?'

Her mother sighed. 'He always kept us all so separate.'

'But he must've realised that this day would come.'

'Yes.' Her mum closed the photo album. The time of happy reminiscing was over.

'When will we know what's happening?' Daisy asked.

'You mean the funeral? The executor said he'd let us know.'

'I'd like to meet them before then. I think it would be less awkward, don't you?'

Her mother didn't look sure. 'Well, it might be. Unless you don't get on and then it might make things worse.'

Daisy hadn't considered that. 'I think I should risk it.'

Her mother nodded and Daisy waited for her to impart some more words of wisdom, but she stood up instead and left the room. It had been a week of such behaviour, Daisy noted. Her mother would suddenly have to do something in another room. Daisy closed her eyes because she could feel the first stirring of tears, but she didn't let them fall because she had something to do.

She was going to call the executor.

'She wants to meet us,' Brenna said, rushing into the living room where Alex and Cordelia were sorting through an oak cabinet full of china and glass.

'Who?' Alex said.

'Who do you think? *Daisy!*'

'She rang you?' Alex's face was ashen.

'No. She contacted Mr Grant.'

'What have you said?' Cordelia asked.

'That I'd talk to you first.'

Cordelia glanced at Alex.

'I don't want to meet her,' he said.

'What?' Cordelia looked surprised.

'I said I don't want to see her. Who does she think she is poking her nose in where it isn't wanted.'

'Our sister?' Cordelia answered.

'*Half!* And that's up for debate.'

'Well, you can't debate it if you don't meet her,' Brenna pointed out.

'Are you seriously even considering it?'

'Yes. And I think you should too. She wants to meet ahead of the funeral. She said she thought it might make everything easier.'

'I agree,' Cordelia said. 'Can you imagine that day otherwise? We'd be distracted looking around for her.'

'God, you'll be asking her to sit with us in the front row next,' Alex said.

'She'd have every right to,' Cordelia told him.

Alex shook his head and mumbled something. Brenna didn't bother asking him what he'd said. She really didn't want to know.

'Just think about it, okay?'

'I've made my decision.'

'Fine!' Brenna said. 'We don't all have to agree. Nobody will force you to meet her.'

'It can't just be two of us!' Cordelia's voice was full of panic. 'How would that look?'

'It would look honest,' Alex said.

Brenna opened her mouth to say something scathing to Alex, but thought better of it. In truth, she wasn't sure how she felt about the unexpected request herself yet, so it really wasn't her place to pass judgement on her brother.

'I'm going for a walk,' she said instead.

'For a change,' Alex scoffed.

'Better than hitting a bottle.'

'Please!' Cordelia cried. 'Let's not fight.'

'I'm not,' Brenna said. 'I'm going out, okay?'

'Let her go,' Alex said. 'She'll be in a better mood when she gets back.'

Brenna caught Cordelia's warning look to Alex before she left the room.

~

Brenna found Blue in an outbuilding. Her hair looked dusty and her cheeks were flushed. She looked beautiful.

'Hey! Good to see you.'

Brenna smiled. Even though she felt ghastly, she just couldn't help smiling when she was around Blue. It amazed Brenna how quickly she'd fallen back into stride with her old friend. It was as if no time at all had passed between them. They were their old selves.

'What are you doing?'

'Trying to patch up a hole. Farm buildings have a lot of holes!'

'So do families. But I don't think they're as easy to mend.'

'Oh, dear. Will an iced bun help?'

'I think it might.'

They headed into the farmhouse. Midge the terrier raised his head but quickly decided that Brenna was friend rather than foe and got on with the business of dozing.

'When do you have time to bake?' Brenna asked as she sat down at the kitchen table.

'Couldn't sleep so got up and made a couple of dozen buns for the B and B guests.'

'Are you okay?'

'Yeah. Just worrying about a section of wall that needs fixing. There's some fencing down too. It's all so expensive.'

'Oh, I'm sorry.'

'I'll work something out. I've actually been thinking about advertising for volunteers. There are sites for that now. Young people who are willing to work in exchange for accommodation and food.'

'If they hear about your iced buns, you'll be inundated.'

Blue laughed as she brought a plate of enormous buns to the table.

'Actually, I think *I'd* be willing to mend walls and fences if you keep the sweet treats coming.'

Blue smiled and the two of them got on with the business of eating.

'So, what's happening?' Blue asked at last, obviously guessing that something was up. 'You look as if you're in the midst of some crisis.'

Brenna sighed. 'Sorry.'

'Don't be sorry. It takes my mind off my own issues for a bit.' She winked and Brenna laughed before telling her about the latest phone call.

'So are you going to meet her?'

Brenna hesitated. 'I... I think so. At least I think me and Cordy will. Alex doesn't want to.'

'He's a grown-up–'

'Well, *that's* debatable!' Brenna interrupted.

'He can make up his own mind. Just don't let it stress you out. You do your thing, Bren, okay? You decide what's right for you.'

She nodded.

'It's rather a lot to cope with all at once, isn't it?'

'Ha! You're not kidding.'

'Still, it can't be as bad as the time we got caught stealing Mr Pomfrey's goat.'

Brenna's face lit up at the memory. 'God, I haven't thought about that for years!'

'You tried to cram it into your dad's car – remember?'

'That's not the kind of detail you easily forget! Father was furious. The car never smelled of anything but goat after that. When he came to sell it, the new owners demanded he knock money off for the smell.'

Blue laughed.

'Why *did* we steal it?' Brenna asked.

'Old Pomfrey wasn't looking after it properly. Its hooves were overgrown and its coat was in a terrible state. But Pomfrey was pretty old and in a pretty bad state himself. I guess he just couldn't do physical work anymore.'

'Is he still around?'

'No. Died years ago.'

Brenna frowned. 'What happened to the goat?'

'We kept her here. His son had something to say about it. Don't you remember? He came after us.'

'Oh, yes! The burly guy with the bad mouth?'

'I've never heard so much bad language!' Blue laughed again. 'Good times!'

'We certainly had some fun together.'

Blue offered her another bun which Brenna gratefully accepted.

'What do you think she's like?' Brenna asked.

'Your sister?'

'*Half*-sister,' Brenna corrected, realising that she sounded exactly like Alex.

'I've absolutely no idea.'

'She's quite close to Cordy in age.'

'What does Cordy think of that?'

'I don't think she was thrilled to learn that she wasn't the youngest child after all.'

'Right!'

'It's a weird one. I guess it's been part of her identity.'

'That doesn't change surely? She's still the youngest in *your* family.'

'But how did Father see her? Where exactly were we in his affections? Did he prefer his Cornish family and life?' She could feel her stomach tying itself up into knots which was not good when attempting to enjoy a second bun.

'Hey!' Blue said. 'Your Father may have had his secrets, but he was there for you, wasn't he? He might have been in Cornwall every summer, but he always came back.'

'I think it was more for his work than for us.'

'Oh, Bren! That's not true.'

'No? I'm sorry, but you don't really know how it was and I guess it's hard to imagine when you had such a good relationship with your parents,' she said, finding it hard not to feel slightly jealous of her friend.

'I guess,' Blue said cautiously.

Brenna frowned. 'What does that mean?'

'Well, Mum could be tricky sometimes. You know how stressful farming can be. I think she was one of life's worriers.'

'You got on well together at least.'

'We did, but we had our moments for sure and I didn't have the same closeness that I felt with Dad. It was always so natural with him. We could work for hours side by side and be so comfortable, you know?'

'No, I don't.'

Blue sighed. 'I'm so sorry, Brenna. You had a rough deal, didn't you?'

'It's hard not to feel bitter sometimes, but I often find myself looking at families and feeling so frustrated that I never felt that kind of closeness with mine. Especially with my father. There was just this massive disconnect with him. I could never reach him. And I can't talk to Cordy about any of this because she idolised him.'

'Then he was obviously capable of emotions,' Blue pointed out.

'Oh, yes. For the chosen few.'

'How was he with Alex?'

'Brusque bordering on cruel most of the time. Alex was always seen as a rival.'

'Really?'

'Father never really encouraged Alex with his art. It was so hard to witness. Alex was always so desperate for his approval and I don't think he ever got it.'

'At least he understands what you're going through.'

'I guess. But he's too wrapped up in his own misery to acknowledge mine.'

'Well, you're lucky to have me then,' Blue said, reaching across the table and squeezing her hand.

'Thanks. It helps to – you know – talk.'

'Well, you know I'm happy to listen. Any time.' Blue took a deep breath. 'You know, I sometimes think we put too much pressure on our families to provide everything we seek from them.'

'What do you mean?'

'I mean – parents – well, they're just people, right? The faults we see in them were probably due to their parents having weird quirks and hang-ups of their own. And *their* parents, of course. When you think about it, we're all just a mass of inherited baggage stretching back generations.'

'What a cheering thought!'

'What I'm trying to say is that we shouldn't put so much pressure on any one individual to supply us with what we need because we're all imperfect and we're always going to disappoint.'

'But you've never disappointed me!' Brenna pointed out.

'Ah, that's because you're not around me all the time. If you were here first thing in the morning when I'm clattering around and cursing as I try to make myself a coffee because I've slept badly the night before, *then* you'd know what I'm really like!'

Brenna smiled. 'No, you're right. Maybe I've expected too much from Father over the years. But some people just get on better with others I guess. Maybe it's different personality types. Introverts and extroverts. Or star signs. *Vibes*. I don't know! But you feel it instantly sometimes, don't you? You know if you're going to get on with someone. And I just never had that with Father.'

Blue gave her a sympathetic look that almost undid her.

She cleared her throat. 'Listen, I'd better get back.' Brenna got up from the table.

'Want me to walk back with you?'

'No. I'm probably better on my own. I'm sorry I'm such bad company.'

'Hey! You're never bad company!'

They hugged and Brenna wondered for a brief moment if she could hide out at Yewdale Farm for a little longer. Maybe for the rest of the month. Or at least until the funeral was over.

'Come back soon, okay?'

'I promise,' Brenna told her and she meant it.

When Brenna got back to Slate House, a stony-faced Alex met her in the hallway.

'I've had a call from the undertakers,' he told her. 'We've got to make a decision about whether we want to see Father or not.'

CHAPTER FOURTEEN

The three of them went through to the living room where they sat together for, perhaps, the most uncomfortable few moments since learning about their half-sister in Cornwall.

'I don't think I can,' Cordelia said. Brenna could see she was shaking.

'It's okay. You don't have to.'

'But are you?'

'I don't know,' Brenna said. 'Alex?'

Alex nodded. 'I feel I should.'

'Okay. Shall I come with you, Alex?'

'Yes. And we should do it now.'

'What – *right* now?'

Alex nodded. 'Get it over and done with.'

Brenna bit her lip. She could see the sense in that, but couldn't help feeling uneasy because she hadn't made her mind up yet. But Alex was on his feet.

'Alex – wait. Let me...' She followed him into the hallway where he was putting on his coat. 'Okay. Let's go.'

Cordelia had joined them and Brenna could see her eyes were bright with tears.

'Are you sure you don't want to?' Brenna asked gently.

She nodded. 'I'm sure.'

Brenna crossed the space between them and hugged her and then she and Alex left.

They didn't talk on the short drive to the funeral home. Alex took charge of everything and Brenna simply followed. She felt a sort of numbness as if she wasn't quite fully present but sort of floating above herself, watching from a safe distance as they met a member of staff and were escorted down a hallway. Brenna tried not to fixate on the framed prints of sunsets that marched alongside her down the corridor. Instead, she looked at Alex's boots, noticing the Lakeland mud on the left heel and wondering if she should say something.

And suddenly, they were there – outside the door that would lead them to their dead father.

Alex turned to her. 'Okay?'

Brenna swallowed. No. she wasn't okay. 'I can't do it,' she told him.

'What?'

'I can't go in there. I'm sorry.' She felt awful – as if she was letting Alex down.

'It's all right.' He squeezed her shoulder. 'It's all right.'

Brenna looked around. There were chairs opposite and she went to sit down as Alex entered the room she just couldn't face. There was a tiny part of her that wanted to peep, knowing this was the only chance she'd get to see her father, but she felt glued to the chair. She couldn't do it. She really didn't want to see him. Her last memory of him was in his studio. She couldn't remember exactly what he'd been doing. Faffing around with his brushes probably. But that's how she wanted to remember him – happy in his domain, surrounded by his art. She didn't want to see him now that his life force had gone and heaven only knew what they'd done to make him presentable. She couldn't bear to think about it and so she stared at one of the awful twee sunset prints on the wall, her vision blurring into the streaks of pink, peach and gold.

Alex seemed to be taking his time. What was he doing in there? She'd thought he'd be in and out. She was feeling increasingly anxious sitting here. There was a tiny window that looked out onto a courtyard but there wasn't much to look at. She closed her eyes for a moment, trying to picture something beautiful and the first thing that came to mind was Yewdale Farm, sitting in its valley full of bracken, blackberries and willowherb. It was a little Eden in a hostile world, Brenna thought. She wished she was there now. She wished she hadn't left when Blue had said she could stay longer. She wouldn't be here now had she stayed. But she knew she couldn't shy away from what was happening. You had to get through days like today. It was part of life.

When the door in front of her opened, Brenna looked up to see Alex, his face ashen. She got up and whether he wanted it or not, she hugged him. She felt his body convulse.

'It's okay,' she whispered. 'I'm here.'

She let him cry, holding him tightly to her.

'It wasn't him,' he whispered after a moment.

'What do you mean?' Brenna asked, her mind racing wildly. Had there been some terrible mistake?

'No. It was him, but not... *truly* him. His essence. It's gone.'

Brenna felt a sudden chill as if a cold wind had ripped through her.

It was then she spotted a pot plant standing on the floor opposite the window. She released Alex from her embrace and stared at it. She couldn't tell what it was. Its leaves were flaccid and some of the tips were dry and looked as if they'd crumble if you took them between your fingers.

'That plant's half dead!'

'What?' Alex turned around, following her gaze.

'Look! Nobody's looking after it.'

He shook his head. 'It doesn't matter.'

'Why would they leave a dead plant in a place like this?' Brenna could feel her anger rising. 'It's obscene!'

'It's just a silly plant!'

'I need to say something.'

'Brenna – come on. Let's just go.'

But she wasn't listening. She was marching. Marching back towards the reception area at the front of the building.

The young woman on reception glanced up, looking concerned. 'Miss Bellwood? Is everything okay?'

'No. No, it's not okay. You have a plant *dying* down there! It's horrible! Why would somebody just leave it to die?'

'A plant?'

'Yes – a bloody plant! Down there – you can't miss it. It's the one with the *dead* leaves!'

'Bren!' Alex had caught up with her now and she felt his hands steady on her shoulders. 'I'm sorry.'

'It's all right, Mr Bellwood,' the receptionist was saying. 'I'll see to the plant.'

'It's too late for it now!' Brenna cried, feeling Alex's firm hand in the small of her back as he guided her outside. 'It's dead!'

The next morning Brenna awoke with a headache. It felt as if an army of soldiers was marching inside her skull. She wasn't surprised. She'd worked herself up into such a state at the funeral home and all over a stupid plant. Alex had done his best to calm her down on the way home and Cordelia had gone into mother mode on their return. Brenna had retreated to her room in tears and she wasn't sure she was ready to come out now even though the September sunlight was bright and seemed to be dancing on her bedroom floor as the curtains stirred. She'd left her window open overnight, feeling that she needed as much fresh air as Cumbria could give her. But now she wanted to hide away from it all, blocking out the sun's rays and the stirrings of the breeze – preferably with her head under her pillow.

It took a gargantuan effort to get out of bed and face the day and she delayed switching her phone on for as long as possible. The truth was she was on edge every time someone's phone rang because she knew it would mean they'd have to face yet another awful task. Alas that morning was no different and a message was waiting for her when she switched her phone on. The owner of a gallery in Keswick had rung to tell her that they had two of her father's paintings left over from a recent show and that they'd need to be collected. Well at least that should be a more pleasant outing than the one she'd endured yesterday, she thought.

After getting washed and dressed, she ventured downstairs to the kitchen. She was dreading seeing Alex and

Cordelia after the scene she'd made the day before, but they greeted her with smiles and eyes that shone with sympathy.

'Are you okay?' Alex asked.

Brenna nodded.

'I'm just making some coffee,' Cordelia said. 'Want one?'

'Two might work better,' Brenna said.

'Did you sleep all right?' her sister asked.

'Yes, but I've got a horrible headache now.'

'Take something for it straightaway and get some food in you.'

Brenna couldn't help smiling at her little sister's forthright tone.

'I've had a call from a gallery,' she told them. 'They want us to pick up some of Father's paintings. I'm going to go and collect them.'

'Are you sure you're up to it? You look a bit ropey,' Alex told her.

'I'm fine. The air will do me good and I'll get us some provisions while I'm out.'

'Good idea. I've actually got a list,' Cordelia said, handing it to her. 'If you're up to it.'

Brenna took it. 'Sure. I'll just have some breakfast and then get on.'

'Where's the gallery?' Alex asked.

Brenna sighed before answering. 'Keswick.'

Cordelia frowned. 'Can't they bring the paintings here?'

'It's okay. I don't mind going,' Brenna told them, catching the look that passed between her brother and sister. 'I'll be there and back before you know it.'

~

Parking in Keswick later that morning, Brenna found her way to the gallery, nodded politely when the owner told her how sorry he was for her loss, collected the paintings and stowed them safely in her car before heading to the nearest shop. However, she didn't make it.

She knew there was always a chance of it, of course, but her head had been so full of her father that she had almost managed to block her mother out completely. Still, Keswick was the place where Lydia Bellwood had lived. In that brief time between leaving Slate House and her death, this pretty Lakeland town had been her home. With him. The Man Who Killed Mother.

Brenna had always done her best to avoid the place, which was hard because it was pretty central to the Lake District, but so much of her past was wrapped up with it and, of course, *he* still lived here.

She'd only ever seen Graham Bartlett a couple of times in her whole life – once when he'd accompanied her mother to Slate House when she was collecting some of her clothes and the other at her funeral, but she'd have recognised him anywhere. It wasn't because he was particularly distinct. In fact he was perfectly ordinary. There was just an aura about him. And it was definitely him approaching her in the street right now.

'Brenna? It is, isn't it?'

'Yes. Hello Mr Bartlett.'

'Graham – please call me Graham. How are you?' he asked, his expression gentle and sincere. 'Silly question!' He shook his head, clearly remonstrating with himself. 'I'm sorry. I've been meaning to reach out to you. I heard the news.'

Brenna nodded, not knowing what to say. 'I should really

be going. I've got...' Her voice petered out and her eyes misted with tears. Traitorous tears at the most inopportune moment.

'Come and sit down for a moment,' Graham suggested.

'But I've got to be somewhere.'

'Well, *somewhere* can wait for a few minutes surely. Come on. You need to sit down.'

Brenna nodded helplessly and Graham gently led her towards a café. It was the last thing she'd expected to happen. She'd told herself that she'd be in and out of Keswick without any drama and now here she was stuck in a café with The Man Who Killed Mother. She watched him as he chatted amiably to the woman behind the counter, pointing to the display and all she could think about was that she was fraternising with the enemy. And yet he didn't seem like the enemy as he walked to the table and placed a tray with drinks and cakes down before her.

'I wasn't sure what you liked so I got a few things. The flapjack is particularly good though.' He smiled gently. Had that been a deciding factor for her mother, she couldn't help wondering, seeing as Father had rarely smiled?

'You shouldn't have gone to all this trouble.'

'No trouble at all. You look as if you've not been eating properly.'

'I've been eating fine!' Brenna said defensively, and then felt she should apologise. 'Sorry.'

'What I meant to say was that you looked as if you could use a sugar hit.'

She sighed. 'Yes. That's kind of you.' She stared at the tray in front of her.

'You choose first,' he said.

She reached for the flapjack.

'Excellent choice!' he said, picking up the chocolate brownie.

She glanced across the table at him a moment later as he stirred sugar into his mug of tea. It was such a simple thing to be doing and yet it filled her with pathos. Here she was having tea with Graham Bartlett when her parents were dead. The thought shocked her. It didn't seem right to be here, sitting so comfortably with the man her mother had left her father for, and yet there was no visible tension etched across his face. He seemed perfectly at ease with her. It was almost as if he'd always known this day would come and that he'd take her to his favourite café and buy her tea and cake.

'How have you all been? Your brother and sister? How are they?'

'They're okay. They're with me at Slate House for a while, sorting things out.'

'And you're still in Cumbria, are you?'

'No, I live in Yorkshire.'

'Ah! Moved across the border, eh? And Cordelia?'

'She lives in London.' Brenna took a sip of her tea. It felt awkward having this sort of light catch-up conversation with this man.

'And Alex?' Graham went on, obviously not picking up on her reluctance to chat or else stoically ignoring it.

'He lives in Greece now.'

'Greece! Your mother would have been astonished, I'm sure. And so proud of you all.'

'Proud? Are you sure?'

Graham frowned. 'Of course.'

Brenna shook her head. 'She left us and never gave us a single thought after that.'

'Brenna, my dear girl! Never *thought* of you? She cried every night for over a year.'

'I don't believe that for a moment!'

'But it's true – whether you believe it or not. You must know that she loved you!'

Brenna shook her head. 'How could I know that? She left us!'

'She was forced to. Your father...' he paused and she could see him wincing visibly. 'Your father made life difficult. He gave her no choice.'

'How? How did he give her no choice?'

'You know the kind of man he was. I know you do. She fought him for years, but she couldn't do it anymore. She was exhausted.'

'But she never tried to see us.'

Graham shook his head. 'She tried to – so many times. But your father made things impossible for her.' He sighed. 'If only you'd been older, it might have been easier for you to see her. I mean if you'd had a car and a bit more independence. Was Alex learning to drive then?'

'No. He was still too young. Anyway, he didn't want to see Mother.'

Graham looked saddened by this revelation. 'I'm so sorry, Brenna. I always put your mother first. Please know that. She was everything to me and I loved her very much.'

Brenna let his words sink in. She knew so little about this man who said he'd loved her mother. She picked at her piece of flapjack, but she wasn't really hungry.

'How did you meet?' Brenna asked after a few moments had passed. She'd never given it any thought until that moment. Graham Bartlett had just existed. She'd never thought of him as a real human being with thoughts and feelings, dreams and desires. He'd just been the man who had taken their mother away from them. But the opportunity to know more might not come again.

'We met at Castlerigg Stone Circle,' he said with a smile. 'I'd gone up to get some shots of it at sunset on the summer solstice. It was a beautiful fiery sky and there were a few people up there. Of course, I wanted to get the shot of the stones without all the crowds and so I waited my turn and, one by one, the people left. Except one. Your mother. She was standing staring at the sky with such ferocity, I knew that I'd have to incorporate her into my shots. So I did. I'm not sure when she became aware of me but, when she saw me, she was horribly embarrassed. I showed her some of the images I'd taken. It was getting pretty cold by then even though it was the longest day of summer. But we just couldn't stop talking. She was a very easy woman to talk to.' He smiled.

For a moment, Brenna reflected on the fact that she'd never been able to talk easily to her mother, but perhaps that had been to do with the situation they'd both found themselves in at the time.

'What happened that day?' she asked at last.

'Castlerigg?'

'No. Derwentwater.'

Graham flinched visibly and she felt cruel for asking him about the last time he'd seen her mother so quickly after he'd described the first time.

'Are you sure you want to know?'

Brenna nodded but then wondered if she truly did want to know because, once she did know, she couldn't *un*know it. That dreadful day would no longer be a bleary sort of smudge in her past; it would be clear and precise.

'I want to know,' she told him.

'Well, we took a boat out on Derwentwater, but I expect you know that much. Your mother wanted to see one of the islands.' Graham smiled at the memory. 'It was early July before the schools had broken up. We thought we'd make the most of the good weather before the worst of the tourist season hit. Lydia had packed a picnic hamper full of goodies and we were looking forward to lunch. I knew she'd make it special. She'd even brought napkins!'

Brenna nodded, remembering the fancy picnics on the lawn at Slate House.

'She loved to swim in cold water.'

'Did she?' This was news to Brenna.

'Oh, yes. But there was no way I was going to get in and she kept teasing me. I dared to dip a toe and it was freezing. I tried to persuade your mother to go after lunch, but she said she'd probably sink to the bottom after eating all the food she'd prepared.' Graham closed his eyes for a moment. 'I wanted to get some photos of the island and told her to meet me back where we'd moored the boat. I was keeping half an eye on her, but I didn't worry because she was a good swimmer.'

He paused and glanced out of the window. 'I really wasn't worried at first when I couldn't see her once I'd got back to our picnic site. I'd taken longer than I'd thought getting the shots I wanted and I thought she might actually have got out of the water and be somewhere else on the island. So I started to unpack the hamper, laying out the plates she'd packed.' He smiled. 'She'd brought her favourite china and I was a nervous wreck thinking I was going to drop something. It was a few minutes after this that I started to wonder where she was. She couldn't still be swimming. It would be too cold. She was only in a bathing costume and, even though she was good with cold water, she wouldn't be in that long surely?

'I remember scanning the horizon, not really imagining that she was still out there. There were some other rowing boats and one of the big tourist boats. But I couldn't see any swimmers. So I walked around the island. The whole island. I called her name and I truly imagined I was going to see her any minute. It wasn't until I got back to the picnic spot that I really started to worry. There was another rowing boat close by and I shouted out to them. But they hadn't seen her. And I couldn't ring her, could I?'

'Did you go into the water?'

He shook his head. 'I thought about it, but I'm not that great a swimmer to be honest. I wondered if she'd got disorientated and had swum out so far that she'd thought I was on a different island so I got in our boat, but I soon realised that the nearest island was a long way off for a swimmer.'

Brenna could feel her throat constrict as she imagined his fear that day. What would she have done in his place?

'Then I had to make a decision and it was the hardest thing I've ever had to do, but I was on my own there. I didn't have a choice. I had to leave without her.'

Brenna saw him swallow hard. His face was pale now as if he'd been physically pulled back to the dreadful moment he was recounting.

'I had to leave and get help because I didn't know what to do. I felt totally lost. That huge body of water seemed to have swallowed her up.'

He looked down at his lap and his shoulders shook.

Brenna reached across the table to take his hand, and he looked up at her, his pale eyes bright with tears.

'She wasn't found for three days. There were divers out looking for her. It was... it was hard. I'd pace along the shores and take a boat out, shouting her name across the water. Why hadn't I been watching her? What happened? Did the cold get to her? Did she get cramp or tangled up in something? Nobody really knows and it kills me every day. And I have nightmares sometimes. I can hear her calling to me, but I can't see her. Do you think she did? Was she calling out for help when I was taking stupid bloody photos of trees?'

Brenna squeezed his hand. She was on the verge of tears and she really didn't want to cry because she wasn't a hundred percent sure she'd ever be able to stop.

'Are you okay?' Graham asked, his voice barely above a whisper now.

Brenna nodded. 'I wanted to know.'

'I thought about writing to you all over the years, but I didn't know what to say. I don't suppose your father would have let you read anything from me anyway.'

'Thank you for telling me.'

'At least you know now. I think it's always best. Even if it's painful. It's good to know the truth.'

'Is it?'

'Yes, of course,' he said.

'Well, we've just been told that Father had another daughter who lives in Cornwall. And I'm sure we'd have been much happier not knowing about her,' Brenna confessed. And then she wondered if she should have shared this with him, but it seemed like a time for confidences.

Graham nodded. And then something occurred to Brenna.

'Did Mother know about her?'

'Yes,' he said simply. 'From what your mother told me, your father wasn't very good at hiding things.'

'Well, he did a pretty good job of hiding it from us!'

'Yes. I'm sorry, Brenna.'

She took a breath. 'How did it affect Mother?'

'To be honest, I think she knew it wasn't working long before...' he paused, frowning. 'Before...'

'Angelina.'

'Yes. Long before Angelina appeared on the scene, I think your mother knew she had to get out. That evening at Castlerigg – she'd got an overnight bag in the car. She told me it was a dummy run to see if she could really do it. Your father had put a lot of nonsense in her head about how she wouldn't be able to cope without him. She had no skills. No talent. And he'd see to it that she had no money either.'

Brenna gasped.

'I shouldn't be telling you this.'

'No, I'm glad you are.'

'Anyway, she'd told him she was staying with a friend for the weekend but she'd booked a hotel in Keswick. She just wanted to gather her thoughts.'

'She told you all this the day you met?'

'Yes. We got each other's life stories. It's that way sometimes with people. Not often, mind, but sometimes.'

Brenna felt completely baffled by this statement. She'd never had that experience. She'd never felt so easy in somebody's company that she'd just open up like that. No, that was wrong. There was one person she felt completely at ease with. Blue. But that was different. They'd known each other for years; they'd practically grown up together so it didn't count, did it?

'But it hurts me to think that you ever doubted her love for you, Brenna. It almost broke her leaving you all. And I don't want to speak ill of your father, especially now. But I think your mother always imagined things being different – easier perhaps – when you and Alex and Cordelia were older. When you could make your own decisions. She was always hopeful of that.'

'We'll never know now, will we?' She couldn't hide the hint of bitterness in her voice.

'But you do – through me,' Graham told her. 'She was always there for you. It's just your father was always standing between you and her.'

Brenna swallowed hard. It was all such a long time ago and yet it still had the power to sting so much. Graham poured them both more tea and they drank in silence. But something had shifted between them now. Brenna didn't feel as tense. Something had been released.

When they left the café together, Graham walked with her for a little way.

'I keep thinking of moving away now that I'm retired and don't have anything keeping me here,' he confessed. 'This place – I sometimes hate being here. I can't even visit the lake now, knowing that it took Lydia from me, and yet this was her last home. It's the place where we made a life together. So, I don't know. I might leave. I might stay.'

Brenna understood his conflict. She felt the same way about Grasmere. It held so many negative memories for her and yet it was still home and the place she'd shared with Alex and Cordelia.

'I think life's like that,' she said. 'There's no one perfect place. The good and the bad – it's all tangled up, isn't it?'

'Oh, yes. All tangled up.' He smiled as they reached her

car. 'Keep in touch, Brenna.' He handed her a card with his number on it. 'Although I don't suppose you will.'

'No, I will!'

They stood for an awkward moment not knowing if a handshake was too formal or a hug too intimate. Brenna made the first move, giving him a single kiss on his cheek. He beamed her a smile.

'You look just like her, you know?'

Brenna's mouth dropped open but he'd turned away before she could ask him more, leaving her to smile and wonder.

CHAPTER FIFTEEN

The hydrangeas were looking so lush and vibrant after the recent rain, Cordelia thought as she made her way through the garden. She spent a little time in their company, sinking herself into their colours, admiring the enormous blue mopheads, the pyramids of pink, the lacy whites and the luminous lilacs. Some were as large as footballs, others were like pretty hats a lady might wear to a garden party. Cordelia loved to see the plants where there were both tight buds and full flowers. They reminded her of something from a fairytale illustration and, as a child, she'd sincerely believed that fairies lived in their garden.

She'd needed to get outside for a while. After Brenna had returned from Keswick and told them about her meeting with Graham Bartlett, she'd needed some time to herself. As if there wasn't enough to cope with at the moment with their father's passing, they were now processing details from their mother's death for the first time. To be fair, Cordelia had only been four when their mother had left. She remembered crying but, thinking about it now, she believed her distress was probably more in response to Alex and Brenna's behaviour than to the physical loss of her mother.

Maybe her mother's leaving was the reason she'd felt closer to their father than Alex and Brenna. They'd been teenagers and at that awkward stage. It must have been hard for their father to placate them whereas Cordelia had been so young. She would have taken love from anyone available to give it.

She often wondered if she'd actually made up the few memories she had of her mother. She'd seen photos of her, of course, but there hadn't been any on display around the house after she'd left, and Alex and Brenna hadn't shared theirs very often.

As she walked down the steps that led to the pond, she thought she heard music coming from the house. A piano. Or maybe it was just the wind in the trees. She stood for a moment and listened. No, it was definitely a piano. Perhaps Brenna was playing.

Cordelia glanced back at the house. How would she feel about it being sold? What would it be like to imagine someone other than a Bellwood living here? She knew Alex and Brenna wouldn't miss it in the same way that she would. They'd left a long time ago, but it was still very much home to Cordelia even though she'd been based in London recently.

She sat down on one of the wide grey stone steps and gazed into the dark green depths of the pond. It was quiet here and she felt wonderfully hidden from the world, but not hidden enough because a mobile signal found its way to her phone. She sighed in relief as she saw Dylan's name and pressed answer.

'Cordy?'

'Hi,' she said, so grateful to hear his cheering voice.

'How are you?'

'I'm just watching a frog in the pond!'

He laughed. 'Listen, I've got some good news. I managed to speak to someone at the auction house and they had a record of the sale of your father's painting. Like we guessed, they couldn't give me a contact name or number, but they've been able to get in touch with the buyer and passed my number on to him. Anyway, he's just called and he's happy for us to go and see him. He sounded nice too.'

'And he has the painting?'

'He does.'

'Where is he?'

'Penrith. And he's around today if that's convenient for you. I could swing by.'

'Are you sure?'

'Absolutely. I'm excited to see it. Aren't you?'

'Yes, of course. It's just...'

'What?'

'I'm a bit scared to now. I didn't expect this to happen so fast,' she confessed.

'Well, we've already gone round the houses a bit with it, haven't we?'

'I suppose so.'

'Let's hope this is it now.'

Cordelia couldn't help smiling. Dylan seemed to have the knack of pulling her out of her darkest thoughts and she was excited by the prospect of seeing the painting at last. Only, what if it wasn't what she was expecting? What if it was a totally different picture from the one she remembered. It was such a vague sort of memory to begin with. What if she'd got it all wrong? Like the memories of her mother – she might just have made it all up.

Dylan was the perfect companion after the stresses of the day. She didn't tell him what had happened to Brenna in Keswick. Instead, she listened to his tales from the gallery, delighting in the amusing stories about his customers – polite ones, rude ones and just plain weird ones. It was a wonderful distraction not only from the revelations about her mother but also the anxiety Cordelia was feeling about the painting.

'Well, this looks like the place,' Dylan said as they pulled up outside a terraced house.

'It's small, isn't it?' Cordelia observed.

'Compared to Slate House, anything's small, I'd say.'

'No, I mean I wouldn't have expected an art collector to live here.'

'After several years in the business, I've learned that you can never make that kind of judgement. You'd be surprised who collects art. It isn't just people in big posh houses with bulging bank accounts.'

'Sorry. I didn't mean to sound snobby.'

'You didn't.'

'I'm just – well – curious.'

They got out of the car and approached the front door, knocking and waiting. The door opened a moment later to reveal a slightly-built gentleman with grey hair and a moustache.

'Mr Hewson?' Dylan said.

'Mr Fenton?'

'Dylan, please. And this is Cordelia.'

Mr Hewson shook their hands and welcomed them inside. It was a modest sort of home with furniture that looked neither cheap nor expensive. The decoration was simple and the colours muted. But the art was wonderful. There weren't many paintings but each one was special in its own way. Cordelia saw several landscapes in oil, a couple of portraits and a few abstracts.

'These are lovely,' Dylan said, approaching a pair of landscapes.

'Picked up in an online auction. Next to nothing,' Mr Hewson told him.

Cordelia couldn't help wondering if her father's painting had been priced so cheaply too but felt it would be rude to ask.

'I think the one you're looking for is through here,' he said, leading them into the dining room.

Cordelia gasped when she saw it.

'Is that it?' Dylan asked her.

Cordelia nodded. She couldn't speak.

'Lovely thing, isn't it?' Mr Hewson said. 'I've often wondered who the family is. Something to do with you?' He turned to Cordelia.

'Yes,' Cordelia managed to squeak the single word as she took a step closer to the painting, taking in the vibrant greens of the garden at Slate House and the vivid colours of the hydrangeas. It was a canvas that captured a perfect summer's day and the perfect family with a mother and children.

'I'd like to buy it,' Cordelia heard herself saying.

'Buy it?' Mr Hewson seemed surprised.

'Yes. Would you be willing to sell it to me? My father painted it, you see. It's of my family.' Her voice sounded fragile, betraying her need.

'Well, I don't know what it's worth, I'm afraid.' Mr Hewson glanced between Cordelia and Dylan, looking decidedly awkward.

'I could help there,' Dylan said. 'If you'd like me to?'

Cordelia stared hard at the painting, wishing there was a way she could have it. She knew she had her inheritance coming soon, but it seemed frivolous to spend it on a painting, and her father's paintings were expensive.

'No, I'm sorry,' she said. 'Forget I said that. I can't really afford a painting like this.'

Mr Hewson scratched his chin. 'Well, now, it seems obvious to me that you really do want the painting. And, to be honest, I can't say that I've looked at it much in the last couple of years. And paintings should be looked at, don't you agree? Why don't you just make me an offer?' He nodded encouragingly at her.

'Really?'

He nodded.

Cordelia thought of the money she'd saved up from her last job which she knew she should be keeping for the future, but when would she get this opportunity again? So she took a deep breath and said an amount, desperately hoping that she wasn't insulting the poor man and making an idiot of herself in front of Dylan.

'Accepted!' Mr Hewson said, extending a hand for her to shake.

Cordelia shook his proffered hand. 'Thank you! I really can't thank you enough.'

'It's my pleasure. Now, I have some bubble wrap if that helps.'

'Yes please,' Dylan said, exchanging smiles with Cordelia as Mr Hewson left the room.

A few minutes later, the painting was off the wall, dusted and wrapped. Dylan then took it out to the car and placed it in the boot, wrapping it in blankets to further protect it for its short journey.

'You've done that before, haven't you?' Cordelia said, watching as he made sure the painting was secure.

'Once or twice.' He winked at her.

After making arrangements for payment, they said goodbye to Mr Hewson, waving as they pulled out.

'I can't believe he sold it to me.'

'You know it's worth at least ten times what you paid the old guy for it?' Dylan told her.

'Really? Well, that doesn't matter. I'm not selling it.'

'I know.'

'You think I should have paid him more?'

'No. He seemed happy enough with the deal, didn't he? He probably got it for a good price at auction too, and I think he was glad it was going back to the family.'

They drove through the Cumbrian countryside and Cordelia gazed down into the blue depths of Thirlmere and up into the golden trees that lined the road, and it occurred to her that this was their last outing. They'd found the painting – the thing that had brought them together – and now she'd go back to Slate House and he'd go back to the gallery. She wondered if he was thinking the same thing. He was uncharacteristically quiet on the journey home. But he wouldn't miss her. He'd probably be glad to get back to his nice normal routine in the gallery without having to drive to all sorts of inconvenient places.

'You must tell me what I owe you,' Cordelia suddenly said.

'What?' Dylan frowned.

'For your time. *And* petrol.'

'Don't be daft.'

'I'm not. We must have driven hundreds of miles across Cumbria by now.'

'It's fine.'

'But I'd feel better if–'

'Cordy – it's fine. I've enjoyed it.' He paused. 'Anyway, if it makes you feel better, I'll claim it against tax. Art business.'

She grinned, relieved.

When they arrived back at Slate House, they sat in the driveway for a moment.

'It's been a real adventure, hasn't it?' Dylan said at last.

'Yes.'

'I'm glad you found it.'

They got out of the car and Dylan opened the boot, removed the blankets and pulled out the painting, safe in its bubble wrap.

'I can take it into the house for you if you like.'

'That's okay. I can manage.'

'You sure? It's pretty heavy.'

'I'm pretty strong.'

He smiled. 'I know you are.'

They stood looking at each other.

'I guess we should say goodbye then?' he said.

She nodded. 'I can't thank you enough.'

'It's been my pleasure.'

There was an awkward pause and a slight movement of his head which made Cordelia wonder if he was going to lean forward and kiss her cheek. But he didn't. Instead, he held his hand out and she shook it.

'Bye, Cordy. I hope everything goes well for you.'

She watched, panic-stricken as he got into his car. Was

that it? Would she never see him again? She'd got so used to their little trips and their chatter and she didn't want that to end. And then she thought of something.

'Hey!' she called, just as he started the engine. He wound his window down. 'Will you be at the funeral? I mean, I don't know when it is yet, but your gallery was important in my father's life.'

'Of course we'll be there.'

She nodded, relieved. 'I'll let you know when it is as soon as we know.'

He smiled and waved and she watched as he drove away, waiting until his car disappeared round the corner where the bluest of the hydrangeas were blooming, and then she headed inside.

'Is that you, Cordy?' Brenna called from the living room. 'Did you find it?'

Cordelia didn't reply. Instead, she focused on getting upstairs to her bedroom with the painting as quickly as possible.

'Cordy?' Brenna was behind her on the landing in record time and followed her into her bedroom. 'Is that it?'

'Yes.'

'Can I see it?'

Cordelia turned to face her. 'It's all wrapped up.'

'I can see that.' Brenna smiled. 'Is it the one you were looking for?'

Cordelia nodded.

'Cordy – are you okay?'

'I'm fine.'

'Well, you're acting strangely.'

'I'm just tired – that's all.'

Brenna frowned, not looking convinced. 'So how come you've got the painting? Has the owner let you borrow it?'

'No. I bought it. The owner wanted me to have it so he sold it cheaply.'

'Are you going to show it to us?'

'No.'

'No?'

'Not yet.'

Brenna looked baffled. 'Why not?'

'It's just... I'm not sure now's a good time.'

Brenna was about to say something else when Alex bellowed up the stairs.

'Mr Grant's on the phone. Needs your input on something.'

Brenna held Cordelia's gaze for a moment longer. 'I'll be right there!' she called back to Alex. 'We'll talk later, okay?'

Cordelia didn't say anything but, as soon as Brenna was out of the room, she carefully slid the painting into the back of her double wardrobe, pulling her winter coats across it.

CHAPTER SIXTEEN

The morning dew was still sparkling on the lawn when Daisy placed her suitcase in the back of the little car she'd only recently been given by her father. It had been her eighteenth birthday present, but he'd made her wait almost a year after her birthday until she'd passed her driving test. Now it was about to be put through its paces for the first time. As was Daisy.

It was a four hundred mile journey from Cornwall to the Lake District and it would take over seven hours. She'd never even left the county before under her own steam and her mother was decidedly anxious.

'I wish you'd take the train,' she told her now as Daisy placed her flask of coffee in the front.

'It would take even longer by train,' Daisy told her. 'Besides, their house is in the middle of nowhere. I'd have to get trains and buses and taxis. It would be a nightmare.'

'But driving all that way–'

'It'll be good for me.

'And on your own!'

Daisy hugged her mother. 'I wish you were coming with me, but I don't think that's a good idea.'

'No, probably not. But you're not an experienced driver, Daisy.'

'And how am I meant to get experience if I don't drive? This is the perfect challenge for me.'

Her mother sighed.

'Didn't you tell me you once drove the length of France and that would have been on the wrong side of the road!'

'Yes, well, I had a few more years under my belt when I did it than you do now.'

'I'll be fine. What's the worst that can happen? Daisy said and instantly regretted it when she saw her mother's face.

'I'll text you every hundred miles, okay?'

'Not while you're actually driving!'

'Of course not!'

They hugged again. 'Good luck!'

'Don't watch me leave. You'll make me nervous!'

'Don't forget those updates!'

'I won't. Bye Mum! Love you!'

'Love you too, sweetheart!'

Daisy got in the car, waited for her mum to retreat inside, and then readied herself. This was a big one. It wasn't just the physical journey that was playing on her mind, but the emotional one once she got there. But she wasn't going to think that far ahead just yet. She was just going to focus on making her way to the first motorway of the trip. That's how you drove four hundred miles – you simply broke it down into stages.

She had thought about an overnight stop but that would only prolong the agony and she was pretty sure she could do it in one day. She'd studied the route endlessly and it looked straightforward enough once she was on the motorway.

Bristol, Birmingham, Manchester. Three cities she'd never been to. The Cotswolds, the Peak District and the Pennines – areas she'd never seen. But there wouldn't be time to stop and visit any of these on this trip.

And then there was the Lake District itself. She'd googled it over the years because she'd known her dad had his other home there, but it was quite another thing to actually be going there herself. She realised what a sheltered life she'd lived. It was one of the reasons why she was determined to make this trip.

Cornwall to Cumbria. It was quite a journey for a novice. But at least her father had chosen two of the most beautiful counties to live in. She wondered which had been his favourite. He'd spent more time in Cumbria, but that didn't necessarily mean he'd favoured it over Cornwall. It was just a pity that they were so far apart. It would be strange seeing the home where her dad had lived. His *other* home. Would it be similar or wildly different? Would she recognise him in the place and be able to imagine him moving through the rooms? Or would it feel alien?

She could only imagine how Alex, Brenna and Cordelia were feeling about her impending visit. But at least they had each other. *She* was on her own. It had been a strange moment when the solicitor had rung, saying that the family had agreed to meet her. She hadn't quite believed it. And then she'd been given the address. She'd immediately searched for it on Google Maps but the camera stopped short of the tiny country lane it was on. Luckily, she'd been sent quite clear directions. Still, she would have liked to have seen the place before actually arriving – just to prepare herself a little more.

Leaving the hamlet on the Cornish creek, Daisy focused on the road ahead. It was going to be a long day, but this was something she knew she had to do.

The sun was slowly slipping from the sky when Daisy made it to her hotel in Kendal. She'd broken up the journey with four breaks which had allowed her to keep her promise to her mother and text updates on her progress. It had been a relatively easy drive with no real delays and only one very unsatisfactory sandwich from a motorway service station to complain about. The motorways had been challenging and she'd found herself hugging the inside lane for most of the journey and had only summoned up the courage to overtake a couple of big lorries when she'd been anxious to get to her next stop. How good it felt to park her car and hit the shower in her hotel room. After a quick bite to eat, she'd rung her mother who'd sounded mightily relieved that her daughter was safely tucked up in her hotel, but it was clear that she was already getting anxious about the return journey.

Daisy had then spent a few quiet moments sitting on the bed. The one person she wanted to talk to was the one person she couldn't: her dad. How she longed to tell him about her epic journey – her car's first real baptism. She knew he'd nod and smile as she told him about the little details of the trip like the tractor she'd got stuck behind on one of the Cornish country lanes and the terrifying speed of the traffic when she'd joined her first motorway. And, yes, the very unsatisfactory sandwich from the service station.

'Can you hear me, Dad?' she whispered into the room. 'I sometimes think you can.' She closed her eyes before the hot tears had a chance to blur her vision.

When she climbed between the cool sheets of her bed that night, listening to all the unfamiliar little noises of a new place, she hoped she'd sleep well, but feared she wouldn't. Today had been a long day, but tomorrow would bring challenges of a different sort.

She was going to meet her siblings for the first time.

'I don't know why we agreed to this,' Alex complained.

'Yes you do,' Brenna told him. 'It'll make things easier at the funeral.'

'Will it?'

'Of course it will, and you've made the right decision to join us in this, Alex.'

He sighed heavily as if he didn't agree.

The three of them were in the living room. Cordelia was standing by the window looking down the driveway, Alex was pacing and Brenna was sitting on the edge of the sofa.

'Shouldn't she be here by now?' Alex asked. 'How far's she coming from?'

'She said she's staying in Kendal,' Brenna said.

'Should we have asked her to stay here?' Cordelia asked.

'No!' Alex and Brenna said in unison.

'And you're sure her mother isn't coming with her?' Alex asked.

'No, it's just her,' Brenna told him.

'God, I feel sick!'

'This isn't about you today,' Brenna told him.

'Yes,' Cordelia agreed. 'Just think how Daisy must be feeling.'

'Wouldn't it have been better to meet somewhere neutral – like a café?' Alex said.

Brenna glared at him. 'We're meeting our father's other child. Don't you think it's right that she sees this place?'

'No I don't. We're not all trekking down to Cornwall to see hers.'

Cordelia saw Brenna shake her head in despair. 'Let's just do our best to get through this.'

'She's here!' Cordelia cried as a small blue car appeared around the corner of the driveway.

'Is that her?' Brenna asked.

'We're not expecting anyone else,' Cordelia said.

'No, but it would be typical of a meter reader to turn up at this exact moment,' Alex said.

'It's not a meter reader.'

They all watched the car closely as it came to a stop.

'It's definitely her,' Brenna said as the woman got out of the car and stared towards the lawn before walking across it.

'What's she doing?' Alex asked.

'Looking at the view,' Cordelia said. 'It is rather wonderful when you've never seen it before. Or even when you've seen it every day for years.'

Cordelia could feel butterflies fluttering in her stomach. It was an odd feeling to know that this person was their *sister*.

Daisy turned and started walking towards the house, gazing up at the gables. They all knew she was only nineteen but she looked even younger and Brenna gasped as Daisy came more clearly into view.

'Oh my god! She looks just like you, Cordy!'

Cordelia had seen it immediately. The long blonde curls,

the pale skin, the delicate features. Even the dress she was wearing looked like something Cordelia might wear.

'You could be twins,' Brenna went on.

'I think it would be polite to go and greet her rather than waiting for her to ring the bell,' Cordelia said, leaving the living room.

Brenna and Alex followed in time to see Cordelia open the front door. And there was Daisy.

For a moment, Cordelia and Daisy stood staring at one another, taking in the striking alikeness.

'This is so weird,' Alex said approaching from behind. Cordelia glared at him and saw Brenna shoving him in the ribs with an angry elbow.

'Daisy?' Cordelia said, doing her best to ignore the antics of Alex and Brenna.

'Hi,' Daisy said shyly and then she turned away. 'The view – it reminds me of home. The way the lawn slopes towards the lake.'

'It's not a lake – it's a mere,' Alex informed her.

'Oh!' Daisy said. 'Sorry.'

Cordelia shot him a look of disdain.

'In Cornwall, the lawn slopes down to a view of the creek.'

Cordelia smiled, trying to imagine it. 'It sounds beautiful.'

'It is. But the house isn't as big as this place though.'

'Come on in,' Brenna said. 'I'm Brenna. This is Alex and Cordelia.'

Daisy nodded and everyone stood awkwardly, wondering whether to shake hands but deciding against it.

'Would you like some tea or coffee?' Brenna asked now that they were all inside.

'Just a water, thanks.'

Cordelia led the way into the living room while Brenna busied herself in the kitchen.

Daisy immediately proved herself to be their father's daughter by approaching one of paintings in the room. It wasn't the largest or the most centrally positioned, but she stared at it in wide-eyed wonder.

'This is beautiful.'

'It was one of Father's favourites. It's the view of Grasmere from the end of the garden,' Cordelia told her.

'It's lovely. The light!'

Alex stepped forward. 'He always captured the light so well.'

'Yes.' Daisy turned to look at Alex and Cordelia noticed a slight softening in her brother's expression.

'Okay,' Brenna said as she entered the room. 'Tea for us, water for Daisy and biscuits for everyone.'

'Thank you,' Daisy said, sitting down in the armchair Brenna nodded towards. The rest of them sat on the large sofa, the tea tray on the table in front of them.

'How was your journey?' Brenna asked, looking awkward at asking such a mundane question.

'Long but okay. First time I've left Cornwall. As a driver.'

'That's some first trip,' Brenna said.

Daisy nodded and sipped her water, declining a biscuit when offered.

There then followed an awkward silence with them all staring at their feet or looking idly around the room.

'I'm sorry,' Daisy suddenly blurted, causing all her siblings to focus their attention fully on her. 'I'm sorry that this came as such a shock to you.' When they didn't respond, she added, 'It did, didn't it?'

'Just a bit!' Alex said.

'I knew about you. For a few years actually.'

'Yeah, well Father wasn't so open with us.'

'No, he wasn't.' She sighed. 'I'm sorry. I don't know what to say.'

'You don't have to apologise,' Cordelia told her gently. 'It's not your fault.'

'I know, but it feels strange.' She shrugged. 'I feel like you might hate me or something.'

'We don't hate you!' Cordelia said.

'Because I know you must blame my mum for your Dad leaving yours.'

Cordelia shook her head. 'Don't say that!'

Brenna leaned forward. 'Daisy – it wasn't right between Father and our mother for years. We knew that. We might not have wanted to admit it, but we saw it. At least Alex and I did. Cordy was so young.'

'But what about all the time he was with us?' Daisy asked.

'Well, didn't you hate us for all the time he wasn't with you?' Cordelia said.

'I could never hate anyone. Especially not my family. Even if I didn't know you.'

'Just for the record – none of us hate you *or* your mother,' Brenna said, her face flooded with concern. 'We're just trying to understand things.'

Alex cleared his throat. 'I hated Father,' he announced. 'When he hurt Mother the way he did. And I hated her for leaving us. I was angry and hurt and I didn't understand what was going on. And there's been an element of that in the last few days since we found out about you.'

Brenna sighed.

'Come on, Bren! Admit it! We'd rather not be dealing with this.'

Daisy sniffed and Cordelia saw that her eyes were bright with tears.

'Well, I wouldn't have put it quite like that!'

'I'm sorry – I shouldn't have come.' Daisy made to stand up, but Cordelia stopped her.

'No! Daisy – listen. Alex is being an idiot as usual.'

'I'm just being honest! Dealing with Father's death is difficult enough without finding out he had a whole other family and that he wasn't working in Cornwall every summer'

'He *was* working,' Daisy corrected him.

'You know what I mean.' Alex held her gaze.

'I know.'

'Look,' Brenna said, 'we're sorry, but this has really hit us hard. It's been a lot to cope with all at once. But we're all in this together, right?'

'Right!' Cordelia agreed, giving Daisy a smile.

'And we're going to get through it.'

Daisy reached into the pocket of her dress and pulled out a tissue, giving her nose a quick blow.

'Sorry – is there a bathroom I can use?'

She got up and Brenna showed her the way, coming back into the living room a moment later.

'She seemed upset.'

'Of course she's upset,' Cordelia said. 'Alex was a *beast* as usual!'

'Oh, for god's sake! We're all upset. There's no need for waterworks, though.'

'Alex – she's nineteen! She's a *teenager* and she's just lost her father!'

Alex looked suitably reprimanded.

'Just be quiet!' Cordelia said. 'She'll hear us.'

'I feel awful,' Brenna said. 'We haven't exactly made her feel welcome, have we?'

'No, we haven't,' Cordelia agreed. 'But there's still time.'

A moment later, Daisy came back into the living room. Her face was a little red, but she looked more composed.

'I should go.'

'No!' Cordelia sprang to her feet. 'We're sorry. We didn't mean to make you feel uncomfortable. And we certainly didn't mean to make you cry.'

Alex stood up. 'I'm sorry, Daisy. I'm not in the best of moods at the moment.'

'You're never in the best of moods,' Brenna said under her breath, just loud enough for everyone to hear her.

Daisy gave a shy smile. The ice was broken.

'Would you like to see Father's studio?' Cordelia asked.

Daisy nodded and the four of them went through to the room at the front of the house.

'We're still sorting it all out so it's a bit of a jumble,' Brenna explained as Daisy walked into the middle of it.

'It's so similar to his one at Creek Cottage,' she told them. 'The big windows and garden view. And canvases stacked everywhere.'

'Is it an artist's prerogative to be messy?' Brenna asked.

'I think it is,' Daisy agreed as she walked towards a stack of paintings and looked through them. 'The colours of the landscape are so different here. Muted, more sombre.'

'That's why I live in Greece these days.'

Daisy glanced up. 'Greece?'

'Skopelos. It's full of lightness and brightness.'

'A bit like Cornwall?'

'Less rain.'

As Daisy and Alex exchanged smiles so too did Cordelia and Brenna.

'Why don't I show you the garden?' Cordelia said. 'Would you like to see it?'

Daisy nodded and the two of them left the house together.

It was good to get out into the garden. It felt less overwhelming than the house.

'I'm sorry about my brother's behaviour before,' Cordelia said. 'He can be a bit gruff sometimes. He's a pussycat really. Well, not really. But he can be *much* nicer.'

Daisy gave a weak smile. 'It's okay. I know it's not easy having me turning up like this, but I thought it was important.'

'It *is* important and we're glad you got in touch. It can't have been easy.'

'I wasn't sure what else to do. It seemed like the right thing. But my mum was a bit anxious.'

'What's she like?'

'She's pretty protective. She was nervous about me driving and made me give her regular updates on the journey. And she demanded a video tour of my hotel room and checked that I knew where all the fire exists were.'

'It's nice to have someone look out for you like that.'

They walked down the steps to one of the smaller garden ponds where there was a stone bench.

'Do you have a photo of her?' Cordelia asked as they both sat down.

'Yeah, somewhere.' Daisy got her phone out and scrolled back through the endless images. 'Here.' She held the phone out to Cordelia.

Cordelia tried not to gasp as she took it and looked at the screen. She might only have vague memories of her own mother, but she'd seen enough photos and paintings of her to recognise her, and this woman – this *other* mother – looked strikingly similar to her.

'She's beautiful,' Cordelia said, quickly passing the phone back.

'Yes. Dad used to paint her all the time.'

Cordelia nodded. 'I'm not surprised. He – he liked painting portraits.'

'Do you have many here?'

'Yes. Quite a few. Self-portraits too.'

'He didn't paint many self-portraits at ours.'

'No?'

'I think he preferred spending time outside.'

'I don't blame him. I bet your summer weather was always a bit better than ours.'

'Maybe.'

They sat in companionable silence for a few moments and Cordelia had to admit how natural it felt. She instinctively liked Daisy and not just because she looked like her. She felt Daisy had an innate sweetness in her and, although Cordelia was only a couple of years older, she felt a little protective of her. So this was what it was like to have a little sister she couldn't help thinking as they sat there together, their hair – the exact same shade of blonde – blowing gently in the breeze and almost knotting together. Was this how Brenna felt towards *her*, Cordelia wondered?

'You've taken my place as the youngest,' she suddenly confessed.

'What?'

'Our father's youngest child. It's no longer me.'

Daisy looked shocked by this assertion. 'I didn't mean–'

'It's okay. It's just an ego thing. But it'll take a bit of getting used to.'

'Sorry!'

'It's all right, really.' Cordelia sighed and they exchanged smiles. This really was the oddest day and the strangest conversation.

After a few more minutes, they got up off the bench and walked to the edge of the garden that looked over the mere below.

'It's really beautiful here,' Daisy said. 'It's so similar to Creek Cottage. I mean, I can see Dad here.'

'You called him "Dad"?'

'Yes. Didn't you?'

'No. He was always "Father".'

Daisy seemed surprised by this.

They turned around to walk back towards the house.

'Are you staying up here until the funeral's over?' Cordelia asked.

'Do you know when it is yet?'

'No, not yet, but we should soon.'

'Well, I might stay. It's a long drive home and back again. I don't know.'

'Is there...' Cordelia paused.

'What?'

'A lot to sort out – in Cornwall?'

Daisy shook her head. 'No because it's our home so it'll stay pretty much the same. I guess you'll be selling this place?'

'Yes.'

'That must be tough.'

'Well, it's more difficult for me, I think. Alex and Brenna

left years ago. But it still feels like my home.' Cordelia glanced up as the gables of the house came into view. She loved how it seemed to grow out of the garden and the landscape around it, its Lakeland slate so robust and yet gentle on the eye.

'We have some of these in Cornwall. Although not as many as you have here.'

'What?'

'These big flowers.'

'Hydrangeas. Father loved them. But our mother didn't, I'm told. Too *in your face*.'

'What do you think of them?' Daisy asked.

'I like them. There are so many different colours – there's one for every mood you're in.'

Daisy laughed. It was the first time Cordelia had heard her laugh and it sounded strikingly similar to Brenna's.

When they reached the house, Daisy stopped by her car.

'I should go.'

'Oh, not just yet!'

'Really, I think I should.'

'At least come back in and say goodbye.'

'I don't know.'

'Come on!' Cordelia smiled in encouragement.

'All right then. Just quickly.'

They went inside together.

'Alex? Brenna? Daisy's leaving.'

Alex and Brenna came out of the studio and Brenna looked decidedly sad.

'Already?'

Daisy nodded.

'You'll keep in touch, won't you?' Cordelia asked.

'That would be nice.'

'Maybe we'll see you again before the funeral,' Brenna said and Daisy smiled, but didn't commit to anything.

They went outside to wave Daisy off, watching as she got into her car. Just then Alex's phone went and he walked back towards the house, the phone glued to his ear.

'Thanks for coming,' Cordelia called as Daisy opened her car window.

And then she was driving away.

'Is it weird for me to not want her to go just yet?' Brenna asked.

'No. Not weird at all,' Cordelia told her.

Suddenly, Alex ended his call and ran after Daisy's departing car.

'Daisy! *Stop!*'

'What's going on?' Brenna cried.

Daisy's car was approaching the first bend. Alex waved his arms madly and she applied the brakes and came to a stop.

Cordelia and Brenna ran to join them.

'What is it?' Brenna asked.

'That was the executor,' Alex told them all. 'We have a date for the funeral.'

CHAPTER SEVENTEEN

Alex had felt awful being the one to break the news to Daisy about their father's funeral, but he'd thought it was as well that she knew at the same time as them all. He'd seen her pale face doing its best not to crumple into tears. Brenna had invited her back in to the house, but she'd shaken her head. She'd wanted to get back and call her mother.

The three older Bellwoods had returned to the house and Alex had spent the next half hour in his room. He'd lain back on his bed, staring up at the ceiling which desperately needed repainting. The walls too. It was pretty shabby these days and hadn't been touched for years. Still, if they were selling, did he need to worry? Or should they invest a bit of money having everything fixed up? It seemed like such a waste when somebody might just come in and redo it their way.

He knew these worries were a deliberate distraction from what he didn't want to think about – his father's funeral. It was finally happening. There was a date in the diary for the end of next week. Did that mean they'd have to finish sorting the house out by then so they could all return to their lives? He guessed that would be the sensible option. And he so longed to return to Greece. Although, if he was perfectly honest with himself, the muted colours of Cumbria were starting to get a hold on him and he was beginning to remember the joy he'd found in the contours of the landscape around Slate House and beyond. It might be good for him to rediscover them.

His mind drifted back to Daisy. He'd been mean to her and he felt awful about that now. She'd looked so fragile sitting in their front room. It couldn't have been easy for her with the three of them bearing down on her like that. It must have taken great courage to drive all that way and enter their family home, and how had he repaid that courage? By sniping at her. He'd hoped they'd had a moment of connection in their father's studio, but goodness knew what she really thought of him.

He caught himself. *Their* father's studio. He was already thinking of Daisy as part of their family unit. It was so strange. But he had to admit that, after his initial rebuff, he'd actually warmed to her. It was hard not to – she was so like Cordy and it was impossible not to adore Cordy as soon as you met her.

He wondered how Cordelia was processing all this. It must have been especially hard for her having this unexpected version of herself turning up. She had seemed to be coping well – inviting Daisy to look around the gardens. And at least she hadn't been rude. Not that it was in her nature to be rude. She was never anything but sweet.

Alex sat up and swung his legs off the bed and sighed. He had been asked if he or his sisters wanted to say any words at the funeral. The thought was abhorrent to him and he'd said an emphatic no on behalf of himself and his sisters. But he realised now that that was wrong.

Going downstairs, he joined Brenna and Cordelia in their father's studio. They'd boxed up some of the art books. They still hadn't decided what they were going to do with them all; there were some beautiful and expensive hardbacks in the collection. Brenna had suggested selling them at auction and that seemed as good an idea as any.

'You okay?' Brenna asked as he walked in.

He nodded. 'I didn't tell you but Mr Grant asked if any of us would be speaking at the funeral.'

'You mean giving a eulogy?' Brenna asked, her whole face creasing into a frown. 'Blimey! I hadn't even thought about that. Are you going to give one?'

'I can't,' Alex said.

'I'm not sure I can either. It just wouldn't feel right. And what would I say? That I hadn't seen him for months?'

'You don't need to say anything,' Alex said. 'Nobody's putting any pressure on us.'

'I'll do it,' Cordelia said.

'Cordy!' Alex felt stunned.

'Are you sure?' Brenna asked.

'Yes. I want to.'

'And you don't mind that we... *don't* want to?' Brenna said tentatively.

Cordelia shook her head. 'You shouldn't feel forced to do it. Not if it doesn't feel right for you.'

'Blimey, little sis is putting us to shame,' Alex said with a tiny smile.

'Don't say that!'

'I'm only teasing.'

'Do you think Daisy's been asked to say a few words?' Brenna asked.

'I'm not sure.'

'Do you think she would want to if asked?'

Alex shrugged at Brenna. 'Maybe I should ring her. Do we have her number now?'

'Yes,' Brenna said. 'Mr Grant let me have it when she asked if she could visit us.'

'Okay, give it to me and I'll call her,' Alex said. 'It would be good to know, wouldn't it?'

Alex decided to make the call out in the garden and sat on a large wrought iron bench where he remembered his father used to place some of his materials when painting in the garden. Indeed, there were still flecks of cerulean blue on the black metal of the bench and his fingers found their way to a piece now, his nail scraping at it idly as he called Daisy's number.

'Daisy?' he said a moment later. 'It's Alex.'

'Hello.' Her voice was shy, almost apologetic.

'Listen – first of all, I wanted to say sorry for my behaviour before.'

'It's all right.'

'No, it isn't. I was mean and crabby and totally out of order. I'm really sorry. Can you forgive me?' There was a pause and Alex hoped with all his heart that he hadn't made her cry again. 'Daisy?'

'I'm here. Thank you. That's kind of you and there's nothing to forgive.'

He sighed. 'There was something else. The executor's

asked if any of us want to give a eulogy at Father's funeral.'

'Oh.'

'Yes, exactly.'

'Are you?'

'I'm not but Cordelia is.'

'And Brenna?'

'No.'

'Okay.'

'You don't have to. There's no pressure. We've got someone taking the service and I think there are a couple of Father's colleagues from the art world who want to say a few words. But you're welcome to if you want.'

'I... probably won't.'

'I don't blame you.'

'It might be a bit confusing if I stand up after Cordelia.'

Alex gave a little laugh. 'I hadn't thought of that.'

Daisy didn't respond. 'Well, I guess I'll see you there,' Alex said and was about to hang up.

'Alex?'

'Yes?'

'Thanks. I hope we can be friends?'

Alex swallowed hard. The sweetness of her voice completely caught him off guard.

'Yes. I'd like that too.'

He hung up feeling so much lighter and walked back into the house to be greeted by his sisters.

'How did you get on?'

'I begged her forgiveness,' Alex confessed.

'Good!' Cordelia said.

'You knucklehead!' Brenna told him.

'Hey! I apologised, okay!'

She grinned at him.

'Is she going to give a eulogy?' Cordelia asked.

'She doesn't think so.'

Cordelia nodded and her bright eyes suddenly glinted with tears.

'Hey!' Brenna saw it immediately and moved towards her. 'It's okay. You don't have to do it either.'

'It's not that!'

'Then what?'

'I just feel sad. I'm not ready to say goodbye.'

'I know.'

Alex wiped his eyes with the back of his hand. He'd been so determined not to cry, but the combination of Daisy's kindness and Cordy's vulnerability undid him.

Brenna opened an arm towards him and the three of them hugged. It was a rare moment of connection and tenderness and Alex felt a little shaken when he withdrew at last and he cleared his throat self-consciously. Brenna mopped her eyes and Cordelia sniffed loudly.

'There's something I should show you,' she said.

'The painting?' Brenna asked. '*Family Portrait*?'

'It's in my room.'

'Why have you been hiding it?' Alex asked.

'I didn't know what to do with it. It's... well, you'll see in a minute.'

Alex and Brenna followed Cordelia upstairs into her room and watched as she reached into the back of her wardrobe and pulled out the painting. She removed the bubble wrap and took the large canvas to the other side of the room where she rested it against the wall. The three of them sat on her bed to stare at it.

'Oh, my god! Look at my face!' Alex complained.

'Looks like you just came out of a fight,' Brenna said. 'But look at my hair!'

They gazed at Brenna's pixie-short cut.

'You look cute,' Alex said to Cordelia.

'Do I?' Cordelia said.

'A babe in arms!'

'Look again.'

'What do you mean?'

'Don't you remember what I said about the painting when I first wanted to find it?'

'No. What did you say?'

'That I thought Father had painted Daisy in the Family Portrait.'

'Why would he paint our mother holding Daisy?' Alex asked, disgust in his voice.'

'That's not Mother,' Brenna said, peering at the painting again.

'No.'

'It's *her*, isn't it?' Alex said through gritted teeth.

'Angelina and Daisy,' Brenna said, 'in *our* Family Portrait.'

'But it's not *our* Family Portrait,' Cordelia pointed out. 'It's *Father's*.'

They all sat staring at it for a moment, this new knowledge settling heavily.

'Did you know all this when you went looking for the painting?' Brenna asked Cordelia.

'Well, I wasn't totally sure, but I thought I'd worked out I wasn't the baby.'

Alex felt more confused than ever. 'Then where are you?'

'Left-hand side.'

Alex leaned forward, looking closer at the painting. 'You're just your dress and a leg!'

'But it captures me at that age – running barefoot around the garden. I can almost remember the feel of the grass under my feet.'

'You can see your hair too,' Brenna pointed out. 'Just a wisp of blonde flying out behind you. It's lovely.'

'I'm glad you like it. I wasn't sure how you'd respond so I hid it.'

'It's still a bit of a shock seeing Angelina and Daisy in it. Are you going to show it to Daisy?' Brenna asked.

'Maybe.'

'I just assumed Mother would be in the painting,' Alex said.

'It must have been painted after she left him.'

'They look similar, don't they? Mother and Angelina? Like you and Daisy look similar.'

'He had a type for sure,' Alex said. 'Slim, fair hair, fair skin.'

Cordelia sighed. 'I can't help feeling that Angelina and Daisy were better versions of me and Mum and that's what Father was looking for.'

Brenna gasped. 'Don't say that!'

'But that's how this feels. Daisy's the Cornish Cordelia!'

'No!' Brenna put her arm around her sister. 'You are the *only* Cordelia! Cordy, Cordy, Cordy!' She squished her nose into her sister's face, making Cordelia giggle.

'He didn't paint himself into any other family portraits, did he?' Alex said, gazing at his father's face in the painting.

'Not that I can remember,' Brenna replied.

Alex nodded. 'I think it's his perfect family. We know things weren't good between him and Mother. What he couldn't find with her, he found with Angelina. And so he's painted us all together here. It's sad when you think about it. He couldn't have all his family together in one place unless it was in a painting.'

'But why did he sell it if it was so precious to him?' Cordelia asked.

'Maybe it was too painful to have around,' Alex said.

The three of them stared at the painting again. A mother. A father. Four children. Two families. One family portrait.

Those few days before the funeral felt like a sort of twilight time. An in between stage the three of them had to get through as best as they could. They had plenty to busy themselves with. Brenna even popped back to her home for an overnight to check her post, water plants and make sure everything was okay with her customers at the shop. She took a few of the smaller pieces of furniture with her – a lamp from her father's study, a wooden chair from his studio and a side table with barley-twist legs. She'd also packed a box from her own bedroom and had chosen some of the paintings around the house. It seemed sad to take them off the walls. Some of them had been up for years and left dark rectangles behind on the wallpaper. But it did feel like they were making progress.

They'd spoken to an antiques dealer who was going to come and assess the larger pieces of furniture and three estate agents were in the process of giving them valuations. Alex had also spoken to a couple of art galleries about doing a retrospective show at some point, and had tentatively spoken about which paintings might be for sale.

Cordelia was uncharacteristically quiet throughout the whole week. She was the only one who didn't leave the house. She used her eulogy as an excuse, hiding away in her room to write it. But Alex suspected that she just wasn't coping with everything. He'd tried speaking to her and had asked if she needed help writing it, but she'd rebuffed him each time.

'I'm worried about her,' he told Brenna when Cordelia didn't come down for lunch one day.

'Me too.'

'What shall we do?'

'I'm not sure there's much we can do,' Brenna said.

Alex hadn't liked that reply. So he did something he thought he'd never do. He turned to his other sister.

'Daisy?' He was outside in the garden, hidden from the house by one of the larger hydrangeas. He wasn't sure why he felt the need to hide, but he supposed he was kind of going behind Brenna's back.

'Alex?'

'Yeah. How are you?'

'Okay.'

'Yeah?'

'Well, you know.'

'I know. It's a horrible time, isn't it?'

'I don't know what to do with myself,' she admitted.

'Are you back home?'

'No. I decided to stay in Cumbria.

'You should have told us you were still here.'

'Do you need help at the house?'

'No. It's not that. But I kind of need help. It's Cordy. She's... well, she's retreated into herself a little. She's writing her eulogy for the funeral and I'm not sure she's coping with it all.'

There was a pause on the other end of the line and Alex suddenly felt foolish for having bothered Daisy with a problem that wasn't hers.

'I'm sorry. I shouldn't have called.'

'No – Alex – wait! I want to help. It's only I'm not sure how.'

He grimaced. 'I'm not sure either. It's just – you're closer to Cordy in age and you seemed to be getting on well together. I don't know. I just thought–'

'Shall I come over? I'm not exactly doing anything.'

'Would you?'

'Sure. Now?'

'That would be great. Only, Cordy will be furious if she knows I've called you.'

'She doesn't need to know, does she?'

'I guess not.'

'I'll say – I don't know – that I decided to stay and see if you needed help with sorting out the house. Does that sound lame?'

'No. Not at all.'

'Okay then. I'll see you soon.'

'Thanks, Daisy – I really appreciate this.'

He hung up feeling mightily relieved and yet horribly guilty.

CHAPTER EIGHTEEN

Cordelia was lying back on her bed, a notebook by her side together with several pages of scrunched-up rejects. She'd started writing her eulogy on her phone, but it just hadn't been working and then she'd remembered something her father had told her.

'Paper and pencil – it's the only real way to gather your thoughts slowly and deliberately.'

And so she'd tried that and the words had flowed for a little while and then they'd knotted and stopped.

Perhaps it was the word *eulogy* that was blocking her. It was such a daunting word full of foreboding. Mind you *speech* wasn't much better. But whether it was a speech or a eulogy, it didn't really matter. The words were not expressing anything close to what she wanted to say.

It was then that she heard the sound of tyres on the gravel drive and, a moment later, a car door was shut and the soft crunch of feet approached the front door. She hoped it wasn't Simon Grant with some more sadness which he just had to bring to their door in person. She'd had enough of him and his rueful revelations. She thought about leaving Alex and Brenna to handle whatever it was, but that felt mean so she got up off the bed, tidied her hair, blew as much self-pity out of her nose as she could and then headed downstairs.

She recognised the voice before she saw her.

'Daisy!'

Alex had let her in. 'Look who's called to see us.'

'I hope you don't mind,' Daisy said shyly.

'How are you?' Cordelia asked, coming forward.

'Okay. You?'

Cordelia nodded.

'Daisy decided to stay in Cumbria and wondered if there's anything she can help us with. Isn't that kind?' Alex said a little too brightly.

Cordelia looked at him closely and then at Daisy. She felt as if something was going on but quickly put it out of her mind because it was genuinely lovely to see Daisy again so soon.

'Brenna and I are just moving stuff around in the study,' Alex told them. 'It's pretty dusty in there, but we could probably use your help with the paperwork in a bit.'

'Okay.'

'Well, shall I leave you two for a while? Maybe Cordy can make you a cup of tea?'

They watched as Alex disappeared into the study.

'Tea then?'

'I'm good actually.'

'Yes. Me too. Shall we make ourselves scarce in the garden?' Cordelia suggested. 'I could do with some air.'

The two of them went outside. There'd been a light shower that morning and the grass was soft and sweetly scented underfoot. The clouds were still low over the fells but the sun was piercing through them, promising a wonderful sunset.

'He's told you, hasn't he?' Cordelia said.

'Told me what?'

'About me locking myself away in my room.'

Daisy's lips pressed together in a tight line across her face, giving Cordelia the answer she needed.

'I was going to call round anyway,' Daisy insisted. 'I'd really like to help you all if I can. I feel so useless holed up in my hotel by myself.'

'It's not your job to help us out here.'

'Maybe not. But I'm offering anyway.'

'That's really kind.'

They skirted the side of the house, the scent of a climbing rose perfuming the air.

'So, how's it going?'

'My speech? Alex told you, right?'

'He might have mentioned it.'

'He's *such* a big brother sometimes!' There was the hint of annoyance in her voice, but she was smiling. 'If you want to know the truth, I've rewritten it so many times and it still doesn't feel right.'

'Do you *have* to write it?' Daisy asked.

'What do you mean?'

'I mean, why not just stand up and speak?'

'With nothing written down? I don't think I could do that.'

'You could make notes – just to jolt your memory. I think it might be less stressful than reading from a script anyway.'

Cordelia mused on this for a while. 'I don't know. But thanks. I'll think about it.'

They walked around the back of the house, up to the

abandoned greenhouse. It was a sad reminder that the place hadn't been loved since Lydia Bellwood had left Slate House. At least three panes of glass were missing and the paintwork had almost completely flaked away over a succession of cruel Cumbrian winters. But the saddest thing was the little tower of terracotta pots which stood so patiently inside, waiting to be planted up with wonders. Cordelia had once spied Brenna picking one up and holding it in her hand. Perhaps she'd been trying to feel her mother's presence in it, she wasn't sure.

'I hate feeling like this,' Cordelia confessed. 'I had no idea it would be so hard.'

'I know.'

'Have you been coping okay?' Cordelia asked as they sat on a bench that overlooked a flower bed full of bright dahlias, their pompom heads seeming to mock Cordelia's sadness.

'Not great. Some days are better than others.' Daisy sighed. 'I always knew he wouldn't be around forever. We were late babies, weren't we? And I knew he was a lot older than my friends' dads. But I hadn't expected to lose him so soon.'

'Me neither.'

'And it feels unfair. I don't feel ready.'

Cordelia reached across the bench and rested her hand on Daisy's. 'It isn't fair. Even if he was older. I don't care if he had a long and good life. Some people get much longer than him.'

'One of our neighbours is ninety-two,' Daisy revealed. 'That's not fair, is it?'

Cordelia shook her head. 'Why do some people get so much more life?'

'I don't know.'

'And Father was healthy, wasn't he? He liked a drink every so often but who doesn't? And he loved life. He really *loved* it, you know? He never stopped seeing the beauty of it – the hills and the rivers, the wildlife and sky. He was always painting it, trying to capture all its moods. Or photographing it. He was always sending me photos – sharing things he'd seen.'

'Me too,' Daisy said.

'And some people – miserable, angry people – are allowed to live right into their nineties.' Cordelia couldn't actually think of anyone in particular, but she bet they existed. It wasn't fair. Nothing was fair.

'Did he use to challenge you to send him a photo of something you'd seen that week that was beautiful?' Daisy asked.

Cordelia smiled. 'Yes! He'd email a picture and expect me to send him one. He'd sulk if I didn't – accuse me of not looking closely enough at the world around me. And it worked too. Even in my busiest weeks, I'd slow down and take a moment to look for something lovely.'

'What did you used to send him?' Daisy asked.

'Oh, I don't know. A photo of a fancy door in a London crescent or a reflection of lights in a puddle.'

'I once sent him a close-up of a seashell – you know the nobbly bit that looks like the inside of an ear, and asked him to guess what it was.'

'Did he guess?'

'Of course. Even though it was blurred. But I loved that he made me look at things. *Really* look at them.'

'Even when you didn't want to,' Cordelia added.

'Yes! I'd be trying to get a sunbathing session in and he'd

insist that I sit up to look at some formation he'd seen in the clouds. It was very annoying!' Daisy said lightly.

Cordelia stretched her legs out in front of her and craned her head back to the sky, looking for clouds now. 'Don't say anything, but this thing with Father – this closeness we shared – Alex and Brenna didn't have that.'

'No?'

'It's really sad and it's hard to talk about my own feelings with them because their experience and memories are so different.'

'How?'

'Well, Alex was the first born and he adored art like Father. But I think they saw each other as rivals. There was always this unease between them. It's really sad because they could have been great collaborators, but that never happened.'

'And Brenna?'

'She's said she always felt more like a secretary than a daughter. Isn't that sad? She never felt close to him. She hates talking about it. I think she's still working through a lot of the issues. As is Alex.'

'But you were close to him?'

Cordelia nodded. 'And you?'

'As close as you can be with a part-time dad.'

Cordelia winced. 'That must have been hard on you. And your mother.'

'It wasn't easy,' Daisy confessed.

'Your mum's coming up for the funeral, isn't she?'

Daisy nodded. 'Do you want to meet her before? You and Alex and Brenna?'

Cordelia wasn't sure how to respond. 'I'm... not sure.'

'That's okay.'

'Maybe after?'

'Sure.'

Cordelia stood up just as the sun disappeared behind a big bank of clouds. 'It's getting chilly, isn't it? Shall we go inside?'

Alex was handing papers to Brenna who was shredding them by the window when suddenly she stopped.

'Look!' She pointed out the window and Alex came and joined her. 'Honestly, it's like they're twins.'

'The resemblance really is something,' Alex said. 'What are people going to think at the funeral?'

'Do you really care?'

Alex thought about this for a moment. 'No, not really.'

'They probably won't even notice and, even if they do, they'll think they're mistaken.'

'They might guess.'

'But Daisy could be anyone. A cousin or niece.'

Alex watched as Daisy and Cordelia walked across the lawn towards the house together.

'Doesn't it feel weird that we've adapted to having her here so easily?' he asked.

'I guess it does,' Brenna said. 'I don't know. It feels kind of right, doesn't it? It's not as if she's a nightmare or making demands or disputing anything. She's just lovely. And Father obviously loved her and we are related. I don't see a problem.'

'If you'd told me a month ago that we'd have welcomed our father's other child into our family, I'd have thought you were crazy.'

'Well, I don't suppose you ever really know how you're going to respond in a situation until you're actually in it.'

'What do you think's going to happen after the funeral?'

Brenna moved back into the study. 'I guess everything will go back to normal. After the estate's settled.'

'Do you think we'll keep in touch with Daisy?'

'I think Cordy probably will.'

'But not you?'

She turned to her brother. 'I really don't know, Alex. I have trouble keeping in touch with you, don't I?'

'Yeah. Sorry about that.'

'We must make more of an effort. In the future.'

He nodded. 'I'd like that.'

They exchanged smiles and then Brenna bent down and pulled a box out from beside a cabinet, opening it.

'Oh my god, Alex! Look what I've found.'

'What?' He came closer to see her discovery.

'It's all our school reports.'

'What the hell did he keep all these for?' he asked, plunging his hand in and pulling one out at random. 'It's one of yours.'

'Don't you dare!'

But Alex couldn't resist. '"Brenna is good at the subjects she enjoys, but Maths is also important."' He laughed.

'Shut up!'

'Oh, listen – this is Art. "Brenna has a steady hand and a good eye for detail."'

'See! Just what I need for my profession.'

'It's just you're crap at balancing your books.'

'Ha ha!'

'What are we going to do with them all?' Alex asked.

'I don't want them.'

'It seems a shame to sling them when Father kept them all this time.'

'But, if we keep them, somebody will just sling them after we've gone. Best to get it done now.'

'You are one ruthless woman!'

'Not ruthless – just efficient.' She winked at him and he moved the box to the side of the room where it joined five others waiting to be taken to the recycling bin.

They'd just pulled out the bottom drawer of their father's desk when Cordelia came into the room with Daisy.

'Anything we can do to help?' Cordelia asked.

'You could pick a filing cabinet and make a start,' Brenna said, smiling and nodding at Daisy. 'We've not even started on those yet.'

The four of them worked amiably together, sorting through ancient yellowing papers held together with rusty staples, and exchanging smiles when they came across something poignant. Alex watched as Cordelia and Daisy chatted. He glanced at Brenna. She was watching them too.

Alex remembered how he'd been dreading coming home to Slate House after hearing of his father's death. He'd felt lonely, frightened and hopeless. But he needn't have feared for he had three wonderful sisters to help him.

CHAPTER NINETEEN

Nicholas Bellwood had not been a religious man. He hadn't even been particularly spiritual although his paintings seemed to be full of the spirit of the places he'd adored. Was that a kind of religion, Cordelia wondered as they entered the crematorium? She thought it could be and she believed she held something similar in her heart. She was truly her father's daughter and she felt the responsibility of that now as she took her seat in between Alex and Brenna at the front of the room. They had sweetly positioned themselves either side of her – kind of like emotional bodyguards, she couldn't help thinking – and she was happy to have them there. She *needed* them there.

She had spotted Daisy as she'd entered, sitting towards the back of the room with a woman whom Cordelia assumed was Angelina. Daisy was wearing a sleek black dress with neat heels and her long hair had been tied back.

Cordelia envied Daisy her seat at the back. At least she didn't have to sit so very close to the coffin. Cordelia did her best not to look at it but it was pretty hard to avoid with the framed photo of her father sitting on top of it.

Music was playing as everyone took their seats and Cordelia knew she'd never be able to hear it again without being back in this very moment.

They had only met the celebrant once before and Cordelia glanced up at him now as he welcomed everyone and said a few words before introducing Cordelia. She'd asked if she could do her bit first because she knew she wouldn't be able to get through the service without succumbing to a serious case of nerves if she didn't get it over and done with as soon as possible.

Brenna gave her arm a little pat as she got up and slowly crossed to the podium where she stood looking down at the floor before raising her eyes to the congregation.

She had three pages in front of her that she'd agonised over for the past few days. She probably knew them by heart now but, as she glanced down at them, she realised that she didn't like any of it. She'd begun with a kind of biography of her father's early years – his schooling, some of the jobs he'd done, and she'd moved on to his work as an artist, listing the awards he'd won and the shows he'd had. It all seemed so dry and didn't seem to capture the person she thought of as her father for it was only one aspect of him. She knew that Brenna would have her believe that it accounted for the whole of him. She was always saying that Father *was* his work and that there wasn't room for anything else in his life. But that hadn't been Cordelia's experience at all. Anyway, everyone here knew about his shows and his awards. They didn't need her to list them.

Perhaps Daisy was right. Perhaps a written eulogy wasn't

such a great idea and she didn't need her notes at all. So she folded them away and looked at the people sitting before her.

They're all friends, she told herself, even though she knew very few of them. So she took a deep breath and just spoke.

'My father loved life. He loved waking up early on a summer's morning and knowing that he had hours of daylight stretching before him. But he loved winter too with its fiery sunsets. When you're a plein air painter, I guess that weather and light are everything. I remember that he hated grey blustery days more than anything and he'd hole himself up in his studio at home and make do with working on canvases he'd started outside.

'He worked hard. Too hard, some would say. And, yes, his paints came with us on family holidays.'

There was a small ripple of laughter at this revelation which gave Cordelia a modicum of courage.

'But then again, I took my dolls and Brenna took her books.' She glanced over at her sister who smiled back at her in encouragement.

'We all, I think, have ways that we escape or find connection. But connection in the real world was harder for Father. He wasn't really a people person, let's face it. And, as much as he loved sharing his vision of the world through his paintings, he dreaded private views. He once told me that they made him feel like a circus animal begin paraded against its will, which might seem a little harsh, but it shows you a little of his personality. He was definitely an introvert, taking pleasure in a quiet life away from the spotlight. He never courted it. I remember overhearing a conversation with a journalist on the phone. "Why would anyone want to know

that *about me?" he asked. I never did find out the question he'd been asked, but he guarded his private life fiercely.*

'I've heard people say that he wasn't a patient man, but I disagree. Anyone that can start a twenty by twenty-four painting and wait to finish it over the course of a week, making sure that the light is just right for continuity – well, they have *to have patience, don't they? And to gather themed pictures together for a show over a course of months takes passion and stamina as well as patience, I think.*

'Anyway, to me, he was patient and kind and loving. He was both mother and father when I lost my mother. He taught me how to ride a bike and – yes – how to paint although my brother Alex inherited the real talent for that. And...

'And I miss him. I... I'm not quite sure what to do with myself. Life seems so strange without him.'

Cordelia could hear the crack in her voice now and tears were threatening, blurring her view of the congregation. A few more words would be her undoing. She glanced around and it was then that she saw Dylan sitting a couple of rows from the back, his face radiating kindness and his eyes bright with sympathy as he smiled at her. It was just what she needed in that moment.

'Thank you. Thank you all for coming today. I know my father is going to be missed by so many of us.'

She picked up her unread notes with shaking hands and left the podium, pausing for a moment by her father's coffin and looking at the flowers and the photograph sitting on top of it. She couldn't bear to think that he was actually inside that box and that she'd never see him again. So she tried to focus on getting back to her seat.

She was so relieved that her moment was over. She couldn't remember a word of what she'd said, but at least she'd managed to get through it. She hadn't cried and she hadn't stumbled.

'Well done,' Alex whispered to her and Brenna grabbed her hand and squeezed it tightly.

There were several other brave souls who got up to say a few words. Cordelia wondered who they all were and if her father had even really liked them. There was one rather pompous man whom she couldn't imagine being his friend at all and yet he had nothing but wonderful things to say about him. How strange it was, she thought, that this stranger held her father in such high regard and had taken time out of his life to pay a tribute to that of her father's.

When the service ended, they made their way to the car which Mr Grant had arranged to take them to the hotel they'd booked for the wake. There followed two hours of agony with small talk and polite nodding and trying to hold the tears back. The food looked wonderful. Somebody somewhere had done a wonderful job, but Cordelia couldn't eat anything. She did, however, manage to down a couple of glasses of champagne. Was champagne appropriate, she wondered? Wasn't that a celebratory drink? Perhaps this was meant to be a celebratory occasion and she should put a smile on her face.

Blissfully, after the second glass, she managed to slip outside and walk down to the nearby lake.

'Cordy?'

She recognised the voice and span around and saw Dylan standing behind her.

'Hello.'

He nodded towards the view. 'Your father painted Ullswater a fair few times, didn't he?'

'This is Ullswater?' she asked.

He looked surprised. 'Yes.'

Cordelia looked around her properly for perhaps the first time. 'Of course it is. Sorry. '

'Well, you did a pretty amazing job at the service. If *job* is the right word.' He smiled awkwardly. 'You know what I mean.'

'Did I really? I can't remember a thing I said.'

'I'm not sure how you did it. I don't think I'd have been able to do that.'

'Well, I wasn't sure I could, but it was strange. Something – some weird kind of energy – carried me through it. I spent *hours* writing and rewriting my speech and then I barely glanced at it. Daisy – you know my half-sister?'

Dylan nodded.

'Did you see her?'

'I think so. I did actually do a double-take when I first saw her because I thought it was you.'

'I know. It's spooky, isn't it! Anyway, she told me just to talk and I didn't trust her. Or rather, I didn't trust myself.'

'But you did it.'

She allowed herself a sad sort of smile as she stared out across the silvery blue expanse of Ullswater. There were boats out on the water and hikers up in the hills. Life was going on all around her and yet she felt completely cut off from it all.

'I feel a little hazy,' she confessed to Dylan.

'Do you want to sit down? There's a bench over there.' He guided her towards it, his hand in the small of her back. She could feel the comfortable warmth of it through the thin fabric of her dark dress.

'Did your father come with you?' she asked.

'He did.'

'That's kind. Where is he now?'

'Sitting in a window seat enjoying a plate of those little sandwiches.'

'Are they good?'

'Very. Haven't you had one? I could get you some now.'

She shook her head. 'I don't think I could eat.'

'You should if you're drinking.'

'You can tell I've been drinking?'

'You are a little bit – erm – hazy around the edges. To use your word,' he said with a grin.

'Oh, dear! I hope I'm not making a fool of myself.'

'Of course you aren't. Anyway, nobody's going to judge you even if you drink every glass in the establishment and dive head first into the lake.'

'I'll try to resist doing that.'

They sat for a moment, the gentle chatter of the guests just audible behind them through the reception room doors which had been opened onto the terrace.

Cordelia felt exhausted and suddenly wanted to go home. Would it be rude to leave already? Where were Alex and Brenna? She turned around, seeing if she could spot them.

'You okay?' Dylan asked.

'Just tired.' She stood up from the bench even though she could quite happily have nodded off there, the sound of the water lapping lightly against the shore. 'I should find Alex and Brenna.'

Dylan stood up and placed his hand on her back again. There was a part of her that wanted to leave with him right now, his hand guiding her away from everything. She didn't want to go back inside and deal with all those sad faces and sympathetic expressions. And she certainly didn't want any sandwiches.

They left the shores of Ullswater and headed back across the lawn. Inside the hotel, the guests were swarming, their voices seeming to hum malevolently. It was the last place Cordelia wanted to be, but she had to look for Alex and Brenna so they could all leave together. She was quite sure they'd be ready to go by now if she was.

As she entered the room, she spotted Brenna in the far corner and waved, but Brenna didn't see her. A man to her left patted her on the arm and started telling her a story about her father which she wasn't interested in hearing. Then a woman she half-recognised blocked her way just as she was about to reach Brenna and started telling her how much she'd admired her father's work.

Finally, Cordelia made it to Brenna.

'Where've you been?' Brenna asked.

'I had to get outside.'

'Have you seen Alex?'

'No. But he's probably at the bar,' Cordelia said.

'Okay, let's look there.'

Cordelia turned to look around the room. 'Oh, no! I've lost Dylan!' she cried. 'Where did he go? I didn't thank him.'

But Brenna was charging out of the room in pursuit of Alex so Cordelia had no choice but to follow.

Sure enough, Alex was at the bar and seemed glad to see them.

'Can we go yet?' he asked. 'I need to get out of here. And out of this goddamn shirt.' He sunk his fingers into the collar to loosen it as best as he could.

'How much have you had to drink?' Brenna asked.

'Not enough.'

The three of them left together in a taxi. Cordelia felt a little guilty for not saying goodbye to anyone, but she didn't think they'd be missed. The only people left at the wake were from the art world and they weren't really interested in Nicholas Bellwood's children.

When they got back to Slate House, they made their way to the kitchen. Brenna put the kettle on and Alex pulled a packet of chocolate biscuits out of the cupboard and proceeded to scoff the lot.

'Well, I'm glad that's over,' Brenna said. 'Who wants a tea?'

Alex shook his head but Cordelia nodded.

'Did that old man with the beard talk to you?' Alex asked.

'I don't think so,' Brenna said. 'Why?'

'He was going on and on about his own bloody paintings.'

Brenna tutted. 'Lovely!'

'I still feel bad about not thanking Dylan,' Cordelia said. 'Maybe I should ring him. Or text.'

'You did so well today,' Brenna told her.

'Yes. You were amazing,' Alex added.

'Thanks.'

'Daisy texted me and said to tell you,' Alex said.

'Tell me what?'

'That you were amazing, of course!'

'That's so sweet! I kind of wish we'd met her mum now.'

'Another time,' Brenna said, handing a mug of tea to Cordelia and sitting down with her own.

They sat quietly for a few minutes, slowly allowing the weight of the day to fall from them. Brenna was the one to speak first, a pained expression on her face.

'I don't like to bring this up now when we're all so tired but I've really got to get back to work pretty soon.'

'Yeah. Me too,' Alex said.

'I can stay a little longer,' Cordelia said.

'But do you really want to be on your own?'

'I might not actually be on my own. Daisy said she'd be happy to stay if we needed help here.'

Brenna smiled. 'I suppose it's better than you rattling around on your own. I don't like the idea of that.'

'Why not?'

'Because you'd brood!'

Cordelia sighed. 'I would not!' She could feel that she was pouting. 'Well, I might a bit.'

'I know I would,' Brenna said.

Cordelia sighed. 'Don't you think it's sad that Father wasn't honest with us all?'

'About Angelina and Daisy? We would have hated him if he'd told us!'

'Maybe to begin with, but we'd have adapted.'

'You think?' Alex said.

'Yes. I do,' Cordelia told him. 'I just can't help thinking that me and Daisy would have loved growing up together. It was pretty lonely here for me sometimes. You two were so much older. I would've liked to have had a little sister.'

Brenna reached across the table and squeezed her hands.

'It just seems sad when I think of what *might* have been,' Cordelia continued.

'You can't think like that.'

'I know. And I guess we're having our chance to get to know each other now. Do you think Father ever thought about that?'

'Well, he revealed her in the will,' Brenna said. 'So he knew we'd all find out about her.'

'Dylan saw her at the funeral,' Cordelia revealed. 'I wonder how many others noticed her.'

'Everyone was too polite to say anything if they did.'

'Anyway, it's over,' Alex said, 'and we don't have to see any of those dreadful people again.'

'Alex!' Brenna admonished.

'What? You couldn't get away from them fast enough.'

'I know, but they were all there for Father.'

'Or the free booze.'

Cordelia giggled. 'Or the sandwiches. Dylan said they were very good.'

'I didn't eat,' Alex said.

'Neither did I,' Cordelia told him.

'I had a strange canapé that looked like an eyeball,' Brenna confessed. She finished her tea and stood up. 'Mind if I head out?'

'Where are you going?' Cordelia asked.

'To Blue's?' Alex asked.

'Probably.'

'You two are getting pretty chummy again,' Alex observed.

Brenna smiled. 'I know. I'm really going to miss her when I leave.'

CHAPTER TWENTY

Once in her room, Brenna quickly got out of her funeral clothes and then pulled on a pair of jeans and a jumper. She combed her hair and immediately felt so much more like herself again.

She really should have taken the car as it was mid-afternoon now, but she figured she could always get Alex or Cordelia to pick her up or she could walk back in the dark. She'd done it countless times before as a youngster and she remembered the thrill she'd got from walking in the lane under a pale crescent moon, her eyes growing accustomed to the soft darkness of a Cumbrian night. It had never frightened her – only thrilled her.

Now, as she walked down the lane that led to Yewdale Farm, she felt safe, almost cosseted by the high hedges and the hills. It was a landscape that seemed to hug the inhabitant and that was intensely comforting.

Blue was in the kitchen when she arrived.

'I was wondering if I'd see you again today,' she said as Brenna walked in the open door after tapping. Midge looked up from his basket, sniffed the air that Brenna had brought inside with her and then closed his eyes again.

'I hope you don't mind me just showing up.'

'Why would I mind? Sit down. I've just boiled the kettle.'

Brenna might have recently had a cup of tea but she wasn't going to turn down another, especially when it came with a plate of ginger biscuits. It felt good to be back with Blue again. There was something so wonderfully normal about her home and Brenna felt grateful to be able to escape here.

'It was kind of you to come to the service,' Brenna said as Blue sat down opposite her.

'I might not have known him well, but he was a good neighbour. And I wanted to be there – for you.'

'Thanks. I'm just glad it's over. You know, one of the first things to go through my mind when I heard Father had died was, *Oh no – I'll have to go to a funeral!* Isn't that awful?'

'Not really. Funerals *are* awful!'

'You know you don't actually have to have one? I just found that out recently. Someone in my village died and I asked a neighbour if there was a funeral and she said no. He hadn't wanted one.'

'Certainly saves money and a lot of angst.'

'I know! I think I'll not bother either.'

'Bren!'

'What? Come on! It would be a massive relief for everyone.'

'You're terrible!'

'Okay, well maybe I'll just arrange for an evening in a nice pub somewhere. No speeches, no wearing black – just a few drinks and some canapés that don't look like eyeballs.'

'Oh, you got one of those too?'

They laughed.

'I don't know how Cordy got through it,' Brenna confessed, sipping her tea. 'She was amazing, wasn't she?'

'She was.'

'Did you see Daisy?'

'There wasn't any missing her. She's a beauty, right?'

'And so like Cordy.'

'Did you speak to her mother?' Blue asked.

'No. She and Daisy didn't come to the wake.'

'So are you going to meet her?'

'Maybe. Not right now though.'

'Well, Daisy's probably enough to be getting on with,' Blue said with a little smile. 'Anyway, how are you?'

Brenna took a moment to process how she was truly feeling. 'I think I'm still coming down from it all. I'm not quite sure I'm back in my body yet. Does that make sense?'

Blue nodded. 'I was the same after my dad's funeral although I suspect the whisky had something to do with it. I found a stash of the good stuff when I was looking for some papers and, well, let's just say I made a good dent in it.'

'It was so strange at the wake. Hearing all those people talking about Father. It was like they were speaking about a person I didn't ever know at all. How can that be?'

'I guess we're different with different people, aren't we?' Blue suggested. 'I don't swear like a trooper when I'm asking my bank manager to extend my loan. And I sure don't wear a nice little skirt and jacket when I'm cleaning the pigs out!'

'You own a skirt and jacket?' Brenna teased.

Blue laughed. 'You saw me in my fine ensemble today!'

'But you know what I mean, right? I know we behave differently around others, but how did Cordy get to have this amazingly warm and fuzzy relationship with Father and I got the strict, grouchy version? And you can't attribute it to a difficult phase he was going through. It was literally *all* the time.' Brenna sighed.

'People are complex,' Blue said with a shrug, 'and I guess it's impossible to get on with everyone.'

'But I wasn't just *any*one. I was his daughter!'

'I know.'

'Am I *so* unlovable?'

'What?'

'I mean that must be it, right? Mother left without so much as a backward glance. And Father wanted so little to do with me – he never even wanted to talk when I mustered up all the courage I had to ring him. I could almost *feel* him glancing at his watch. He must have hated me and done his best to avoid me!'

'Bren – stop! You can't think like that.'

'Then how am I meant to think?'

Blue reached her hands across the table, grabbing hold of Brenna's. 'Let me tell you this – you are *so* lovable! You're smart and kind and beautiful! You're one of the best people I know. No – you're the *best* person I know!'

'You're just saying that because you're kind.'

'Ahem! When have you ever known me to lie? Huh?'

Brenna shook her head. It was true. She had never known Bluebell Daker to tell a lie. Even when they'd been caught red-handed – quite literally – having eaten most of the blackberries Blue's mum had picked.

'We were hungry!' Blue had said simply. Of course, they'd had to go out and pick three punnets full to make up for the deficit and they'd had awful bellyaches later from overdosing on fruit, but Blue hadn't lied. She hadn't blamed her friend or the dog or denied having any knowledge which many kids would have done in her position. She had owned the truth.

'But you're my friend,' Brenna insisted. 'It's your job to tell me I'm lovable.'

Blue swore quite colourfully, making Brenna laugh.

'What do you want me to say – that you're a royal pain in the backside? Well, you are that too – *obviously!* But you are also the sweetest person I know.' Blue's hands were still holding Brenna's captive and she lifted the one in her right hand to her lips and kissed it.

The two women stared at each other across the table and then Brenna freed her hands, stood up and looked out of the window into the yard.

'Where's Linnet?' she asked, suddenly realising that she hadn't seen or heard the young girl.

'At a friend's house. She's having a sleepover.'

'I remember those!'

'Me too. Want one tonight?'

'A sleepover? Here?' Brenna said.

'Of course.'

Brenna smiled. 'I don't know. Aren't we a bit old for those now?'

'Well, we might be too old to play with dolls and mess around with make-up,' Blue said. 'But I'd really love you to stay.'

Blue joined Brenna at the window and reached a hand towards her, gently brushing a strand of hair out of her face, her fingers lingering close to her mouth.

'You're so beautiful,' Blue whispered.

'I'm not.'

'Yes, you *are*.'

Brenna felt completely relaxed in that moment. Assured.

Loved. And she wasn't a bit surprised when Blue leaned forward and kissed her fully on the mouth.

When she opened her eyes, Blue was so very close to her, so she spoke in a whisper.

'I'd better let Alex and Cordy know.'

'Know what?' Blue asked.

'That I'm staying the night.'

Cordelia was going through some of her father's paintings in his studio just as the afternoon light was beginning to fade. There were so many at all different stages of completion. Alex had told her she could take whatever she wanted. He was only going to be able to keep a couple.

'Don't break your heart over them,' he'd told her. 'We can't possibly keep them all. Just pick your absolute favourites.'

And that's what she was doing now only she wasn't just doing it for herself. There was somebody else she had in mind as she gazed lovingly at the muted tones of autumnal landscapes and the brilliantly bright light captured during summer in the Lakes. It was so hard to choose just a few for herself, but she was determined to be practical about it. After all, Brenna had been taking photographs of the paintings so they'd have a record of them and she already had *Family Portrait* safe in her keeping.

As she flipped through the boards stacked up against one of the walls, she pulled out one painting of the garden in late spring. It was a simple image with Grasmere in the distance, but it had managed to capture that glossy green glow of spring when the morning dew sparkles on the grass and the leaves on the trees are almost transparent. She put it to one side, knowing she couldn't part with it.

She picked a couple more from various stacks around the room. There was one of a Cumbrian village she recognised, its cottages huddled among the hills, and a stream running under a stone bridge. And, in contrast, she also chose an oil painting of Wastwater – just because that was so evocative of the Lake District at its primitive best, its dramatic scree slopes, its dark peaks lost in a swirl of clouds, and the steely blue waters of the deepest lake in England. It inspired awe, fear and adoration.

There was just one more painting she wanted. It was a view of Blea Tarn with the Langdales in the background – soft and serene. She took all four up to her bedroom, keeping one of the paintings separate from the others. And then she made a call.

'Hi. It's Cordy. Can we meet? I have something for you.'

CHAPTER TWENTY-ONE

It felt strange and yet perfectly natural to wake up at Yewdale Farm. Brenna took a moment to soak it all in – the beautiful white sheets contrasting with the rough tartan wool of the blankets, the pillows smelling of lavender and rosemary and the light flowing in from the open window. She stretched out and stared up at the ceiling, not wanting to move, not wanting this hazy, crazy feeling to end and yet knowing it must.

Getting washed in the adjacent bathroom and pulling on her clothes, Brenna ventured down the stairs, her feet finding all the old creaks in the wood. Blue was in the kitchen, but it was obvious that she'd been up and outside and had probably walked a mile and wrestled a dozen sheep already.

'Morning!' Brenna called, not wanting to startle her.

'There you are!'

'What's the time?'

'About ten.'

'No way! Why didn't you wake me?'

'I thought you could do with a rest,' Blue said. 'You looked so peaceful.'

'I've not slept that well for weeks.'

'I kind of figured that.'

They exchanged smiles.

'Coffee or tea?'

'Tea please.'

Blue nodded and turned around to make it and that's when Brenna crossed the room and wrapped her arms around her from behind.

Blue laughed.

'Thank you!'

'What for?' Blue asked.

'For saving me. Countless times. For being there. For loving me.'

Time seemed to stand still for a few brief moments in the ancient farmhouse kitchen. Happily so.

'So, what's on the cards for today?' Blue asked at last.

'I'm not sure I want to think about it,' Brenna confessed. 'I might just hide out here, give Midge a tickle, scratch a pig or two, pick some blackberries and make a crumble.'

'Sounds good to me.'

'There's still so much to sort out. I've taken a few bits back to mine already and we'll auction the bulk of it, but there are some things Cordelia wants to keep for the future. She can't have them now because she's in a tiny shared flat in London, but she doesn't want to lose it all. Storage is so expensive, though, isn't it? I think she'll probably pay more for storage than the pieces are actually worth.'

'She can keep it all here.'

'No! You don't want a lot of old stuff cluttering up your place.'

'I want to help,' Blue insisted. 'And I have rooms that aren't being used. Honestly, it's no bother.'

'Well, that's very kind of you. I'll let Cordy know.'

'Good.'

Tea made, the two of them sat at the kitchen table together.

'Can I ask you something?' Brenna said.

'Sure.'

'When did you know?'

'That I was in love with you?'

'Yes.'

Blue's gaze was direct and unflinching. 'Always.'

'But you never said anything.'

Blue's face softened with a gentle smile. 'I didn't think you were ready to hear it.'

Brenna nodded. 'I wish I didn't have to go.'

'Then don't.'

'But it's late. I should get back to help. Alex will be wanting to leave soon and–'

'I mean, *don't go*.'

'What?'

'Stay. Stay with me.'

Brenna frowned. 'You mean...'

'Yes.'

'With you and Linnet? Here?'

'Right here.'

Brenna's mouth fell open in surprise. It was something she'd never considered and yet it sounded like the loveliest invitation she could ever receive.

'Let me be absolutely sure,' Brenna said. 'You want me to live here – with you?'

'Yes! Emphatically *yes!*'

Brenna laughed.

'Is that a *good* laugh?' Blue asked.

'I think so! There might be a bit of surprise in there too though.'

'Surprise is good! I can work with surprise. Just say yes, Bren!'

Brenna laughed again, her very soul feeling suffused with light and joy as she sang out her reply.

'Yes!'

As Brenna walked back to Slate House, she knew that everything had changed. Her world had shifted on its axis and she felt a clarity that she'd never felt before. It was as if she could truly breathe for the first time in her life.

She smiled as she thought of Bluebell. Her best friend for so many years. Her sweet, funny, wise friend. And, now, so much more than a friend. Brenna felt so blessed. But what would everyone think? How would Linnet respond? She seemed like a sweet, easy-going little girl, but how would she truly feel about somebody moving in to her home to live with her mother? And what would Alex and Cordy say? The truth was Brenna didn't feel ready to tell them just yet. She wanted it to be her and Blue's wonderful secret for a little while longer.

It was then that something occurred to her. She'd been feeling anxious about selling Slate House. Even though she had never been completely happy in the house itself, she still felt enormous affection for Grasmere and it pained her to know that, by selling Slate House, she'd be cutting off her ties with the place. But, if she were to live at Yewdale Farm, it would mean that she could inhabit a place she loved without the shadow of Slate House falling upon her. She had always felt so at home at Yewdale Farm and now she realised why – it had been her true home all along.

Cordelia had left Slate House after an early breakfast and was now getting off the bus with just a short walk to take her to her destination. She felt a little anxious which was silly. Still, she couldn't control that and she gave herself permission to feel whatever she wanted. It had been an emotional few weeks, she told herself. It was absolutely normal to feel anxious or sad or angry or anything else for that matter.

Her hand tightened around the handles of the large bag she was carrying, its bubble-wrapped gift inside nice and snug as she approached the gallery. She stopped outside the window and looked inside. Dylan was behind the counter on the phone, his head nodding and a smile on his face which made Cordelia smile in return. She waited a moment, giving him time to finish the call, and then she entered.

'Cordy!' he said, coming out from behind the counter to greet her.

'Hello.'

'How are you?'

'I'm okay. Tired.'

'I can imagine.'

'I'm so sorry I didn't get to say goodbye to you properly yesterday.'

'That's all right.'

'No, it isn't. Not after all your kindness. I wanted to thank you.'

'You really don't need to.'

'Yes, I do.' She took a deep breath and then handed the bag to him. 'I hope you like it.'

'This is for me?'

'Of course!'

He took the bag from her and reached inside, taking the bubble-wrapped gift out and placing it on the counter behind him. Cordelia watched as he uncovered the painting inside, his smile slipping.

'Oh, dear! You don't like it?'

'Cordy!'

'I can swap it for something else if you'd prefer.'

He looked up. 'I *love* it!'

'You do?'

'But it's too much!' he protested. 'You can't just give this to me.'

'Yes I can. And it's nowhere *near* enough for all the kindness you've shown me.'

'I – I really don't know what to say.' He looked up at her. 'Except thank you.'

'I know it's not the scene of Wasdale you remember, but I hope it's close enough.'

'It's stunning. A real masterpiece. I love it!'

'You can sell it if you want.'

Dylan's head snapped up immediately at her startling statement. 'You're joking! I'm *never* selling this.'

Cordelia smiled. She was pleased he wasn't going to sell it although she hadn't wanted to give a gift with stipulations attached to it.

They both spent a few moments admiring the landscape and then Dylan turned to her.

'There's something I've been hoping to ask you.'

'What's that?'

His bright eyes widened a fraction. 'What happens next?'

Cordelia felt a little flutter somewhere deep inside her. 'What happens next?' she repeated. 'I'm not sure...'

She didn't have a chance to finish her sentence because Dylan stepped forward and cupped her face gently in his hands, kissing her tenderly, his lips warm and firm.

'I've been wanting to do that for a very long time,' he whispered.

'I've been hoping you would.'

He frowned. 'Really?'

'You sound surprised!'

'I am!' he confessed. 'I wasn't sure how you felt about me.'

'You could have asked.'

He shook his head. 'I didn't think it was the right time.'

Cordelia rested her hands on his chest and looked up at him, smiling. 'But it is now.'

His smile was wide and totally infectious and, for a moment, they just stood staring at each other laughing.

'I daren't ask, but I expect you'll be heading back to London pretty soon,' Dylan said at last.

'I guess, but not just yet. Alex and Brenna have to get back, but I'm staying on for a bit. Actually Daisy's offered to stay at Slate House with me.'

'Yeah?'

'It'll be good to have her company. Don't tell Brenna I'm

admitting to this, but it is a bit spooky being there on your own.'

'And can I visit you? When you *do* return to London?'

'I'd be disappointed if you didn't.'

They kissed again and Cordelia tried not to worry about the future and how the logistics of all this would work with her living in London and Dylan in Cumbria. She just knew in that moment, with his arms around her and hers around him, that it *would* work.

CHAPTER TWENTY-TWO

Alex, Brenna and Cordelia spent another week together at Slate House and it was as they were sorting through one of the last cupboards in their father's study that Cordelia discovered something that surprised them all.

'Brenna – look!'

'What is it?'

Cordelia handed her a sheet of A4 paper on which was a drawing in felt tip pens of a scene that looked very much like their garden.

'It's mine, isn't it?'

'Well, it isn't mine,' Alex said with a smirk.

'No, but I think this one is,' Cordelia said, reaching back inside the cupboard and bringing out a small framed painting. It was a landscape in oil.

'You're right – that is one of mine,' Alex said, stepping forward and taking it from his sister. 'This is from my first ever show. The one where I only sold one painting. I had no idea Father bought it. Why didn't he tell me?'

'And I had no idea he'd kept this,' Brenna said, staring at

her childhood drawing. 'I don't understand. What does it mean?'

'I think it means he cared,' Cordelia said simply.

'Nah,' Alex said. 'It means he felt sorry for me when my show was such a flop.'

'Well, that's still a kind of caring, isn't it?' Cordelia said. 'Anyway, I seriously don't think Father bought paintings that he didn't absolutely love.'

'Then what's it doing hiding in a dingy cupboard?'

Cordelia shrugged. 'He didn't want to hurt your pride.'

Alex seemed to consider this for a moment as Brenna looked in the cupboard and pulled out an old shoe box. Opening it, she revealed a messy medley of small items. There was a football trophy that Alex had won as a teenager, a school certificate Brenna had been awarded for a science project and a funny little clay figurine that Cordelia had made in an art class. There were also random photos from family holidays, old postcards the three of them had sent home over the years and birthday cards.

'I didn't know he kept sentimental things like this,' Alex said, picking up one of the postcards and reading his own messy scrawl on the back from at least two decades ago from when he'd been on a school trip to France.

'He wasn't a sentimental man,' Brenna said.

Cordelia's eyebrows rose. 'You see! You never can tell, can you? Just because someone doesn't show certain emotions, it doesn't mean that they don't feel them.'

'Yeah, well, he still could have been nicer,' Brenna said with a self-righteous sniff. 'Keeping a few oddments in a box doesn't make up for years of bad behaviour.'

Cordelia couldn't help feeling a little wounded at

Brenna's blunt statement so she did her best to ignore it as she rifled through the box.

'Look!' she cried a moment later, pulling out an envelope full of photographs and fanning them out for the others to see.

'It's Mother,' Alex said. 'Look, Bren – she looks just like you there.'

Brenna nodded and Cordelia could see that her sister's eyes were misting with tears.

'He kept them even though they separated years ago,' Cordelia said. 'Doesn't that tell you something?'

'That he forgot the photos were there?' Brenna said as she blinked back her tears.

'No!' Cordelia said in frustration. 'It tells you that he never stopped loving her. And there *was* love between them. Just look. Look at her face here.' She held out one the photos of their mother smiling into the lens of the camera.

'She looks so young,' Alex said.

'And so in love,' Cordelia added. 'You can just tell.'

The three of them looked through the rest of the photos, pausing at one of their parents together, arms around each other, the soft green water of Grasmere behind them. And it was completely undeniable that Nicholas and Lydia Bellwood had once been totally in love with one another.

It was after they'd finished emptying the cupboard and were just about to make a light lunch that Brenna took Cordelia to one side in the hallway.

'Cordy, what would you think if I didn't leave Grasmere?'

'You want to stay here?'

'No. Not exactly. Nearby.'

Cordelia looked bewildered, but then understanding dawned. 'You mean...' she paused. 'At Bluebell's?'

Brenna nodded, her stomach tight with knots at how her sister would respond. 'She's asked me to live with her.'

A smile spread across Cordelia's face. 'And you said yes!'

'I did.'

'Does Alex know?'

'Not yet. How do you think he'll react?'

Cordelia considered her answer for only a split second. 'Like he's always known it would happen.'

'*Really?*'

'Yes really!' Cordelia told her.

'But *I* didn't even know.'

'Oh, I'm sure you did, didn't you? Deep down?'

Brenna nodded and the two sisters hugged.

'You're not the only one, you know?' Cordelia said. 'I think me and Dylan are definitely going to be seeing a lot more of each other.'

Brenna gasped. 'I *knew* it!'

Cordelia laughed. 'So that just leaves Alex.'

'Yes. I've been thinking about that actually.'

'You mean Aimée?'

Brenna nodded just as Alex came into the hall.

'Are your ears burning, Bro?' she said.

'No. Why? What's going on?'

'I was just thinking. Isn't it time you rang Aimée?'

His face clouded with a frown. 'But she hates me.'

'I don't think so. I think she hated what you'd become, with the drinking and – dare I say it – all that self-pity. But you're through that now, aren't you?'

Suddenly, Alex looked like a little boy standing there

before them. So vulnerable. So unsure of himself. But with so much to give.

Brenna gave him an encouraging smile. 'Call her.'

There was only one thing left for the Bellwood children to do, and the three of them set out early on their final morning together, the air apple crisp, the leaves of the trees shimmering in shades of gold, amber and russet.

They'd talked only a little about the place they would choose and they said even less as they walked there from the house. But they all knew the spot. Quiet, hidden and beautiful. Nicholas Bellwood would have approved.

EPILOGUE

It was a warm spring morning in late April when Brenna drove down the lane towards Yewdale Farm. There were lambs in the field and primroses starring the grassy banks. Everything looked glossy and new.

Slate House had been sold and Brenna had been organising her own home so she could rent it out on a long-term basis. She'd also been arranging her business so that she could work more from home – or rather from the farm. Blue had said one of the outbuildings would make a perfect framing studio for her, and Brenna couldn't wait to get to work there.

She got out of the car, inhaling the sweet Lakeland air, and made her way into the farmhouse through the door which had been left open to welcome her.

'Hello?' she called. 'Anyone home?'

The sound of little feet on floorboards came from upstairs and, a moment later, Linnet appeared, her red hair tied high in a ponytail and her hands behind her back as if she was hiding something.

'Hi Linnet. How are you?'

She gave a shy smile. 'Mummy said you're coming to live here with us.'

'And is that okay with you?' Brenna dared to ask, anxious as to the reply she'd receive. But she needn't have feared. Linnet nodded and then presented her with the fistful of primroses she'd been hiding.

'For me? *Thank* you!'

The little girl ran out into the farmyard and Brenna made her way into the kitchen to put the flowers in some water. As usual, Midge was in his basket. But, rather than just sniffing the air and going back to sleep, he did something wonderful and rather unexpected. He got up, stretched his front legs out before him and then trotted towards her, his paws tapping lightly on the stone floor.

'Hello, Midge!' Brenna said, bending to tickle the old dog behind his ears.

It was then that Blue entered the kitchen.

'Well, don't you look right at home!' she said as she surveyed the scene.

Brenna, still surprised by both Linnet and Midge's welcome, turned to face Blue.

'I think I've been accepted!' she said.

Blue smiled before wrapping her up in a big warm hug. 'You'd better believe it!'

ACKNOWLEDGEMENTS

Huge thanks to the regular team: Roy, Catriona and Jane. And to my loyal readers who make sure I don't keep them waiting *too* long for the next book!

ABOUT THE AUTHOR

Victoria Connelly is the bestselling author of *The Rose Girls* and *The Beauty of Broken Things*.

With over a million sales, her books have been translated into a dozen languages. The first, *Flights of Angels*, was made into a film in Germany. Victoria flew to Berlin to see it being made and even played a cameo role in it.

A Weekend with Mr Darcy, the first in her popular Austen Addicts series about fans of Jane Austen has sold over 100,000 copies. She is also the author of several romantic comedies including *The Runaway Actress* which was nominated for the Romantic Novelists' Association's Best Romantic Comedy of the Year.

Victoria was brought up in Norfolk, England before moving to Yorkshire where she got married in a medieval castle. After 11 years in London, she moved to rural Suffolk where she lives in a pink thatched cottage with her artist husband, a springer spaniel and her ex-battery hens.

To hear about future releases and receive a **free ebook** sign up for her newsletter at www.victoriaconnelly.com.

ALSO BY VICTORIA CONNELLY

The House in the Clouds Series

The House in the Clouds

High Blue Sky

The Colour of Summer

The Book Lovers Series

The Book Lovers

Rules for a Successful Book Club

Natural Born Readers

Scenes from a Country Bookshop

Christmas with the Book Lovers

Other Books

The Way to the Sea

The Beauty of Broken Things

One Last Summer

The Heart of the Garden

Love in an English Garden

The Rose Girls

The Secret of You

Christmas at The Cove

Christmas at the Castle

Christmas at the Cottage

The Wrong Ghost

The Christmas Collection - Volumes One and Two

A Summer to Remember

Wish You Were Here

The Runaway Actress

Molly's Millions

Flights of Angels

Irresistible You

Three Graces

A Weekend with Mr Darcy

The Perfect Hero (Dreaming of Mr Darcy)

Mr Darcy Forever

Christmas With Mr Darcy

Happy Birthday Mr Darcy

At Home with Mr Darcy

Escape to Mulberry Cottage (non-fiction)

A Year at Mulberry Cottage (non-fiction)

Summer at Mulberry Cottage (non-fiction)

Finding Old Thatch (non-fiction)

The Garden at Old Thatch (non-fiction)

Introvert Abroad

VICTORIA CONNELLY

Bestselling author of *The Beauty of Broken Things*

The WAY *to the* SEA

The past is never far away.

When Cate Rivers leaves her husband in the middle of the night with their young daughter, Eliza, she has no idea what the future holds. Taking a live-in position at Hollow House on the Dorset coast, she determines to make a new life for her and Eliza.

But Cate's new boss, fossil hunter Charles Thorner, could do without the problems of a couple of runaways under his roof. He's got enough worries of his own, including a painful past which still holds him prisoner today.

As the two of them learn to work alongside each other, secrets are shared and a new closeness is found, but they soon discover that you can only hide from the past for so long...

MILLION SELLING AUTHOR
Victoria Connelly
Introvert Abroad
Feel the fear and travel anyway!
World Travel A Guide to Greece

Feel the fear and travel anyway!

Author Victoria Connelly hasn't been abroad for fifteen years, but a sudden longing to see the world hits her hard and she decides it's time to venture forth from her peaceful country cottage.

But what's it like travelling as an introvert who's battling menopause, chronic nerves and Google Maps?

Join Victoria as she visits Amsterdam with a friend, Sicily with her brother, Belgium with her husband and Crete – on her own!

With over 20 colour photos, *Introvert Abroad* is a delightful memoir full of inspiration and humour, proving introverts everywhere can feel the fear and travel anyway.

Printed in Great Britain
by Amazon